THE *kiss* PRINCIPLE

A HAZARDVERSE: SIDETRACKS NOVEL

GREGORY ASHE

H&B

This is a work of fiction. Names, characters, places, and incidents either are the product of the author's imagination or are used fictitiously, and any resemblance to actual persons, living or dead, business establishments, events, or locales is entirely coincidental.

The Kiss Principle
Copyright © 2024 Gregory Ashe

All rights reserved. No part of this book may be reproduced in any form, stored in any retrieval system, or transmitted in any form by any means—electronic, mechanical, photocopy, recording, or otherwise—without prior written permission of the publisher, except as provided by United States of America copyright law. For permission requests and all other inquiries, contact: contact@hodgkinandblount.com

Published by Hodgkin & Blount
https://www.hodgkinandblount.com/
contact@hodgkinandblount.com

Published 2024
Printed in the United States of America

Version 1.05

Trade Paperback ISBN: 978-1-63621-104-6
eBook ISBN: 978-1-63621-103-9

1

"Keep it simple, stupid."

Augustus sounded like he was trying not to laugh. "That is a terrible name for a life plan."

"It's not a life plan, sugar-tits." It took me a moment to come up with: "It's a life philosophy."

"It's terrible either way."

"Sorry, Augustus. Not all of us had the opportunity to enroll at Dong Knockers University."

"I have no idea what that means, but I'm going to take it as a compliment."

"It's not. It's a dig about you being a dong knocker."

On the other end of the call, Augustus sighed. Then his voice changed, and he said, "I'm talking to your Uncle Fer."

"Is that Lana? Put her on the phone."

"You want to say hi?" Augustus said, still speaking to Lana. "I don't know, sweetheart. He's pretty busy."

"Give her the phone, monkey balls!"

"All right, here you go."

Fumbling and scraping noises came, and then Lana said, "Hi, Uncle Fer." Her voice was flat, but even the diminished affect couldn't hide her excitement. It made me smile. "Papi's taking me snorkeling."

"Swimming," Augustus said in the background, and I could hear the smile in his voice.

Lana then launched into a convoluted explanation of...something. It had to do with the pool and with another girl and I thought maybe there was something in there about *Finding Nemo*. Finally, Augustus's voice came closer as he said, "Okay, let me talk to Uncle Fer now."

"Bye, Uncle Fer!"

"Bye, princess."

"You never had a cute nickname for me," Augustus said.

"What's a cute nickname for a crotch fungus you can't get rid of?"

In the background, Theo said, "Did I hear 'crotch fungus'?"

"Fer," Augustus said.

Theo made an understanding noise.

"Tell him to shut the fuck up," I said.

"He says he loves you," Augustus said.

"No, I didn't, dick-snot."

"Hi, Fer," Theo said. "I love you too."

"Tell him he's an infected ulcer." Genius struck. "An ass ulcer."

"He's got a new life plan," Augustus said. "He's going to keep his life simple."

Theo laughed way too long about that.

"I am going to keep my life simple, fuckwad."

"You should hear him," Augustus said, still talking to Theo. "It's adorable."

"You know what's not going to be adorable? When you and Theo send out Christmas cards of you swinging on an ass hook in your sex dungeon."

"You're talking about our asses a lot today."

"That's because that's prime real estate for you two butt pirates."

"Do you think about our asses a lot?"

"This is what I'm talking about. This is the kind of shit I'm not going to have to deal with anymore."

"Oh Fer."

I chose to ignore that. "You're off my hands now because you're officially the responsibility of the senior living center you call a home."

"That wasn't one of your best ones."

"And Mom's getting married at the end of the year."

"God, I hope not."

"He's barely older than a cumstain, but he seems like he's serious, and that means she'll be out of my hair too." Augustus's silence was unhappy, so I hurried past that part. "Chuy is doing his usual fuck-all, but he's clean, and that means he's officially not my problem either."

"I don't think you're supposed to say clean. I think you're supposed to say he's not using drugs."

"And now that I actually have a chance to live my own life, I'm going to keep it simple. I'm going to smoke a lot of weed. I'm going to watch whatever I want on TV. And I'm finally going to be done with fucking pharma sales." I didn't want to sound like an enormous geek like Augustus, but I couldn't keep myself from adding, "I've got a fucking fantastic chance at a new job."

"What? Fer, that's amazing. What job? Where?"

"Do you remember Lou?"

Augustus groaned.

"Knock it off," I told him.

"Are you serious?"

"She's got one of the biggest grows in the county. Business is fucking booming."

"I'm not worried about her business."

"She's my friend."

"She gave me panties for my sixteenth birthday. In front of all my friends. Before I was out."

"That was a compliment. She said you had the ass for them."

"She said my wedding photos would be me getting gangbanged by a crew of roughnecks."

"That was a compliment too. Like, stamina. And a willingness to please."

A (horrified) pause. "What is wrong with you?"

"What's wrong with you, you ungrateful little shit?"

"Why do I ever talk to you? Why do I pick up the phone?"

"It's a great fucking job, Augustus. Head of sales for the entire fucking grow. It'd mean a pay cut at first, but that business is going to keep getting bigger, and I can swing the pay because—"

"You're going to keep your life simple," Augustus said drily.

"Fuckin' A."

"Okay. I guess we'll see how that goes."

"What the fuck does that mean?"

He sounded like he was grinning when he said, "Bye, Fer. See you tomorrow."

2

When Mom started screaming the next morning, I turned on the shower.

Three more hours, I thought. Less if I'm lucky.

The sound of the spray swallowed her voice. Almost. I leaned against the vanity, my back tight and aching, and waited for the water to warm. That was an old trick, the shower. Or the vacuum cleaner. Or turning on a fan and telling Augustus if we put our faces right next to the grille, we could talk like Darth Vader. And the nice part was, it worked for all sorts of things. When Mom was fighting with the nineteen-year-old child she was fucking. Or when Mom was doing one of her productions—*No one will ever love me* always got rave reviews. Or when she came home with her head screwed on backward, and the bozo she brought with her kept looking at Augustus like the Big Bad Wolf. Slide the dresser in front of the bedroom door and turn on the fan, easy peasy. I checked the water; hot enough to sting. I got under the spray and let it needle my aching back.

Three more hours and I'd be on a plane. And because, as Augustus liked to put it, I was *seriously messed up* and because there was, in Augustus's words, *something wrong with your head*, my first vacation in—God, how many years? Three? Four?—wasn't to an all-inclusive resort in Mexico where I could pound drinks, blaze up, and, if I were lucky, have a string of meaningless fucks to refill the well. (We were beyond a dry spell. This was the fucking Dust Bowl.) No, instead, I was going to visit my fuckhole of a baby brother. And his partner, the dinosaur. In Missouri. The fact that I was so excited told me how fucked-up my life had gotten.

Mom's voice rose, the words shrill and indistinct over the hiss of the water.

Of course, I had to survive the next few hours first.

As my back loosened up under the heat, I got to work cleaning myself, and from time to time I took a swig from the energy drink on top of the toilet. That's called multitasking, bitches. On a bad day—and I'm only talking every once in a while—you can swap it out for a beer. Makes it easier to slide into a Monday. There'd been a time when Augustus was always posting "life hacks" on TikTok. Stupid stuff like *tape a dryer sheet over your AC unit to make it smell better* and *take a picture of business cards in case you lose them* and *use a hanging shoe rack to organize cleaning supplies*. Give me a break; when was the last time Augustus organized jack shit, let alone cleaned something? Energy drink on top of the toilet, that's a good idea. And here's a tip: all soap is soap, so you can use your body wash for your face and hair and butt and stuff. Oh, and—in a pinch—to jerk off. Follow me for more life hacks.

By the time I got out of the shower, the screaming had stopped. Everything's fine, I told myself. She got it out of her system. I dried myself off. She probably sent him to play outside, and she's cooling off, and everything's going to be okay. I ran a comb through my hair. Or she's on the floor, I thought, sobbing. Or she's gotten into Mommy's special candy again. I checked the mirror and told myself—for the millionth time—I was going to get back to the gym. For my back. I turned sideways, though, and thought, Jesus Christ. As soon as I'm back.

She only has safety razors, I thought as I let myself out into the hall. Maybe she's hyping herself up. Maybe she's getting ready for a matinee performance of *My life is over and nothing matters*. I listened, but I still didn't hear anything. And another part of me said, She knows how much this means to me. She has to know. She wouldn't fuck it up now.

Towel wrapped around my waist, I rapped on Chuy's door. He didn't respond, so I shouted, "Get your ass out of bed."

I dressed in my room. Jeans that were too tight. T-shirt that had shrunk in the wash. My luggage was already packed. As I pulled on socks and sneakers, I shouted, "Chuy, get up or we're going to be late!"

Still nothing. I hammered on his door again.

A cat yowled, and for a moment, I thought someone was screaming. The sound startled me. My heart pounded, and pins and needles ran down my body. As though on cue, my back tightened, and pain sparked. The damn cat was still going, the noise high-pitched and unrelenting. I made my way down the hall and knocked on Mom's door.

"I'm in the middle of something," Mom said breathily.

"Hurry up, or we're going to be late."

Mom said something too low for me to hear, and the boy toy laughed, and then Mom moaned.

We had an electric oven, otherwise I'd have opened up the gas and stuck my head inside. Maybe I could drink bleach, I thought. What was the right way to go out after hearing some Gen Z micropenis finger your mom?

You are so strange, said the voice that sounded like Augustus. *You are seriously so messed up.*

Don't I know it, I thought as I made my way across the living room. That horrible yowling scream was getting louder and louder, and I was starting to think it was inside the house. Another of Chuy's fuckups. Some stray he'd picked up while he was high, and I'd be the one who had to take it to the animal shelter. Or he'd left the back door open—that had happened more times than I could count—and a tom had wandered in. I had a vision of dragging Chuy out of bed, making him catch the damn thing and put it outside. But forcing Chuy to do anything always ended up taking more energy than doing it yourself, which was why—

I stopped in the opening to the kitchen.

On the table, in a car seat, a baby was screaming its head off.

3

The baby couldn't have been more than a couple of weeks old, with a tiny swatch of dark hair, and still with that old man look that newborns have. I remembered Augustus when he'd been that age, so small I'd been afraid to hold him, convinced that as soon as I picked him up, I'd drop him, and he'd break like an egg. I'd gotten over that pretty fast, but I'd never forgotten it. This baby was pinker than Augustus had been, and as the baby screamed, the pink deepened to red.

Not a cat, a distant part of my brain observed. Chuy had left the door open, and a baby had wandered in.

But that wasn't true, of course. The car seat. A diaper bag. Someone had brought this baby into the house. And then, apparently, left.

The infant's screams penetrated the fog in my head, and I looked around. Someone had to be here, right? Somebody this baby belonged to. I jogged to the windows in the living room, but there was nobody parked out front. I opened the back door and stuck my head out. Nothing. The baby was still screaming, and I raced the length of the house and threw open Chuy's door.

His bed was empty.

Drawers hung open, clothes spilling out of them.

I stared for a moment, as though Chuy might pop out and yell, *Surprise!* But this wasn't the first time he'd packed a bag and bolted, and I recognized the signs. He was gone. The piece of shit junkie motherfucker was gone. And he'd left a baby.

It was like something out of a fairy tale, out of those Golden Books I used to read Augustus. Or something out of a nightmare.

"Mom," I shouted, "I need you!"

She didn't answer, but maybe God was being merciful because the baby was screaming too loudly for me to hear whatever was happening inside her room.

The baby's desperate cries finally jarred me into action. Nobody was here. Nobody was going to do this but me. I went back to the kitchen. I unbuckled the car seat straps—I didn't remember Augustus's being this complicated, and it took me a few tries, but that also might have been because my hands were shaking. I got the baby out, caught a whiff of pee, and touched wet fabric. The plain white onesie was soaked through.

"Okay," I whispered as I shifted the baby to one arm. My body remembered this, the movement that was somewhere between rocking and bouncing as I pawed through the diaper bag with my free hand. "You're okay. Hey, somebody's got a good set of lungs."

Somebody was trying to puncture my ear drum.

By some miracle, the bag held not only a clean diaper and wipes but a bottle and a container of formula. Diaper first, I decided. I stripped the baby out of the onesie, tossed it on the floor, and threw the dirty diaper in the trash. That answered one question: the baby was a she. It took me a few fumbling tries to get the clean diaper on—I swear to God, they'd moved the little tape-tab things, because it definitely hadn't been this hard with Augustus—and then, for lack of anything better, wrapped her in a clean towel. She was screaming even harder now, if that was possible.

I heated water in the microwave and, somehow, got most of it into the bottle. I scooped. I measured. It was starting to come back to me, and I even screwed the top of the bottle into place one-handed. I shook it, and then I tested it against the inside of my arm. Maybe a little on the cool side, if anything. Better than burning her mouth.

When I brought the nipple to her lips, she let out a final, whimpering cry and took it into her mouth. Then she ate like an animal, still shaking now and then as the force of her crying slowly drained out of her body. I held the bottle, rocking her slowly as I walked around the kitchen. It was easier than I remembered; I'd been a lot smaller when it had been Augustus, and he'd felt heavy even when he'd been a newborn. This little girl hardly weighed anything. I'd need to burp her, I thought, but it was like thinking through a haze. And she'd need to sleep. How long had she been in that car seat, wet and hungry? How long had she been alone? How long since Chuy had put her there like a sack of groceries and then shoved his shit in a bag and run?

The click of a door opening made me step into the living room. The boy toy emerged from Mom's room first, his face and neck still flushed from his nut, a nineteen-year-old's cocky grin plastered across his face, the kind of look teenage boys have, like they invented fucking. He spotted me, and his grin widened. A mop of blond hair under a Dodgers snapback, a white T-shirt, black shorts. His Vans looked new, but like he'd tried to make them look well worn. "What up, Fer?"

I looked past him. "Mom, get out here."

"Yo, where's my hug at?" the boy toy asked as he came toward me.

"Fuck off. Mom!"

She appeared a moment later. Gabby Lopez was beautiful; she ought to have been, considering how much of my money she spent to look that way. Out of all of us, Augustus probably looked the most like her; the little turd had good luck that way. Today, she wore a green romper, and she bent to adjust one strappy sandal, one hand on the boy toy to steady herself. When she straightened, she said, "What is that?"

"It's a baby, Mom. You squirted three of them out of you, remember?"

The boy toy snickered. Mom gave me a look, and then one for the boy toy, and I wondered if he noticed how similar they were. "I meant, is it yours?"

"Yeah, it's mine. Surprise. My imaginary girlfriend and I couldn't wait to tell you."

"Thank God. We have enough mouths to feed already."

While I was still trying to figure out the *we* in that sentence, the boy toy said, "Bruh, babies are so dope."

"You'll be able to share toys," I said. "How's that fucking sound for dope?"

"Watch your language in front of the—" Mom apparently didn't want to say the word. Maybe she was worried it was a disease and she might catch one herself. I made a mental sign of the cross; I couldn't raise a second Augustus, I honestly couldn't.

"You know what?" The boy toy's eyes lit up. "You could, like, totally get a girlfriend with that baby. Bruh, then she wouldn't be imaginary!"

I opened my mouth to tell him what I thought of that particular brainfuck, but before I could, Mom said, "Cannon, my suitcases are so heavy."

"I'll get them!"

With zero regard for the fact that I had to witness it, the two of them gave each other a tongue bath. When they finally separated, Mom moved over to a mirror and touched up her lipstick.

"My suitcases are so heavy," I said.

Mom made a dismissive noise. "He likes having something to do. Honestly, it's a bit refreshing; his mother raised him right. I wish my own children were more like Cannon."

"Sure, those three darling children you raised yourself: Bookshelf, Doorknob, and Wonder Bread. Mom, what the fuck are we going to do?"

She gave me wide-eyed dismay. "Well, I don't know."

"Someone has to stay here and deal with this, and it's not going to be me."

"I can't cancel my trip, Fernando. The reservations are non-refundable."

"Who cares? I paid for it. I'm telling you that as soon as I can get an Uber, I'm going to the airport, and I'm going to see Augustus."

"No, dear, Chuy is driving us."

"Chuy is gone!" It was a whisper-shout, one I barely managed to tamp down. "And he left us a fucking baby!"

The baby fussed, and I started rocking her again.

Mom cooed a little and came over and touched the baby's head. "See? You're a natural."

"No. No way. I haven't had a vacation, a real vacation, in years, because I've spent every minute either getting Augustus to college or from college or keeping him alive while he was at college. And I deserve a break. I deserve some time to myself. I am not going to be saddled with this." I held the baby out in demonstration.

"But you're only going to see August again. And you can go see him anytime, and we got such a good deal at the Bellagio, and you don't know how hard it is to get into this little spa I found. Why don't you call human services?"

"What the fuck is human services?"

"Call the police then."

"No, you are—"

"I don't see why I should be the one who stays."

In a strangled whisper, I managed, "Because you're this child's grandmother."

"Fernando!" She glanced at the hallway. "Keep your voice down. And anyway, we don't know that. Not for a fact."

Cannon chose that moment to stagger out into the hall, only to immediately get jammed when he tried to roll two full-sized suitcases through the doorway at the same time. He tried again. And then he tried a third time, making straining noises.

A hint of a blush rose in Mom's cheeks, and she murmured, "He's a tad enthusiastic."

"I heard him being enthusiastic at three in the fucking morning. Dumbass! One at a time!"

Sure enough, Cannon got one of the suitcases through the door. He laughed and said, "No way."

"Either you call them and cancel," I said, "or I will. I am not giving up my vacation."

The first changes were so small that it was hard to name them: the softening around her mouth and eyes, a slackness in her cheeks. Then she blinked rapidly. Turned her head away. Her eyes shimmered.

"Not going to work," I said. "Augustus is gone, and I've got zero fucks left to give. I'm sure boy toy will help you unpack."

The boy toy in question had gotten himself jammed again in the hallway because, again, he was trying to wheel the suitcases side-by-side.

"All right," Mom said. She caught a tear before it could fall and stared at it on her finger. "All right. You're right."

"You're goddamn fucking right I am."

"I'm sorry we make your life so hard, Fernando. I'm sorry we've always been a burden for you." She touched her eyes again. "I want you to be happy. You deserve to be happy; you've sacrificed so much for this family."

The baby fussed some more, and I held her to my chest. Her little head settled on my shoulder, and she made a noise that told me I'd need to invest in some burp cloths sooner rather than later.

"And you're right: you deserve to have a vacation. That's something I can give you." Her voice was thick as she added, "My perfect, perfect son. I don't know where any of us would be without you." She kissed my cheek. "Cannon, take those bags back into my room, please. We've got a change of plans."

Somehow, she unwedged the jackass, turned him around, and got him moving again. I carried the baby into the kitchen, bouncing her slowly. Her breath was soft against my neck, and she had that newborn smell I'd forgotten. She was so little. And I remembered how it had been, Augustus crying for a bottle because Mom was too busy rehearsing or doing her makeup or talking to a "friend." One time, she had lined a laundry basket with a clean blanket and put him in the closet. She had been doing her scales, I remembered tiredly. My back was tight as a motherfucker as I rocked the baby against me. That was when she was going to be a singer.

I dug out my phone, looking out the window at the deck, the haze of pollution over the valley, the hard little tin-stamped city. Lots of people wanted to be actors, I thought as I typed out the text to Augustus. Lots of people wanted to be singers. And somehow, the world kept turning.

Something came up, I wrote. *Change of plans.*

4

Two days later, I was late for an appointment, and the nanny still hadn't shown up.

More importantly, the baby was crying.

Those two days had flown by. Mom and Cannon were, according to her texts and, more importantly, my credit card bill, having a fantastic time in Vegas. I'd spent those days trying to (in no particular order) get settled with the baby, reschedule appointments and meetings, and find my junkie brother so that I could, once and for all, murder him myself.

It had been twenty-five years since Augustus had been an infant, and apparently, a lot had changed. Part of that was probably the fact that I was an adult, that I could go to stores and see what there was to buy—we'd never had money growing up, and basically everything Augustus had was either a hand-me-down from me or Chuy, or something a neighbor or friend had given us. It was eye-opening (maybe a better word would be ball-shattering) to walk down aisle after aisle of expensive strollers and car seats and pumps and swings and diapers and formula. Everything looked and sounded great—and was seriously fucking expensive. It was overwhelming. I caught myself in a kind of fugue state, stalled out in the car seat aisle, reading the specs on the tags and comparing crotch buckle depths (great name for a band, or for the next time I needed to yank Augustus's chain), when I finally realized I was in over my head.

That first day, I bought pretty much everything I could put my hands on: diapers, of course; my weight in wipes; some clothes (those I got off the clearance rack—they had about eighteen of these hot dog onesies, and I bought all of them); a crib; crib sheets; blankets (I refused to call them blankies like the woman at the register); a baby monitor; a waterproof changing pad; a sleep sack, which was apparently a straitjacket for babies; bottles; a bottle brush; a bottle drying rack; baby wash; baby shampoo; a baby tub; baby nail scissors; burp cloths (I'd needed them, desperately, the day before); and so much goddamn formula.

I could return all of it, I figured, once I tracked down Chuy and found the baby's mother.

The rest of that day, I moved or canceled all of my appointments, and I spent the time putting together the crib, figuring out the car seat (okay, figuring out *both* of the car seats—I bought an extra because the crotch buckle thing threw me), and reacquainting myself with the types and quantity of things that come out of babies. She had three blowouts, I shit you not. No pun intended.

I'd forgotten about the nights. I swear to Jesus Christ himself, every forty-five minutes she woke up again. She didn't want to eat every time. She wanted to be awake. And have me be awake. Every. Forty-five. Minutes.

But even with the brain fog, day two was actually easier. Things started to click, my body (and my brain) remembering little things that had worked with Augustus—how he'd liked to be rocked, or the best way to burp him (honestly, trying to replicate any of Neil Peart's drum solos worked like a charm), or the fact that sometimes babies were fussy and nothing you did would make them stop crying. I remembered the blessedness of naps, and we shared a few of those. And, of course, I spent a lot of time on my phone, reading, because I realized that there were probably some better ways to take care of a child than whatever an eight-year-old had cobbled together. I also spent a lot of time on the phone, trying to get a nanny, which turned out to be harder than expected. I ended up having to agree to an outrageous service charge ("rush processing" like I was calling QVC, for fuck's sake), but it was worth it, because I had to get back to life.

The next night, she only woke me up three times, which I considered a win.

Only now it was the morning of the third day, and the nanny still wasn't here.

I changed the baby. I got her dressed and fed. I burped her, and only after I was sure I'd cleared the danger zone did I jump in the shower and get ready for work. She watched me from the floor as I buttoned up my shirt.

"You've got your dad's eyes," I said as I scooped her up. "Let's hope that's all you got from that miserable son of a bitch, huh?"

She fit right in the crook of my arm, which was perfect for pacing and looking out the window and, every five minutes, calling the nannying agency and getting a busy signal.

I was getting ready to call Dr. Phan and cancel (which would be better, in the long run, than not showing up) when a knock came at the door. I threw it open, a few choice words already rising in my throat. I was pretty sure that ripping someone a new asshole and then entrusting them with a child wasn't the best course to follow, but that advice occupied a small part of my brain in the moment.

Then I forgot what I was going to say because a dude was standing on the doorstep. He had surfer hair—windswept, dark except where the sun had lightened it, a perfectly tousled mess of texture that was long enough to cover the tops of his ears. He was tall and well-proportioned, athletic, but toned instead of bulky. Almost as dark as I was, I thought, but I couldn't tell how much of that was the sun. In the cool of the April morning, he wore a Baja jacket and board shorts, and where the shorts hit him at the knee, I could see an angry red scar.

"Hi," he said, a hint of an accent that marked him, for me, as Latin. "My name is—"

"Don't care," I said and pushed the baby into his arms. "I'll be home by five. She just ate. You should have everything you need, but if you think of something—" I checked the curb and saw a weathered Buick LeSabre (maroon). Its tires were bald, and paint was peeling off the hood, and something about the car, even motionless, suggested the possibility of sudden and complete spontaneous combustion. "—get it delivered, and I'll reimburse you. Phone number is on the fridge. Call me if there's an emergency."

He stared at me, and I figured he fell into the same category as most boy toys: pretty and a bit touched in the head. But he was rocking the baby, and he seemed to know how to hold her, and the agency had sent him.

"Mister—"

I checked my phone; I could still make the appointment with Dr. Phan if I drove like Satan was eating my ass. I sprinted toward the garage and called back, "Only if it's an emergency!"

The last thing I saw when I looked back was the nanny—I guess they called them mannies—standing on the porch, cradling the baby and staring after me. Well, there was a reason he was a manny, I decided. A bit simple. And maybe he was only a temp.

On the drive out of our neighborhood, something felt off. The Escalade was too quiet, so I turned on the radio, got a talk station with what sounded like a man shouting inside a phone booth, and turned it off again. I tried Spotify, and because Augustus wasn't within a hundred miles of me and my back was bitching at me and I'd had my life turned upside down and gotten approximately twenty-seven minutes of sleep over the last three days, I put on Destiny's Child. The sky was a wide, clear plate of blue, and the day would be dry and mild. Relax, I told myself. Relax. You don't have a baby to feed or change or snuggle. You don't have laundry to do. (My God, how many clothes and towels and blankies—blankets—could one child go through?) You don't have anyone to take care of except you. So, relax.

But then I hit the dregs of morning traffic, cars piling up ahead of me, some jackass trying to shoehorn himself in. The sun off the glass started to give me a headache, and the Escalade was too hot now, so I buzzed the window down and fought a wave of nausea.

What the fuck, I thought, was wrong with me?

I'd shoved the baby into the arms of a total stranger. I'd run off like a maniac—why? To keep an appointment with a doctor who was, admittedly, nice, and who had also told me she had no intention of buying from me?

Not a total stranger, I argued with myself. Not some rando off the street. The agency vetted him. Approved him. Trained him. He'd looked comfortable with the baby in his arms. Not quite all there, maybe, but he didn't have to be a rocket scientist. He had to be careful with her, make sure she was changed, fed, warm, safe.

A call came in on the Escalade's system.

"Mr. Lopez? This is Brigitta with Not So Nanny. I am so sorry we missed your call."

"It's fine," I said. "It all worked out."

"I'm so happy to hear that. Now, I know we weren't able to accommodate your needs today, but I do have Zora lined up for the end of the month, and if it's a good fit, I believe she'll be interested in discussing the possibility of a long-term arrangement."

My brain cycled around Zora. Does she wear a mask? That was a knee-jerk thought, the kind of dumb joke that would have made Augustus groan. And then the rest of that sentence freight-trained through my head.

"What do you mean?"

"Well, typically a nanny likes to meet a family before committing—"

"What do you mean you weren't able to accommodate—what do you mean? He's there. He's there right now."

She made a vexed little noise. "I'm sorry, but I don't see anything on your paperwork. Let me put you on hold."

He'd rung the doorbell. He'd rung the fucking doorbell, and I'd—

The way he'd stared when I'd put the baby in his arms.

The way he'd tried to say something.

A rash of sweat broke out across my forehead, my face, my chest. I spun the wheel and whipped the Escalade around.

5

The drive home, parking, running into the house—they were all a blur. I was distantly aware of the flush of heat roaring through my body, the way my hands trembled, how far off the house seemed, like I was seeing it through a telescope. I had to try twice to get the key in the lock. Then the door swung open, and I stared.

He—whoever he was—was sitting on the couch, rocking the baby in his arms as he sang quietly to her. He glanced up at me, and some of that tumbling mass of hair hung in his eyes, but he didn't speak. He turned his attention back to the baby, still singing. It wasn't Spanish. Portuguese, maybe; it had the sound of Portuguese, anyway.

The song ended. With a grunt, he scooted forward on the sofa, shifted the baby to one arm, and used his free hand to get to his feet. He glanced at me again and then down at the baby. She was asleep, her tiny chest rising and falling slowly. When I held out my hands, he passed her to me, and I carried her into her room—Augustus's room—and laid her in her crib.

He was standing by the door when I got back to the living room. I stared at him, trying to think of what to say. How to explain. To myself as much as to him. The exhaustion. The desperation. The brain fog.

But before I could put words together, the rush of adrenaline faded, and exhaustion rolled in. I rubbed my eyes, and a yawn caught me. That made him smile, but it was gone again in an instant.

And instead of anything I'd planned, what I said was "Holy Christ, I need a beer."

"It's nine o'clock in the morning." The words were quiet and held that faint accent I'd heard the first time.

"You're right. I need to smoke." I found my vape and hit it. The spiky, earthy taste filled my mouth, and I held the vapor in my lungs for as long as I could before I blew it out again. I held the vape out to him, and he shook his head.

"I don't think you should do that. Not in the house. Not with the baby."

I scratched my eyebrow. "No," I said, and a laugh unraveled inside me. "No, I guess I shouldn't."

And then it all hit me at once: Mom and Cannon and Chuy, the surprise of finding the baby, the disappointment, yet again, of giving in and giving up. The exhaustion of the last couple of days, the fog inside my head, the memory of standing there, staring at the two different car seats, trying to make a decision and wanting to cry because my brain seemed to have shut off. Everything from this morning, from the moment I'd opened the door and seen him standing there, and how badly I'd screwed up. I remembered being eight years old and Augustus wouldn't stop screaming and I didn't know what to do.

"So," I somehow managed to say. "You're not the nanny."

He shook his head.

That ought to have made me laugh. "I thought—" But I had to stop because my throat tightened. I fought to get the words free. "I thought, you know—" I had to stop again, and I choked the last words out. "Wow, I am really fucking everything up today."

He stared at me. He shifted his weight. I blinked to keep the tears from spilling. Tears, I had learned a long time ago, didn't help.

The weed started to hit me, and that helped. The familiar waves of warmth rolled through me, and I could feel myself getting heavier, like my body was more solid. When I had myself under control again, I managed a rough "All right" and cleared my throat. "I'm sorry about that. About all of this. I'll, uh, pay you for your time."

He pushed back some of his hair, and his lips curved in a half-smile. "It looks like you need help."

I barked a laugh. "I bet."

"When was the last time you got some sleep?"

"Does it count if it's when I'm in the shower?"

This time, I got the full smile, unrolling lazily across his face. "When was the last time you ate something that didn't come out of the microwave?" He must have seen the question on my face because he shrugged. "I looked in the fridge."

I shook my head.

"Come on," he said. "I'll make you something."

"Huh?"

"You need to eat something."

"No. You don't—huh?"

Hands on my shoulders, the touch light but confident, he steered me into the kitchen. After settling me in a seat at the table, he went to the fridge. He didn't limp, not exactly, but each step seemed cautious. He rummaged around and came up with the bag of kale Mom used for her smoothies, some of those precooked strips of chicken Mom keeps around the house when she goes keto, and a bottle of lemon juice.

"Olive oil?"

"You don't have to make me something to eat. I'm fine."

He waited.

Eventually, I pointed.

After washing his hands, he went to work. He stripped the kale, and then he added olive oil and salt. He worked each piece of kale between his fingers. He had strong hands, the knuckles defined and prominent, and the oil glistened on his skin.

"What are you doing?"

"Massaging the kale."

"Why?"

"Because it's worked hard all week."

"Ha."

A smile turned the corner of his mouth as he continued to work. "It breaks down some of the fibers, makes it tender. And less bitter."

I didn't know what to say to that.

When he finished with the kale, he washed his hands again. The sound of the water was pleasant, but it felt startling loud after nothing but the scrape of the bowl across the counter and the rustle of the kale between his fingers. He added some of the precooked chicken. Then lemon juice. Then more salt.

"It's better if the lemon is fresh," he said as he brought the bowl over to the table.

I took a bite. The lemon juice was a bright note against the richness of the olive oil, and although the kale was still bitter—he'd said less bitter, I reminded myself—it still tasted better than any kale I normally ate. The chicken tasted like refrigerator chicken, and all in all, it wasn't a masterpiece of culinary invention. But it tasted clean, if that made any sense, and the simplicity was actually part of what made it so good. It probably didn't hurt that the weed was working now—I wasn't high, or not very, but every bite tasted so goddamn good.

Before I had time to feel awkward about eating in front of a total stranger, I had finished. At some point when I'd been devouring the salad, he'd sat at the table, and now he had his phone out and was looking at it.

"Thank you."

He looked up and reached for the bowl.

"I'll wash it," I said.

"I don't mind."

I gripped the bowl. "No." And then I forced myself to add, "Thank you."

We sat there, silence filling up the space between us. I was full of salad (which was strange, considering it wasn't even ten yet), and my body was clearly appreciating the protein and veggies, because I felt like I could put my head down and sleep for a week. The weed probably wasn't hurting either. And he sat there, looking at me, not saying anything.

"Who are you?"

"Zé Teixeira. Well, José, but I go by Zé."

"Why did you knock on my door this morning?"

His jaw tightened, and he looked at the floor. "I go door to door." And then, in a rush, "Offering massages."

"What, like the kale?"

His eyes came up.

I arched my eyebrows.

After a moment, a wry smile touched his mouth.

"For real?" I asked. "Door-to-door massages? Do you get a lot of customers at eight-thirty in the morning?"

"You'd be surprised," he said drily. "Can't start much earlier or the husbands are home."

I raised an eyebrow.

A blush caught fire under the dark brown skin. "Oh God, no, that's not what I meant."

"Uh huh."

"No, I promise." His blush deepened. "I'm gay."

The pause was interesting, like he was building himself up to it. And the fact that it made him blush. This was southern California, and nobody cared if you were gay. They cared if you were ugly, and that definitely wasn't this guy's problem.

I gave him another look; now that I had some food in me, I felt like I was thinking clearly. Or more clearly, anyway. The board shorts had been expensive once, but they looked well worn. Same with the Baja jacket. He wore Hurley slides that were starting to crack along the sides. His feet were like his hands: big, masculine, strong. So, either he didn't care about appearances (a possibility), or he didn't have money. I thought about the beater he was driving. And I thought about the fact that he didn't have a massage table, didn't have a flyer or a business card to leave with prospective clients, about the fact that he was going door to door even though he'd clearly had some sort of surgery to his knee. All of which meant he was broke.

The baby started to cry. Zé pushed back his chair, but I waved for him to sit. I put the bowl in the sink and made my way to the baby's room. She was unhappy about being wet, she told me—loudly—so I changed her. I rocked her for a few minutes in case she was ready to go back to sleep, but she kept crying.

"She might be hungry," Zé said from the doorway.

"She's always hungry."

But we made our way back to the kitchen, and he sat again, wincing slightly as he stretched out his leg. He held out his hands, and after a moment of consideration, I passed him the baby. It would be easier to make the bottle while I wasn't holding her, and—

And she stopped crying. Immediately.

"You son of a bitch," I said. "What did you do?"

Zé wasn't doing anything, as far as I could tell. He held her in the crook of one arm, her face resting against his chest. Looking up, he let out a quiet laugh.

"I'm serious. What the fuck kind of bullshit is this?"

He covered her ear with his free hand. "You can't talk like that around a baby."

"Fuck that. Trust me, she's heard worse. How did you make her stop crying?"

"I didn't make her stop crying," Zé said. He rocked her slowly. "She just stopped."

"Because you're holding her."

I got the full smile again. Almost a smirk.

"Fuck that," I said again. "That is so fucking unfair."

"Don't worry," he said softly, combing her hair with one finger. "She still loves her dad." The grin flashed out again. "She just happens to also have great taste in men."

"I'm not her dad," I said. "She's my brother's. I think. It's a long story."

Zé was quiet for what felt like a long time before he said, "You're taking care of her. I think that makes you her dad in any way that counts."

"It makes me a sucker, that's what it makes me."

He looked at me, and I couldn't read whatever was written in his eyes, so I turned my back on him and got the water running.

"You thought I was a babysitter," Zé said.

"A nanny. Uh, manny. Look, I'm sorry. And I will pay you."

"I have two younger sisters." The words burst out of him. "And a younger brother. I know how to take care of babies."

I turned around.

It was another new expression, a strange mixture of defiance and—what? Vulnerability? Fear? "I could take care of her."

"Are you licensed?"

"Nannies don't have to be licensed in California." Some of that dark ruddiness came into his cheeks again. "I checked."

"Are you a serial killer?"

He didn't seem like the eye-rolling type, but he was clearly tempted. "And you need the help. You can't do everything yourself."

I opened my mouth, and then I closed it again.

He wasn't wrong about that; the thought of reliving the last three days made me want to run into traffic. And while part of me knew that I could, in theory, do this—there were single parents all over the world who did this—another part of me realized that most of those people managed because they had some kind of support system. And what did I have? Chuy was gone, and even if he was here, I wouldn't trust him alone with an infant.

Mom would be gone for at least a week, and I still had a vivid memory of when Augustus, who was crawling, pulled her curling iron off the counter. The nanny service wouldn't be able to provide anyone until the end of the month, and that's assuming whoever they found was willing to take a long-term position with me. Zé, at least, seemed unfazed by my particular brand of crazy.

You already left her alone with him, I thought, and what did he do? He got her ready for her nap, like you told him. He rocked her. He sang to her. She wouldn't stop crying until he held her again. And he was worried about you. He made you a salad. When was the last time anyone did anything for you?

"Please," Zé said, his voice small. His shoulders curved in, and he looked as tired as I felt. With something like a start, I realized he was young. He might not have been any older than Augustus. He must have taken the silence as a negative, and it was like a cloud moving across his face. His voice was stiff, as though he were fighting for every word. "I need this."

I thought about how early he must have gotten up so he could drive out here from wherever he lived. About going door to door. Making his pitch over and over again. And, if they said yes, the casual humiliations. He was handsome. Plenty of people would expect more than a massage. I thought about what I'd want someone to do if it were Augustus.

"You have to pass a background check."

"Yes." His voice was husky with emotion. "Of course."

"Fingerprints, the whole deal."

"I can do that. I've never been arrested. I'll pass. I promise I'll pass."

"Drugs?"

"Huh? Oh, no. I don't use anything."

"Not even weed?"

"You offered me a vape."

"I asked you a question."

"No, not even weed."

"A Xanax you got from your friend, and it's only this once, and you need it to calm down. You never do addies, but you're so tired, and so this one time it'll be okay. You hurt your back, and your mom never finished her pain pills from when she had surgery."

He shook his head. "I don't use any drugs."

"I'm serious, Zé. If you're on a prescription, we can talk about it, but otherwise I do not want that shit in my house. I don't want any connection to that shit. It's bad enough my brother—" But I stopped myself. "This is your last chance."

His face was hard, and I realized, with a kind of shock, how much I'd pressed him. "I don't use."

"All right. Then we'll see about the background check." I didn't know how to do one myself, but I knew someone who did. "I can pay you twenty dollars an hour, and I'd need you here from eight to five on weekdays."

His jaw sagged. And then, maybe because he didn't have anywhere else for the emotion to go, he hugged the baby to him and nodded as a tear slid down his cheek. He shouldered it away. He was smiling, and he didn't seem to know it, and somehow, that made the smile go through me like an arrow.

"Thank you. Thank you. I'm going to take such good care of—"

He hesitated and looked up at me.

I stroked the baby's hair, and my fingers brushed his. I didn't mean to say it; a part of me knew I was making a mistake. But the words slipped out anyway. "Isabela. It was my grandmother's name."

6

"You look like shit," Lou said when I got out of the Escalade.

She was a big woman, as tall as me and barreled with muscle, and she wore her dark hair chopped short. The ends of it bristled out from under a John Deere hat. When her mother had named her Lourdes, she'd probably been hoping for good little Catholic girl, maybe even one who would grow up to be a nun. Which goes to show that it's stupid to hope for things, especially when other people are involved.

Leaning on a wheelbarrow, Lou gave me a closer look as she pulled off her gloves. We'd known each other in college, and we'd stayed in touch even though we'd taken different paths. I'd finished my degree via night classes as soon as I got a job. She, on the other hand, now ran one of the largest grows in the county—acres of hoop houses lined up one next to each other, each of them full of cannabis, until the fields gave way to scrub and stunted, dusty pines. The air held the muskiness of the crop, mixed with a dark, loamy earthiness. Near the road, a massive steel framework mounted on a concrete foundation told me that Lou's plans for an indoor grow facility were underway.

"Look who's talking," I said. "Dakota lets you out of the house like that? Dressed like Paul Bunyan about to go fuck Babe?"

"Dakota's visiting her mom, and fuck you, and what the fuck happened to you?"

"Long story," I said. "What the fuck are you waiting for? I'm fucking starving."

"Fuck off. Fucking pansy-ass wearing your fucking white Lacoste tennis shoes to a fucking farm like a fucking idiot."

I mimed jerking off.

"Yeah," she said as she pushed off with the wheelbarrow. "You're a pro at that."

I almost laughed, but that would have ruined everything.

She headed for the barn, and I made my way to the house. It was frame, white clapboard, and built sometime in the 1930s. To hear Lou tell it, the first farm, all the way back when somebody had first broken open the ground and started working this land, had been hemp. She liked telling people that. Wouldn't shut up about it, in fact. Particularly the part about how now a couple of lesbians were making a fortune with a legal grow.

Boards creaked as I went up onto the porch. The door was heavy and had a tendency to stick in the frame, and inside, the house was clean, but old lady curtains and a lot of junk made the place feel small and dark. Part of that was the old-fashioned layout, with lots of little rooms. And part of it was the fact that Lou was basically a hoarder, but she specialized in literally anything she thought she might use to fix something on the farm. One room was full of two-liter bottles she'd saved, don't ask me why.

The kitchen, though, had the curtains open, and the window looked out on all that beautiful grass. The linoleum was worn down to the backing, and the furniture looked like it was as old as the house (even the refrigerator looked like it predated Eisenhower). But the room was full of light, and it smelled like curry and pepper and cauliflower.

Lou's heavy footsteps announced her passage through the house.

"Dakota's going to kill you for wearing your boots inside," I said.

With a grunt, Lou moved past me and got two mason jars full of cold water from the fridge. She handed me one, opened hers, and drank deeply.

"You know, it's a real fucking shame that the only people I know with literally unlimited weed happen to be a couple of vegan lesbians who won't even keep beer in the house."

"And it's a real fucking shame you've got a gut and you're losing your hair and you smell like snatch from eating out doctors all day," Lou said. "Life's full of disappointments."

"One day, Dakota's going to run you over with the baler, and I'm going to help her get rid of the body."

"What are you going to do, princess? Paint her nails for her?"

The smile slipped out before I could stop it. Lou didn't smile back, not exactly, but her eyes crinkled at the corners. She pointed to a seat, and I sat, and she went to work: pulling dishes out of the refrigerator, lighting the ancient gas stove (which still required a match), dropping a pad of vegan butter in the skillet. It hissed, and a moment later, garlic followed.

Lunch with Lou was a standing appointment. We saw each other once a month. I reminded her that human beings bathed more than once a week and that she might want to scrape the shit out from under her nails before fingering her lovely wife. And she had all sorts of pleasant things to say about my personality. In the craziness after Isabela had appeared, I'd forgotten about the appointment, but once Zé came into the picture, well, things had changed.

"What's wrong?" Lou asked. "Where'd you stick your dick? And how long are you going to be on antibiotics?"

"Real fucking classy."

"Is it the drip?"

"Yeah, it's the fucking drip."

Tofu sizzled when she dropped it into the pan. Then she turned around and folded her arms.

"It's Chuy," I said, slumping in the chair. "It's a fucking mess."

When I finished telling her everything, she said, "You need to go to the police."

"I thought about that."

"Then why didn't you? Because in case I misunderstood something, there's a baby in your house, and you don't know who it belongs to."

"Chuy—"

"He's a junkie! For all you know, he stole that child so he could trade her for a score!"

Lou moved the pan around on the stove, attacking the tofu with a turner. The only sounds were the scrape of metal on metal and the occasional sizzle and sputter.

"I'm worried," she said in a softer voice. "About you."

"The baby is his."

Lou shook her head as she worked the pan back and forth over the flame.

"She's his," I said. "And I'm not going to abandon her."

"Of course you're not. That's the whole problem."

"What do you want me to do, Lou? Put her with some foster family?"

"She has a mother, dumbass."

"Yeah, what a great fucking mother."

"You don't know the first thing about her."

"Neither do you! But I know Chuy, and even though Chuy is a fuckup in about every way that counts, he wouldn't hurt a child. Especially not his child. He brought that baby home for a reason."

"Yes." Lou turned around fast, waving the turner at me. "Because he knew this is exactly what would happen."

"Don't start with that."

"Every fucking time, Fernando."

"I said don't start."

"You've been cleaning up his messes since you were twelve years old."

"Somebody has to."

"Yeah? How's that working out?"

"What the fuck was I supposed to do? Leave her on the table crying? You talk this big fucking game about tough love and consequences and all that bullshit, but tell me what the fuck you would have done if it'd been you."

She pulled the pan from the stove, and the only sound was the hiss of the gas feeding the burner. She turned that off. Then it was silent.

"Where's your mom?"

"Playing reverse cowgirl in Vegas."

"Jesus, Fer."

I shrugged.

"I'm about to eat," Lou said.

"You told me my mom is hot. I'm the one who was scarred for life."

"Your mom is hot. I still don't want to picture straight-people sex."

She pulled down plates and served the food. The tofu had some sort of chili-maple glaze, and we ate it with a cabbage salad that was crisp and cold from the refrigerator. For a while, our forks and knives clinked against the plates.

Then, in a different voice, she said again, "I'm worried about you."

"I'm a big boy."

She snorted. "Remember when you blasted that dick pic to the whole class?"

"I didn't—"

"I guess big is a relative term. What are we talking? Big compared to those little swinging peanuts?"

"That wasn't my dick! And that was Robbie's idea of a fucking hilarious prank!" I tried to stop. "And the angle on that picture was terrible!"

"The little head was so cute. It had a lot of personality."

I stared at her. "This is why I'm so fucked up. This is what Augustus is always yammering about. It's because of you. Why do I ever talk to you?"

"Because I give you free weed."

"There is that."

The rest of the meal passed more easily, and as I carried the dishes to the sink, Lou asked, "So, what are you going to do?"

"I don't know. I've got something. Maybe. A nanny."

"How big are her tits?"

"For fuck's sake, Lou."

"I'm asking." She cupped her chest. "Stop me when I get there."

"I have other friends. I have other people who I can talk to about things."

Her hands were still moving. "Wait, seriously? Tell me when I—Fer, Jesus, you're kidding me. There's no way—"

"I can pay for weed. That's what I should start doing. I have a job. I'll buy some."

"I'm starting over. Are we talking apples? Cantaloupes?"

"He's a guy, dumbshit."

Lou grimaced. "Come on. First you tell me about this super-hot nanny with giant tits—"

"I never said that!"

"—and now all of a sudden he's a dude. What's wrong with him?"

"What?"

"Is he gay?"

"Wait, hold on."

"I knew it. 'Oh Fernando, I keep dropping everything.'" She mimed bending over. "Oh Fernando, help me. Oh Fernando, if it slips in on accident, it's not gay."

"How can you literally be the most homophobic person I've ever met?"

Another snort. "I heard you on the phone with Augustus last time you were here. I think the phrase was 'Cum-drunk monkey slut' and there was something about getting stuck on Theo's knob."

"Yeah, but that's okay. That's Augustus."

"Is he cute?"

"No, Augustus looks like a Mack truck collided with a camel's vagina."

"The manny, shit-for-brains."

I stressed each word. "He's a guy."

"I know. I heard you." She gave me a considering look. "Why him?"

"Well, he's the only candidate, so he's got that going for him. Oh, and Isabela is already obsessed with him. And he watched her while I slept for four hours yesterday, and I swear to God, it was better than sex."

An expression I couldn't name flickered in Lou's face when I named Isabela, but all she said was "If that's not an exaggeration, something is wrong with your dick."

"He even made dinner and straightened up the house."

That same expression darted across Lou's face again. "So, what's the problem?"

"I need to run a background check."

"Easy."

"Seriously? You'll do that?"

"We do background checks on everyone we hire. Get him up here, and we'll do it. I'm not letting some pervert jack off in my niece's crib."

I pressed my thumbs against my eyes. "Jesus Christ."

"That was only an example."

"No more lesbians. I'm going to find a lot of straight guys. Probably white guys. Bros."

"Yeah," Lou said, "that'll work out great."

The conversation shifted to the grow, and as usual, I was impressed. Lou's operation was growing steadily, which made sense—she'd known what she wanted to do since we were in college, and as soon as California legalized cannabis, she'd poured everything into the farm. After updating me on the new strains she was trying, as well as loading me down with enough to get me through the month, Lou walked me to the Escalade. The breeze rippled the poly of the hoop houses, and it snapped and rustled as the familiar, musky scent filled my nose.

I almost made it out alive.

"What's going on with Bea?" Lou asked when we were ten feet from the SUV.

Only ten feet. I could make it.

"You piece of shit," Lou said.

"Give me a fucking break!"

"You didn't text her."

"Things came up."

"You promised me you were going to text her. I told her you were going to text her."

"I had a baby dropped into my lap. My universe imploded. I'm so fucking sorry for not texting your friend."

"That was this week. It's been four weeks, Fer—what happened the other three?"

"Believe it or not, I'm busy."

"Sitting in front of the TV every night after work?" Lou asked. "Getting loaded in your underwear?"

"I have a life. I go out with friends. I go mountain biking."

"You go out with friends," she said in disgust. "When do you go mountain biking?

"Well, not since I hurt my back."

"Are you for real right now? I'm trying to help you. You're fucking miserable in that house, spending every minute being a fucking clean-up boy for those two human disasters—" Lou stopped, but too late. Some of the color left her face, but she managed to hold my eye as she mumbled, "Sorry."

I opened the Escalade's door.

"Fer, come on," she said. "I'm sorry. We want you to be happy."

"Hey, look at that—turns out, I'm fucking ecstatic."

"It's—" Indecision made her voice waver, and then she burst out, "Aren't you lonely?"

"You don't understand," I said. "And I don't need you to understand. But I do need you to keep your fucking opinions to yourself."

"Fer."

I almost said, They need me. I almost said, I have to search Mom's room after every breakup. I almost said, Chuy got stabbed, did you know that? And who had to change the bandages and drive him to the doctor and get his prescriptions refilled? I almost said, When? When was I supposed to walk away? When I started college, and Augustus hadn't even hit middle school? And I wanted to say, How? I don't know how.

But, softening my voice, I said, "It was nice of you and Dakota to try to set me up. I'll text her. What's her name? Betty?"

Lou's eyes were shiny with tears, but she said, "You are an asshole."

I got behind the wheel. "We're, uh, still on, right? The job, I mean."

"We're still straightening everything out. A couple of guys on the senior leadership team are dragging their heels." Maybe she saw the worry on my face because she added, "It's going to happen, Fer. I might need you to schmooze a little, help them realize you're perfect for this. Everybody will be here in a few weeks for some meetings, and I want you to get some face time."

"I can do that."

"I know you can. Make sure you clean the shit off your nose."

I opened my mouth to—well, *fuck you* wasn't technically a way of saying thanks—but my phone buzzed. I took it out of my pocket. A message from Zé. It was a picture of Isabela propped against the sofa in one of the clearance onesies I'd picked up—one of the hot dog ones. The text said, *Igz misses you.*

Igz, I thought, staring at that tiny, old man face and the little tuft of black hair.

Then I texted, *That is the stupidest nickname I've ever heard.*

Another picture came through in response: a photo of Zé holding Igz—God, it sounded absolutely awful, but now it was stuck in my head. He'd used some kind of filter, and they both had big, bushy black mustaches.

When I looked up, Lou was watching me, and I realized I was smiling.

"What?" I asked.

In a thoughtful voice, she said, "Have I ever told you that you're an idiot?"

7

"Dinner is on the table," Zé said as he grabbed his keys. "And Igz had a bottle right before you got home."

The last part, I probably could have figured out on my own. Igz—Isabela—had a dreamy look on her face that told me she was deep in a milk coma. She lay against my chest, breathing softly and slowly. She fit there. Everything, it seemed was starting to fit. Zé, in his Quiksilver tee (so old that the collar was frayed and there was a hole under one arm) and his board shorts and the same cracking Hurley slides, fit. What had seemed like pure chaos not so long ago was now routine.

Over the last couple weeks, everything had started to come together. Zé's background check had come back clear, like he'd promised. He'd started watching the baby full time, and true to his word, he arrived on time every morning, and from what I could tell, was doing a great job. Igz—Isabela—was happy (and obsessed with him), the house was cleaner than it had been in a long time, and more often than not, he made something for dinner before he left. He didn't have to do that; I'd told him that more than once. But he nodded, agreed, and then did it anyway. We'd even made it through our first doctor's appointment together (Zé had gone along for moral support), and Igz (God damn it: Isabela) had come through with flying colors.

Along the way, I'd started to learn more about the guy who was currently the second-most-important person in my orbit. Zé had grown up in Brazil until he was thirteen. On the coast, he said. A town called Saquarema, near Rio. Then he'd come to the States with his family. He'd done some school, but nothing had grabbed him, and he'd stopped taking classes instead of continuing to pour money down the drain. He was twenty-five, and every day he had on a variation of the same outfit, and his hair always had that effortlessly windswept look that made me want to choke somebody. He was thinner than he should have been, and when he thought I wasn't looking, he took his weight off his injured knee. He wasn't a fanatic about sports, but he'd watch the Dodgers with me. He did yoga. He read a lot on his phone, he said, when I asked him what he did during the day. Read what, I asked. Whatever I want. He had a way of saying things like that, things that could have sounded petulant or defensive or rude, so that they seemed authentic, sincere, unselfconscious. Whatever I want. Wouldn't that be nice? He was a giant goof (exhibit A: the dance he choreographed for him and Igz; when he sent me the video during a work meeting, I'd started laughing and had to excuse myself). He did yoga, did I mention that? And he offered to teach me, like I could so much as touch my fucking toes. Once, I'd come into the kitchen in the morning when he'd been feeding Igz. The way he was holding her had rucked up his shirt to expose the small of his back, and the fabric was tight over his shoulder blades.

Zé shifted his weight, stretching his leg and knee. "Anything else before I take off?"

I shook my head, adjusting Igz (well, fuck it, I give up) against my shoulder. She'd be in her milk coma for a while, and I'd eat whatever Zé had left me (in front of the TV, obviously), and then we'd go to bed. Mom had gone straight from Vegas to—I wanted to say Aspen, but who the hell knew anymore?—and in spite of a lot of phone calls, I'd been unable to track Chuy down. I'd have the house all to myself. Again.

Before I knew it, the words were slipping out my mouth: "Do you want to stay and eat?"

Zé grinned and shook his head. The textured mess of hair fell in his eyes, and he brushed it away. "Already ate, thanks. I know you like some time to yourself."

Igz made a few discontented noises, so I shifted her higher on my shoulder and rubbed her back. "You know that, huh?"

"Kind of figured it out that time you told your brother to stop crawling up your ass for five minutes while you ate dinner."

"Jesus Christ, you weren't supposed to hear that."

And that was the truth; since Zé had started working for me, I'd been making a concerted effort not to spook him with what Augustus called *your particularly heinous brand of verbal diarrhea*. I was polite. I kept the language moderately clean. I even smiled. Sometimes.

"It's not that big of a house."

But he was smiling, and I laughed in spite of myself. He shifted his weight again and put his hand on the door handle.

"Hot date tonight?"

A little furrow appeared between Zé's eyebrows.

"You're in a hurry," I said.

"Oh. No, no dates. A—a meeting."

"Your knee?"

"Oh. No."

The vagueness was about as close as Zé would ever come to telling me to mind my own fucking business, so I nodded. "Have a good night."

"You too." He opened the door and paused. "Is everything okay?"

Aren't you lonely?

"Yep. Thanks, you know. For Igz."

Zé's smile was uncertain, but a moment later, he stepped out of the house and pulled the door shut behind him.

I carried Igz into the kitchen. True to his word, Zé had left food for me: an on-the-small-side portion of lemon-pepper salmon, hot and crispy from the air fryer; and a mountain of roasted broccoli.

"He's not exactly subtle, is he?" I asked Igz.

Instead of another night sitting in front of the TV, I took a chair at the table. I could have put Igz on the floor or in her crib or in the swing (one of Zé's few requests). But I'd gotten used to holding her, and she was warm, and there was something pleasant about her sleepy weight. I ate the salmon. Then, because I was still hungry, I ate the broccoli. I wondered if I was supposed to give Zé a performance review. Would it be fair to dock him points on something that wasn't technically his responsibility? Not that the broccoli was bad. It was great, actually—roasted until it crunched, bringing a slight sweetness out of the vegetables, and then lightly salted. The *lightly* part would be another note in his file.

After I cleaned up (which meant putting my plate and silverware in the dishwasher, because Zé had already done everything else), we moved into the living room. Igz's eyes were open, but she was quiet. The house was quiet. I turned on the TV. Since I was a responsible adult, or a reasonable impersonation of one, I didn't smoke around Igz, which meant I'd been watching a lot more television—and a lot more of my life—through sober eyes. It turned out a lot of things sucked when you weren't high enough to take the edge off. We found some show with people singing, and half of them sounded like cats getting their scrotes stretched. I told Igz, and she didn't appreciate the language.

Aren't you lonely?

Well, no. I wasn't. I shifted around to find a more comfortable spot. I adjusted Igz on my chest. ESPN, ESPN2, MTV, CBS. I stalled out on a commercial. Some guy was doing ballroom dance with what looked like a plastic bag.

"Stick your head in," I told him. "See if there's anything in there."

Igz didn't approve. She fussed and squirmed on my chest. The baby version, I thought, of beating me up.

Was I lonely?

It wasn't a question I'd had to consider before. Before, I'd been busy. That had been my default state. Busy taking care of Augustus and Chuy, because Mom always had an audition, or she was burned out and needed to see a friend, or it was an important party that could help Mommy get a job. Once Augustus had been old enough for me to leave with Chuy (who, until he'd started getting high at twelve, had been reliable enough), I'd started mowing lawns. And then I'd had a series of jobs. And school. And Augustus. And coming home, at the end of a shift, to do as much homework as I could before I fell asleep. The impossible days.

I stroked the back of Igz's head and told her, "I'm glad those are over."

There was nothing good on TV—a big-eyed woman, who seemed to straddle the line between housekeeper and wife, couldn't get the bad smells out of the kitchen, but don't worry, somebody was going to sell her something that would help—so I took out my phone.

Sure enough, a few weeks back, Lou had sent me Bea's name and number.

Hi, I texted. *This is Fernando.*

As the message zipped off, a voice that sounded like Augustus said, *Seriously, what is wrong with you?*

So, I sent a second message: *Lou's friend*.

And then: *Lourdes*.

Lourdes Amador.

I'd seen slow-motion car accidents before. Videos, you know. People like that stuff for some reason, and you watch it, and it looks like there's all this time to change course. But there's not. When you're on the inside, all you can do is watch it happen.

Somehow, I managed to drag myself away from explaining further. Instead, I opened the text thread with Augustus. His profile pic was from when he was ten, at Disney, looking like a Disney kid himself: sun-streaked bangs and a huge white smile. Even back then, he'd been a wiener. I wrote, *What do people text each other these days?*

But that wasn't right, so I erased it and tried, *What am I supposed to text someone to introduce myself?*

I erased that too.

What should I text this girl?

When Augustus was happy, his whole face lit up, and his nose got a little crinkly. The ten-year-old version of it was staring back at me. I thought about his face if I sent that text. And then I thought about the years and years I'd have to spend cutting him down to size again.

I was still waffling over sending the message when Bea replied: *Hi! Good to hear from you!*

Sorry, I wrote back. *Things have been weirdly busy.*

Lou told me about the baby??!!!

After that, it was easier. At first, the texts were short, and I focused on talking about Igz, because it was easier. But slowly the chat moved on to other things. She was a biochemist at Caltech, which immediately put her about eight leagues out of reach, and she loved scuba diving and swimming and, in general, being in the water as much as she could. I managed not to make myself sound like a total tool, I think, but *I do some mountain biking* sounded pretty limp-dicked compared to her last vacation, diving the Great Barrier Reef.

I was surprised, when she told me she needed to call it a night, how much time had passed. Igz was getting fussy, and it was time for both of us to go to bed (for approximately three hours, before Igz screamed me awake). I told Bea goodnight, and then I carried Igz and laid her on the floor in the hallway while I peed, brushed my teeth, and washed my face.

I changed into my pajamas—this ratfucker T-shirt that said BIBLE EMERGENCY HOTLINES, and then a list of things like STRESSED and LOSING HOPE and SINNED, each one with a Bible verse, and then at the bottom, TOLL FREE – TWENTY-FOUR HOURS. Augustus had given it to me because he still thinks he's hilarious. He'd given me the shorts too, which made me look like I was ready for somebody to swing me from an ass hook in his dungeon, but I couldn't stop wearing them because they were literally the most comfortable thing ever.

I bent over to pick up Igz and stopped. She was breathing fast, what I would have called hyperventilating. And then, as I watched, she stopped breathing entirely. She looked like she was struggling to get any air, her tiny nostrils flaring. She was pale.

"Oh my God," I said, dropping onto my knees.

My first thought was that she'd somehow grabbed something and put it in her mouth and was now choking. I opened her mouth as gently as I could and, using my phone as a flashlight, tried to see if something was blocking her windpipe. Not that I could see anything. Not that I knew what I was looking for. I wondered if I was supposed to do the Heimlich.

By that point, though, she was breathing again—those rapid, frantic breaths. I'd done enough safety trainings to know not to try the Heimlich if someone was breathing. I scooped her up and staggered through the house, grabbing my keys and wallet, shoving my feet into a pair of sneakers. Her little face was full of struggle as I fumbled with the buckles on her seat.

"Go in, go in, go the fuck in," I said.

Why hadn't I practiced? Why hadn't I spent more time doing this?

Somehow, I got her secured, and then I bolted for the SUV. I backed out of the driveway so fast we bounced off the curb, and a voice inside my head told me to calm down before I made things worse. I took a deep breath as I shifted into drive, and I accelerated more carefully down the street.

Orange County was a patchwork of light and dark: streetlights, security lights, neon lights buzzing on and off. The sky ended in a low, flat ceiling of clouds. I called Mom, and she didn't pick up.

"Call me back."

I hesitated. Who next? Augustus? But he was two thousand miles away, and, more importantly, I hadn't told him about Igz yet. It wasn't the time, and there was no point telling him something that would upset him until we knew what was going to happen long term.

Before I had time to reconsider, I placed a call to Zé. This one went to voicemail too.

"It's Igz." My voice broke, and I had to struggle to shore up that place inside myself before I could say. "Sorry. I shouldn't have—I'm sorry."

I disconnected.

The drive to the closest urgent care felt like a lifetime: my hands slick on the steering wheel; my back aching as I twisted around, every fifteen seconds, to make sure Igz's eyes were open, that she was still breathing; the storm inside my head of *what if what if what if*.

It was a corner unit in a stucco strip mall, with a wall of windows and an illuminated sign in red and white letters. Then I couldn't get the car seat out of the base, and a scream started building at the back of my throat. Press this button, then press—

With a click, it came free.

I ran.

The lobby was empty, and the white woman behind the safety glass was missing her front tooth and had a tattoo of an anchor on her forearm, like a cartoon sailor.

"She's not breathing. She can't breathe."

The woman's expression changed. She said something I couldn't hear into a walkie and then motioned me toward the door that connected to the rest of the facility. I jogged over to it, and the door opened. This woman was Black, her hair in beaded braids, and she wore a white lab coat with a name tag that said Ferguson. She glanced at me before bending over Igz.

"Her name's Igz," I said, and that place inside me threatened to break open again. I fought back tears. "She's a month old, and she—and she—" I knew there was more I was supposed to say, but it was like I'd reached the end of the tape, and there wasn't anything left.

The doctor ignored me. She had a stethoscope out, and she was listening to Igz's heart. Then she slipped an oximeter onto Igz's big toe. She checked the display. After what felt like an eternity, she said, "All right. She's breathing, and her oxygen saturation is good. Her heart rate is a little accelerated, but it's not in the danger zone." She straightened, looked me over again, and said, "She's not in any danger right now, sir. Let's get you set up in an exam room, and we'll see what's going on."

After *not in any danger*, I barely heard the rest of it. My knees didn't literally buckle, but my body did feel a million times lighter, and I had this strange sensation that someone had turned up the lights, that the ceiling was higher than it had been a moment before. There was this whooshing sound in my head, and I heard myself think, Oh shit, am I going to pass out?

But I didn't. Instead, I sat in the exam room, trying to fill out paperwork. I didn't make much progress because every time the doctor moved, I looked up to see what was happening. But from what I could tell, it was a more thorough version of the exam Igz had gotten in an abbreviated form a few minutes earlier, not that far off from what she'd had when we went to her one-month checkup.

"Has she had an episode like this before?" Dr. Ferguson asked.

"No, never."

"Any complications in her health history?"

I shook my head.

"Walk me through what happened tonight."

So, I told her about it—eating the dinner that Zé had made, watching TV together, texting Bea, getting ready for bed. From a long way off, a part of me recognized that I was babbling (Dr. Ferguson's mouth twitched while I was using my hands to show how much broccoli Zé had left me). But she let me get it all out.

Then she asked, "Have you noticed any changes in her behavior?"

"Nothing."

"Her feedings?"

I shook my head.

"Do you have a lot of air fresheners in the house? Or candles? Do you or your partner typically wear strong colognes?"

"No, Zé's not—" And then I remembered the day I'd met Zé, how stupid I'd been taking the vape out of my pocket, using it in the house. Since then, I'd taken my recreational shit outside, but that was a recent change. I'd been vaping in that house pretty much every day of my life for years. I'd smoked, too. And Chuy had done God only knew what. What kind of particles were floating around? "Oh my God, this is my fault. I vape—I used to vape inside the house. That's what it was, wasn't it? Oh my God, I did this to her. Did it damage her lungs? Is this like asthma, is this how babies get asthma? What the fuck is wrong with me?"

"Take a breath." She smiled softly. "Pun intended. Igz is a healthy baby. There's nothing wrong with her lungs as far as I can tell. Do you still vape in the house?"

"No. God, no."

"That's good. Do you still vape?"

When I'd been twelve, Mom had wanted to try a megachurch, and I remembered the long-faced white pastor clutching my shoulder, his breath close and hot in my face and smelling like peppermint as he asked, "Fernando, do you touch yourself?"

"Uh."

Dr. Ferguson was too professional to roll her eyes. "Since you're an adult, I'm sure you know that vaping is not a healthy lifestyle choice."

"I've been thinking about quitting."

Okay, maybe she wasn't too professional to roll her eyes. "Like I said, you're an adult. But I do recommend that you do it outside the house, and not anywhere near your daughter."

I almost said, She's not my daughter. But I didn't.

"You don't need to beat yourself up," Dr. Ferguson added. "As far as I can tell, this was a minor respiratory episode. That's what we call them when we don't know exactly what caused them or why. It could be an allergen. It could be dust. It could be that her throat got dry. This kind of thing is common in newborns."

I looked up at her.

"Yes," she said with a smile. "Really. Keep an eye on her, and if it happens again, or if the symptoms are worse, you'll need to do more testing. You did the right thing bringing her in tonight. You're a good dad."

Finishing the paperwork took almost as long as the exam itself, but I didn't mind. Igz fell asleep on the drive home. I went slow. I took the turns carefully. I stopped at a red light with a Taco Bell on one corner, and I stared at the illuminated Taco Bell sign, and it felt like my head was empty—this big, open, empty place. Then my vision blurred, and I sank down in my seat and fought to keep from coming completely undone. When the light changed, I snuffled into the Bible hotline T-shirt and let the Escalade roll forward.

Zé's car was parked in the driveway when I got home. That was unusual; he always parked on the street. Sometimes, I didn't see his car at all, and he'd say he parked up the block because he wanted some exercise. A lie, maybe, because he was embarrassed to admit he'd needed a ride. But Zé wasn't a liar, so it was probably the truth.

Tonight, though, his car was in the driveway. When the garage door rolled up, he got out of the car. I only caught a glimpse of his face, a mesh of shadow and worry, as I parked in the garage. By the time I got out of the Escalade, he was already coming toward us. His knee must have been hurting worse than normal because he was limping.

"What happened?" he asked. "Is Igz okay?"

"She's fine," I said. "I, on the other hand, am not. I am still freaked nine fucking ways from Sunday." As I got the car seat out of the base (zero problems now, of course), I added, "I'm sorry I ruined your night. You didn't have to come."

The yellow light from the garage painted the side of his face and left the rest in shadow. He moved some hair off his forehead. When he spoke, I didn't understand what I heard in his voice, but all he said was "You called me. Of course I came."

I told him what happened. And then he had to check Igz himself, even though she was still asleep. He tried to go down on his knees, but then he wobbled, and he only caught himself by throwing out a hand and grabbing the side of the house. It was hard to tell in the weak light, but I thought his face was red.

With my free hand, I steadied him and helped him stand. The spring night was cool, and the air smelled like Calla lilies from the Hensons' garden. It smelled like sage, like the wild parts of the world that lay out there in the dark, beyond the reach of streetlights and subdivision. It smelled like a warm body, like coconut wax and something earthier that made me think of driftwood. A warm male body. And even though the night was cool, I felt warm too.

"Come on," I said, surprised by the roughness of my voice. "Igz and I will walk you to your car."

Zé let me walk him a pair of steps before his whole body locked up. When I tried to tug him forward, he wouldn't move.

"I'm okay," he said, and for the first time since I'd met him, I heard panic instead of his usual calm. "I'm fine. You need to get Igz to bed. Let me help you—"

My first thought was junkie. And then, liar. Chuy was both, and I'd spent enough time with him to recognize the flailing effort to redirect, to avert.

And so I did what I always did with Chuy: no fucking mercy.

"I don't need help getting Igz to bed," I said, and I gave another, harder pull. It was cheating because I was using his bad leg against him, but I didn't care. He was lying to me. About something. Somehow. I had a sixth sense for it. And all my fear, all my adrenaline, everything that still needed an outlet—it flared up in the white-hot heat of my anger. "I want to make sure you're okay." Yank. "In your car." Yank.

Zé was taller, but I had more muscle (well, more mass, anyway), and more importantly, he was off-balance. He made a few objecting sounds, but all he could do was stumble along.

I stopped at the car. Enough light filtered in from the street that I could make out the interior. The sleeping bag. The jugs of water. The clothes piled on the passenger seat.

How long, I wanted to ask. And why didn't you tell me?

"All right," he said, and his voice was an imitation of its usual easy happiness. "I'll see you guys tomorrow—"

"What the fuck is wrong with you?" I shook him by the arm. And like that, two weeks' worth of struggling to keep my mouth shut flew out the window. "You should have told me, you stupid nut-rabbit!"

I don't know if he was trying to get free or if I simply shook him too hard. Whatever the reason, he stumbled back a half-step, and then his knee folded, and he let out a sharp breath.

"Zé, Christ—"

"I'm okay. Oh shit. Oh shit, my knee."

Holding on to him turned into holding him upright. He wouldn't—or couldn't—put any weight on one leg.

"I need to sit down," he said, fumbling in his pockets. "Could you open the door—"

"For fuck's sake, you're coming inside."

"No, I'm fine—"

"No, you're right. It's a fucking fantastic idea for you to crawl into your fucking car and be left alone right now."

He ran the back of his hand across his mouth. The reflection of the streetlights made it hard to read his eyes, but I could feel how pain tightened his body.

"Inside, jack hole. Right fucking now."

Maybe I couldn't read his eyes, but they definitely got a little wider.

We made our way inside, the three of us—me balancing Zé on one side, and Igz swinging against my leg on the other. She didn't help at all, of course; after nearly giving me a heart attack, she was sleeping peacefully.

I got Zé to the sofa, helped him lie down so that he could keep his knee straight, and retrieved an ice pack from the kitchen. He propped himself up on one elbow, mouth open to protest, so I said—a little too loudly—"Oh, I'm sorry, did you have another great fucking idea?"

He shrank back down to the cushion.

I sat next to him and placed the ice pack on his knee. Then I didn't know what to do with my hands. It felt strangely intimate, sitting so close to him, touching him. The Quiksilver tee rode up to expose a band of smooth skin and the hint of his treasure trail. His belly rose and fell slowly. His arm came up, and he put his hand on my thigh. He doesn't know what to do, I told myself. He's scared, and he's touching you because he's hurting.

But I didn't see pain on his face. Or fear. I saw something unreadable. It made me think of sun catching the snowpack.

"Let me get Igz back in the SUV," I said, "and then we'll go to the hospital."

He shook his head.

"Yes, absolutely. If I fucked up your surgery—"

"I'm okay."

"You're not okay. You couldn't even stand."

His hand rubbed my thigh slowly. It was like someone stirring up sparks from a fire; it had been a long time since someone had touched me, even like this. "You can take the ice pack off."

I peeled it away.

He sat up and scooted until he was propped up by the arm of the sofa. Then, slowly, he tested his knee, bending it, straightening it again. A hint of dusky color came into his cheeks. "It's okay," he said again. And then, more firmly, "I'm okay."

"This is all very fucking convincing."

He laughed very quietly. "I'm sorry. I thought I felt something, and I was so afraid—" He stopped, and then, to my total amazement, he blinked away tears.

"Zé."

"No," he said thickly, shaking his head at whatever I might have said. "I'm fine, I promise. It's just been a lot."

I didn't know what that meant, but when the silence stretched on, I asked, "What kind of surgery was it?"

"My ACL."

"Ouch. What happened?"

"That's the stupidest part. I was messing around with some friends. I slipped, tried to catch myself, and pop."

I winced, but I was only halfway concentrated on his story. His hand was slowly rubbing my thigh again. And the little dicklet shorts that Augustus had bought me left a lot of bare skin for him to chafe.

Once again, the silence had gone on too long. I opened my mouth to say something, but Zé spoke first. "I'm glad Igz is okay."

I made an agreeing noise.

"You realize the shirt and the shorts are sending a mixed message, right? All those Bible verses. And then—" He plucked at the hem of the shorts, high up my thigh.

"That's because I've got a gayball brother who also thinks he's a comedian."

In that quiet voice of his, he said, "You have a lot of pictures of the two of you. You must love him a lot."

"Oh no. Nice fucking try."

He closed his eyes.

"You're living in your car?"

"Don't yell; you're going to wake Igz."

"Don't yell? I'll yell if I want to yell." But I did lower my voice because I wasn't an idiot. "What the fuck kind of shit-slurry do you have for brains? What have you been doing every day when you walk out of here? Where do you go? Tell me, right now. And you'd better not try to lie to me."

He opened his eyes, and they were silver with tears. He couldn't quite blink them all away, and the ones that fell traced their way down his cheeks. "Are you firing me?"

"What? No. God, no."

"I'll be here on time every day, like always. I'll be rested and focused, and I'll take good care of Igz. I don't steal food. Sometimes, I've showered here, but only after I do yoga. And if you want me to stop, I won't do it anymore."

"I don't steal food," I said. "Give me a fucking break."

"I don't know what you want me to say!"

"I want you to answer my goddamn questions!"

He shrank back. His hand fell from my thigh. He's young, I had to remind myself. He might be taller than you, he might be knitted out of all that long, lean muscle, but he's Augustus's age, which means he's practically a kid, and he's hurting, and he's alone, and he's trying to do everything on his own.

"Yes," he finally said. He wouldn't meet my eyes. "I sleep in my car."

"Where?"

"In my—"

"No. Where do you park your car?"

After a pause, he shrugged. "There are places."

"Jesus fucking Christ. Donkey balls, you are going to get yourself killed."

"I can take care of myself."

"You're doing a great fucking job of it so far."

Then his eyes did come up to mine, and for the first time, I saw him angry. "If you're not firing me, and it's not affecting my work, then it's none of your business."

"Of course it's my business."

The best he could come up with, apparently, was a baffled, "Why?"

"Because you are in my life, and that means I'm responsible for you!" My face heated as I heard my own words, and I hurried to add, "And because I have no fucking idea what I'd do with Igz if something happened to you, you big sackless wonder."

The corner of his mouth turned up, and in a tone I didn't recognize, he said, "You big sackless wonder."

"This is how I talk. Is that going to be a problem?"

It was definitely a smile now. He shook his head. "What's a nut-rabbit?"

"What do you fucking think? And it's not because you're gay. And it's not sexual harassment since I said it out of a place of anger."

"And how can I have donkey balls and be a sackless wonder at the same time? Is it because I have a shit-slurry for brains?"

"Look, I didn't mean—I can try not to, I don't know, say stuff like that. But I can't promise anything about the swearing."

Zé shook his head. He still wore that tiny, unreadable smile. "I kept wondering what you were holding back. You'd get so mad at something on TV, or that time someone knocked over the trash can, or when you stepped in that dogshit, and I could see it building. And then you never let it out, and I wondered what it was."

"If those two brainfucks would keep that fucking dog behind their fence—" I drew a deep breath. "I, uh, will work on it."

His smile canted. It was something else now. Deeper. More, if that could be a thing—if a smile could be more. "You don't have to work on it, except maybe around Igz." And then, with nothing to explain what the fuck he might possibly mean, he added, "It's cute."

I was suddenly aware again of our positions: his long body stretched out on the couch, propped up by the armrest, the tilt of his head that displayed the strong lines of his neck. That ridiculous hair hung in his eyes again. We were so close that I couldn't help noticing the freckles sprinkled at the hollow of his throat, or the stubble that accented his jaw, or that his lips were slightly chapped.

"Yeah, well," I said, "we've gotten off topic. You're not sleeping in that car anymore."

Zé opened his mouth. "I don't need—"

I spoke over him. "I'm not going through the hassle of finding Igz another nanny. Manny. Whatever. I will blow my fucking brains out before I have to deal with that again."

"Fer, I'm fine. Thank you, but—"

"It's not a discussion. This is a new condition of the job."

"You can't do that!"

"Can. Did. I'm exclusively looking for a live-in nanny. Manny. God, why does that sound so fucking stupid when I say it? I don't expect you to take care of Igz in the evenings; your nights and weekends will still be your own. But I need you here because we may occasionally have to flex your hours. And because I have this strange thing where I like knowing that my manny isn't going to be gutted and tossed in a dumpster by a band of murderous hobos."

"I'm getting an apartment. I'm waiting for the lease to roll over."

"What did I tell you about lying to me?"

I didn't expect the resistance in his face, but maybe I should have. I remembered how much it had cost him to say please, to ask for the job in the first place. How hard it had been to admit that he needed it.

"Say yes, jackass," I said in a low voice. "It's a bedroom. A place to sleep. I'm not asking you for anything else."

"Fine." Then he rubbed his face, and I thought I saw tears again.

"What do you need from the car?"

"I can—"

"Try getting off that couch. See what happens."

He let out a wet laugh and wiped his face. The struggle was there again. And then he whispered, "Thank you."

I pushed some of that windblown hair away from his forehead, and he smiled. It was a nice smile. And then I realized what I'd done. I pulled my hand back and stood, and my voice sounded rough when I said, "And you need a haircut."

But, of course, that only made him laugh.

8

April turned into May. Mom and Cannon came home, and while I expected some kind of explosion, Mom had, instead, been thrilled. Which, in hindsight, I should have anticipated.

"We have a manny. Oh my God, Courtney is going to be so jealous!"

Meanwhile, Zé had settled in nicely. After that first, kind-of argument about moving into the house, Zé hadn't shown any kind of discomfort or resistance. I cleaned out Chuy's room and got him set up in there. He didn't bring many personal belongings into the house. His clothes, his phone and charger, his toiletries. No pictures of family or friends. No…junk, for lack of a better word. No clutter of trinkets or mementos.

In the mornings, he was up before I was—he did yoga on the deck, then he showered, and then he started the day. The only reason I knew was because one day, Igz had woken up earlier than usual. I'd carried her into the kitchen, and there he'd been: in nothing but a pair of tiny shorts, dawn glowing on the defined muscles of his arms and back and legs as he moved himself through the poses. Sweat glistened on his shoulders. It gathered at the small of his back. A lock of hair clung to his temple in a curl. This early, the day was so quiet, and the sky above the valley was white softening to blue. One of the jacarandas had started to bloom, the purple blossoms barely starting to open, and they trembled in the light breeze. I thought I could feel that breeze. I thought something was trembling inside me too. I'd stood there, watching him as I fed Igz, until he scooted off the mat and started to roll it up. And then I'd realized I was being a creep, and I'd hurried out of the kitchen and pretended to watch TV.

Even though I'd told him—repeatedly—that he didn't have to take care of Igz until eight and that he was off duty at five, Zé refused to listen. He'd say, "I don't mind," and "It's fine," and "I'm happy to do it." One time, I sat him down and asked him if he thought he had to do extra duty because he was staying here now. He burst out laughing and went into the kitchen to make dinner.

When Mom was home, Zé often retreated to his room after dinner. But more often than not, Mom was out with Cannon, or she was seeing Shannon, her life coach, or she was getting drinks with Courtney and Kelli and Sara. Those nights, Zé didn't go to his room. We ate dinner together—more and more frequently at the kitchen table, instead of in front of the TV. He told me what Igz had done that day. He asked me what I had done. Since I worked from home, sometimes there wasn't much to tell, but he was smart and curious, and he asked good questions, and he wanted to know about the doctors I visited, and how I pitched a new drug. Every once in a while, I'd realize I was boring him. I'd be in the middle of saying something, and he'd be staring at me, and I could tell he wasn't hearing a single word coming out of my mouth. So, I'd ask him about his day, or about Igz, and he'd blush and stammer something, and then things would feel normal again.

He was still a giant goof. He gave himself and Igz shaving cream beards one day, and thank God I had muted my Zoom because I almost shat myself laughing. Or one time, he was giggling uncontrollably while I was trying to make a presentation. And then, out of nowhere he shouted, "Oh my God!" When I got to the kitchen, he was still holding a bubble wand, the bubble solution dripping onto the floor as he stared at Igz.

"What?" I asked. "What happened?"

He glanced at me, as though he'd forgotten I was still there. And then a grin bloomed on his face, and he blew a bubble. He looked at me again. Waiting for something.

And then I saw it.

Igz was smiling.

"Holy fucking shit," I said.

He laughed.

"Holy fucking shit!"

The rest of the day was bubble day.

Bea and I continued texting, which was something of a minor miracle. Before long, we'd agreed to meet, and to my surprise, Bea suggested dinner.

"I thought she'd want to do coffee," I told Zé as I buttoned up a shirt. He lounged on the bed, tickling Igz's stomach as she lay next to him. "Why would she pick dinner?"

"Because she likes you."

"But she's never met me. What if I'm an asshole?"

"What if."

"What the fuck was that?"

Zé pulled up the collar of his Rip Curl tee to hide a smile.

Examining myself in the mirror, I said, "This looks terrible, right?" I started to undo the buttons. "This is a disaster."

With one last tickle for Igz's tummy, Zé stood. He flicked through the clothes in my closet, sliding the hangers along the rod. He glanced at me as I slid out of my shirt, and then his eyes went back to the closet. Then he pulled out an oxford. The front pocket and the collar were a different color than the rest of the shirt; there was probably a name for that kind of thing.

"Where are your dark jeans?"

"What dark jeans?"

"Oh my God, Fernando."

He rummaged through my dresser—mercifully skipping the underwear drawer—and tossed me a different pair of jeans. Then he grabbed Igz and stepped out of the room. I changed into the jeans. I buttoned up the shirt. I checked myself in the mirror. I didn't look like I was going to embarrass myself, but hey, I hadn't had a chance to open my mouth yet.

I found Zé in the living room. He was putting Igz in the car seat, explaining to Mom how the buckles and straps worked.

"What's going on?"

"I'm going out for a quick bite with the girls," Mom said. "They are going to die. You know Sara's daughter can't have a baby, right?"

"Real nice, Mom."

"I think I'm going to call her Ava. Do you like that, Ava?"

"Her name isn't Ava. It's Igz. And I don't want you taking her to a bar."

"We're not going to a bar. We're going to a perfectly lovely bistro. You're going to love it, aren't you, Ava?"

"Igz," I said. "You said you were going to stay home. You said you were going to watch her so I could go out."

"I am going to watch her, Fernando. I'm taking her with me, aren't I?"

"I don't want other people holding her."

"Oh my God."

"I don't want them to get her sick. I don't want your weird friends breathing on her and touching her and getting in her face."

"Your uncle is rude sometimes," Mom said to Igz. "It's because he's nervous about his date."

"I'm not nervous," I said. "I don't want them vaping around her either. She's got sensitive lungs."

"Ava and I are going to my room," Mom said. "Until a certain grumpypants leaves."

And, true to her word, she picked up Igz in the car seat and carried her down the hall.

"I know you heard me about the vaping," I called after her.

Zé had watched the whole exchange without saying a word, his face unreadable.

"Well?" I said.

"Auggie got you that shirt."

"Thanks a fucking lot."

His smile slipped out, and he studied me for a moment. Then he undid the topmost button of my shirt.

"I'm not Magic Mike," I said.

"Why am I not surprised you've seen that movie?"

"What the fuck is that supposed to mean?"

He ducked his head as he took me by the wrist, but the smile was bigger now. He cuffed one sleeve. His hands were steady and warm, and he took his time.

"I saw the previews, that's all."

"Bull. Shit."

I laughed in spite of myself, and he was grinning as he worked on my other sleeve. I couldn't think of anything to say, so I listened to his breathing and the rustle of the shirt.

"Don't you have any friends?" I asked.

His hands stopped moving, frozen in the act of adjusting my sleeve. Then he said, "A few."

"Shit, that's not what I meant."

When he looked up, his face was unreadable again. He smoothed a hand down my chest. I was painfully aware of the belly I was carrying around, how it pulled the shirt out. He followed the curve of my body, and when he reached the hem of the shirt, he straightened it. Then he stepped back and said, "You look handsome."

"I meant—I don't know, I was thinking about how nice you were being, and I don't have any friends because I'm an asshole, like this ripped-open, plundered asshole, and so then I thought but you're nice, so you should have friends, but you're here most nights, and you're here weekends, and I was trying to ask if you needed more time off."

"No," Zé said, "you weren't."

"Well, I thought of it when I was trying to cover my ass, so it still technically counts."

"Did you say 'plundered'?"

"I figure that's pretty close, right? Like an asshole, but an asshole that's tore up. Wrecked. Shredded."

He was fighting a smile; you could tell because the corner of his mouth gave him away. "I don't like it when you talk about yourself that way."

"I was literally an asshole to you five seconds ago."

"You asked me a question without thinking about how it sounded, Fernando. I'm not made of glass. Trust me, you'll know when I'm upset."

But I thought maybe he was upset. Not with me. But the question had bothered him, and now that I'd said it out loud, it bothered me too. He was young. He was undeniably attractive. He was sweet. He was a dick-balls nerd. And he was gay. Why wasn't he out partying? Why wasn't he out hooking up and trolling for dick and living Augustus's wet dream (or what had been his wet dream before he'd found his pet dinosaur)? He'd make someone happy; the thought came through like the first clear note of a bell. Like this, sharing a life together, he'd make someone incredibly happy. Happy to come home and spend an hour hearing about his day with Igz. Happy to come home and spend the next hour telling him every fucking thing that was wrong with the Dodgers' current lineup. Happy to look over on a commercial break, to see him falling asleep at the end of the sofa, the way his lips were parted and his breathing was smooth and slow, and tell him to get his ass up and go to bed. And instead, he was here.

For a moment, I felt confused by the thought. Of course he was here. He was supposed to be here.

"You have friends," Zé said, and at first, I didn't understand what he was saying. Then I remembered the conversation; it felt like it had happened hours ago. "Lou loves you. And it sounds like her wife loves you too. And I'm sure you have other friends."

"I don't."

"I'm your friend."

I didn't know what to say to that.

He laughed. "I wouldn't hang around and listen to an hour-long story about the best edible you ever tried if I didn't want to, Fernando." A grin sliced across his expression. "Not unless I was on the clock."

"You cunt-weasel!"

"Uh, technically, because I'm gay—"

"You little ferret fucker! That was a good story! I drew you a diagram—"

I cut off—in horror—because the little shit was laughing, and doing a poor job of covering it by pretending to scratch his cheek. Through the laughter, he managed to say, "The diagram was cute."

"It wasn't supposed to be cute. It was supposed to be—no! No, I am not doing this. Next time, don't bother listening. Next time, you can go shove a Slim Jim up your chute and ride a fucking meat stick."

What I'd said came back to me, and who I'd said it to, and the inevitable lawsuits. I had a feeling like I'd stepped off a cliff.

But Zé only laughed harder. Not loud—he was, I was starting learn, never loud. But he had tears in his eyes, and he had to sit on the arm of the sofa and wipe his face as he continued to laugh.

"The diagram was cute?" I bellowed.

He slid onto the sofa and covered his face with his hands.

Down the hall, the sound of a door opening came, and Mom said, "What is going on out here?"

"Nothing," I snapped.

"Ava and I are practicing our song," she said. "So, we'd appreciate a little quiet."

"What song? She's not even two months old."

"This is why I wanted girls," Mom said, her voice growing fainter as the door closed. "Or a gay son."

"A gay son? What the fuck does that mean? You've got Augustus, and he's gayer than Christmas!"

But the door clicked shut.

Zé drew himself up, no longer laughing, although his face was lit up with—what? Happiness? Contentment? Amusement? All three, maybe. I liked how it looked on him. I hadn't realized, until now, that while Zé was always kind, always in a good mood, always pleasant, I wasn't sure he was always happy. He met my gaze, and for a moment, I thought he was going to say something. And then, instead of—well, I wasn't sure what—he said, "You're going to be late."

"Shit." I grabbed my wallet and keys. At the door, I stopped, because it felt like I ought to say something. The best I could come up with was "Thanks for, uh, all this."

He smiled crookedly. "What are friends for?"

9

The restaurant was called Industria, and it was, according to the blurb I'd read online, a post-industrial deconstruction of traditional Italian cuisine. Which meant, I was pretty sure, it was going to be expensive as fuck and leave me hungry enough to stop at a taco cart on the way home. When I got there, the look of the place confirmed my suspicions. It occupied an enormous, high-ceilinged space, and it leaned into the industrial look with exposed ductwork and polished concrete and lots of rivets or bolts or whatever the hell they were supposed to be. No white linen tablecloths. No stuffy maître d's. No candles, even—each table had a little origami LED light that changed colors constantly.

Bea arrived about two minutes after I did. I'd seen pictures, of course (and no, you pervert, not that kind of picture). She was petite, blond, and she looked more like a yoga instructor than a biochemist. You could tell she'd had her lips done, but that didn't exactly make her stand out in a crowd. What made her stand out in a crowd was when she opened her mouth—she was smart, she was funny, and it took me about five seconds to realize my first assessment had been wrong. She wasn't eight leagues out of reach. Put it closer to fifteen or twenty.

The hostess sat us, and Bea ordered a bottle of wine, and we held our menus and made small talk. She played tennis. She ran. She was heading up a new project at work, but she couldn't talk about it because it was a Big Secret (she told me "capital letters for both words").

"But you get bonus points for asking," she said with a laugh. "Most guys like to pretend they didn't hear me when I bring up work."

"Most guys have the emotional maturity of a bag of dicks."

Her eyes got wide.

"God damn it," I said. This was Zé's fault, I decided, because he always acted so goddamned amused, and I'd been letting my filter slip. (Okay, maybe I hadn't let my filter slip. Maybe my filter was hanging ass in the wind.) "I'm sorry, I—"

But she cut me off with a wave of her hand as she laughed. "No, you're right. They do. And God, think about how all those dicks would threaten their fragile heterosexuality?"

I grinned. "No homo."

"Oh my God," she groaned. "I hate that phrase so much."

That led us, somehow to Augustus, and before long I was talking about the consulting work he did, digital marketing, all the obstacles he'd overcome, and the fact that he was, despite every sign to the contrary, apparently going to become a fully functioning adult at some point in the near future, instead of the human cum-bucket I thought he'd been destined for.

I left that last part out—believe it or not, I did manage to put my filter back into place. Well, mostly. And Bea, to her credit, rolled with it. In hindsight, I should have realized that any friend of Lou's must have been able to hold up pretty well to that woman's rent-a-fuck caliber of verbal battery; anything I dished out would be child's play in comparison.

The conversation was easy, and as I relaxed, I found myself having fun. She was pretty, although I wouldn't have said she was my type. My type ran more to—dark eyes, I thought, maybe. Dark hair. With some texture. Salt and wind and sun. Not that I had a type, these days. You had to go on more than one date a year, I was pretty sure, to be able to say you had a type.

The food came, and even though my prediction had been right—one reimagined meatball, sir, lightly dusted with nutritional yeast, in a tomato-free chutney—I was surprised to find I was having a good time.

That, of course, was when my phone started to go off. I ignored it the first time. The second time I reached to silence it, I checked the screen. It was Mom. I let it go to voicemail, and she called again.

"If you need to take that…" Bea said.

I hesitated. Say no, a voice told me. Turn your phone off and pay attention to this intelligent, attractive, interesting woman who did not run for the hills when you said you'd seen micropenises bigger than the breadsticks they served in this place.

"Fernando, if it's important, you can answer. In fact, this is the perfect chance for me to run to the restroom."

"Thank you."

She waved the words away.

"I'm sorry," I said. "My mom. She's called four times now."

"Take the call," she said as she set her napkin aside. "I promise it's fine."

As soon as Bea was a safe distance away, I accepted the call and whispered furiously, "What the fuck is such a big fucking emergency that I can't have one night to myself?" And then it was like a trapdoor had opened inside my head. "Is Igz okay?"

"She is not okay!" Mom's voice was high and thready. "She is ruining my evening! She won't let the girls hold her, and she's been fussing nonstop."

"I told you I didn't want them—"

"And do you know how embarrassing it is to be turned away at the door? I mean, my God, Fernando, when did they stop letting you take a baby into a bar? This is still America, isn't it?"

"You took her to a bar?"

"Not inside because they wouldn't let—"

"What the fuck is wrong with you?"

My volume slipped on that one, and the question was an explosion. Conversations around me dimmed, and other diners turned looks of cow-eyed curiosity on me, still sucking down their fucking polenta foam made with air imported from the Mendocino Farm.

"She ruined my night out," Mom said. "And Zé won't pick up his phone, and I don't think that's right, do you? I mean, he's living here, isn't he? Shouldn't he be available to help every once in a while?"

"What are you—" I managed to rein my voice in. "What the fuck are you talking about?"

"They're at the Blackbird, Fernando. You know that's my favorite."

"Let me get this straight: after you promised to watch Igz tonight—promised, Mom—so that I could go on a date, now you're calling me, telling me how a baby ruined your chance to drink vodka tonics with your stupid friends at that stupid bar, and I'm going to guess that, since Zé is enjoying his night off, you want me to come home and watch her."

The question flashed through my mind even as I said it: enjoying his night how? A date? Did guys his age go on dates? Or maybe a hookup? Did he have Grindr or Prowler or any of those apps? Or maybe, I thought as reason reasserted itself, it wasn't any of my business. For all you know, he's getting the oil changed in his car, jackass. Sure, I thought. All that pumping and thrusting and lube. And what the fuck right did he have to go off and fuck around when—

When what? When it was his night, and he was free to do whatever he wanted? With whomever he wanted?

Mom, of course, picked up on that opening right away. "Oh, would you, darling? That would be wonderful. Thank you."

"No, I surely fucking will not. I'm on a date, Mom. I'm allowed to have a night to myself. And you promised—"

In the background, Igz was crying.

Mom made a vexed noise. "Do you hear that? How am I supposed to put her to sleep now?"

"No," I said.

"You're right, Fernando. You deserve a night out." She gave a little laugh. "I raised three children all by myself. We'll be fine."

"No, Mom. Don't you dare put her to sleep and then leave for that fucking bar."

The call disconnected. I called Mom back, but she didn't pick up. I called again.

"Everything all right?" Bea asked.

She'd do it. She'd done it so many times before. In Mom's mind, nothing could go wrong if you waited until the children were asleep before sneaking out of the house. And that's probably because, as far as she was concerned, nothing had gone wrong. She wasn't the one who had to wake up to Augustus screaming his head off because of the night terrors. She wasn't the one who had to put out the fire Chuy started in the closet. She wasn't the one who had to make breakfast in the morning and pretend everything was okay even though nobody knew where she was, and hold it all together because somebody fucking had to.

I glanced around, found our server, and raised my hand. "I'm so sorry," I said to Bea. "Family emergency."

"Oh God. Is everyone okay?"

"Kind of." I tried for a laugh, but it didn't sound right. "I don't know. My mom—it's a lot to go into."

She made a sympathetic noise. "Go on. I'll get the check."

"No, please let me."

"I invited you—"

But at that moment, the server swooped down on us. I held up my card and waved her off.

"You didn't have to do that," Bea said.

"It's my pleasure. And I'm sorry for running out on you like this. Like I said, it's a family emergency."

"It's okay, Fernando. Life happens."

"It sure does," I said. Life happens. Family happens. If it's not Mom, it's Chuy. If it's not Chuy, it's Augustus. If it's not Augustus, it's Igz. It keeps happening.

We said an awkward goodbye at the curb, and she got into her car, and I drove home.

Igz was asleep in her crib. Mom was touching up her lipstick in her bathroom.

"Didn't anyone teach you to knock?"

I stood there, breathing. The anger came on me so quickly that I started to shake. "What the fuck is wrong with you?"

"Your language, Fernando." She turned her attention back to the mirror. "Did you have a good time?"

The house had the kind of stillness that only came late at night. I wiped my hands on my jeans; they felt slick with oil.

"Do you know what Kelli told us tonight? She said her son, Rogan—do you remember Rogan?—she said Rogan's getting divorced. He's got two children, you know. And I felt like such an idiot because I'd been telling everyone how wonderful you've been about Ava. All night long I was telling them how I couldn't have done this without you. They all know how wonderful you've been." Her voice was soft as she said, "My perfect boy. They all know how perfect you are."

I shook my head.

She made a kissy face to the mirror, turned, and patted my cheek. "Since you're here now, I'm going to catch up with the girls. You should have seen what Courtney was wearing—I swear to God, the waiter could see her fanny." She considered me for a moment and added, "Get some sleep, dear. You've got bags under your eyes."

Then she was out the door, and the sound of her car faded into the night.

I checked on Igz, and she was doing fine—breathing evenly as she slept. I turned on the baby monitor and went out to the living room. As usual, there was shit on TV, so I ended up watching highlights from the Dodgers game. It went to commercial, and the King from Burger King got stuck going down a slide. Because of that huge plastic head. I watched him struggling to get free. Kids were running around, laughing, playing, oblivious to him shouting for help. I turned the TV off.

For a while, I tried to think about what to text Bea. I wrote something. I rewrote it. I deleted it. I started over. I ended up with pretty much the same thing I'd started with, only now I was more convinced than ever that I was a fucking moron.

Sorry again for leaving. I had a nice time, and I'd like to see you again.

I waited. My screen started to dim. I tapped it to keep it awake. Still nothing. I lay on the couch. I watched my phone. I tapped the screen. And eventually, I let it go dark.

The sound of a key in the door made me bolt upright, and I realized, in a disoriented heartbeat, that I'd fallen asleep. The lights were still on, and it was still dark outside, and it could have been minutes or hours. My phone said it was barely eleven. Still no message from Bea.

When Zé stepped inside, something was different about him. The way he held himself. His vibe, if I wanted to sound like Augustus. Solemn was the first word that came to mind, and I rejected it. Because Zé was quiet, but he was a goofy kind of quiet. Serious, maybe. Although that was only a few inches from solemn, so maybe I'd been right the first time.

"I thought you'd still be on your date," he said, and then he smiled, and he was Zé again. "How'd it go?"

"Where were you?"

He turned his keys in his hand, and they jingled.

I rubbed my face and counted to ten. From behind my hands, I said, "Sorry. None of my business."

He made a noise that could have meant anything.

I let my hands fall and said, "If it makes you feel better, that was ninety percent automatic. It kind of becomes a habit when one of your brothers is a shit-for-brains addict, and the other one is Augustus."

He jingled the keys again, and I couldn't make out his tone when he said, "Only ninety percent, huh?"

"It's your night off. You're free to do whatever you want, and you certainly don't have to tell me. You're an adult—"

Zé laughed, and after a moment, I made a face and flipped him off. Then I laughed too. I was still laughing until he came across the room and sat on the couch. His knee brushed mine. He was still in the surf bum clothes he'd been wearing when I'd left, and I wondered if that was what you wore to a gay hookup. Maybe. Some guys wouldn't mind, I was sure. Not that it mattered with Zé. He could have been wearing a Barney-the-dinosaur costume and done fine for himself.

"Was that hard for you?" Zé asked. The words sounded like they were meant to be light, but he said them with that same unreadable tone.

"First time I've ever been able to say that. Chuy is most definitely not an adult, and neither is my mom, and God only knows with Augustus."

Zé sat there for what felt like a long time. "I saw the calls from your mom."

"Fuck her. She knew it was your night off."

"I had my phone on silent. I wasn't ignoring her. But when I called her back, she didn't pick up, and she didn't leave a message, and you didn't call…"

"Zé, it's fine. You're allowed to have a life." But I thought about that. About his phone being on silent. Why would his phone have been on silent? A movie, maybe. But people put their phones on vibrate in a movie, right? I had this picture in my head of his phone face down on a nightstand. He was young. He'd need to get it out of his system somehow, right? Drain the pipes and all that.

"Is everything okay?"

"Igz is fine."

He shifted on the couch to look at me. "Fernando, what happened?"

For a moment, it was like a dam about to break: everything, all of it, building behind the wall I'd built, the pressure growing and growing. I shook my head and pushed up from the couch. "Long night, I guess. I'm going to hit the sack."

Zé struggled to his feet; it looked harder for him than usual, and maybe that was only because he was tired. He followed me down the hall.

"She called you," he said. "That's why she didn't pick up."

"It's fine."

"She ruined your date."

"Give me a break, Zé. It was dinner with some girl I've been texting."

"That's not fair. She shouldn't have done that."

I stopped in my bedroom doorway. The lights in the hall were off, and against the glow from the living room, Zé was a silhouette. I held up my phone as evidence. "It's not a big deal. Apparently, I managed to fuck it up all by myself, since she didn't respond to my text."

"Fernando."

"Get some sleep. I bet you need it."

I surprised myself with the sting in those last words, and he must have heard it too because he shifted his weight, and he was silent again. I thought about apologizing. Instead, I started to step into my bedroom.

"You are a great guy, Fernando. Anybody would be lucky to have you in their life. I'm sorry that tonight didn't go the way you wanted, but you can't give up. Maybe we can work on a dating profile for you—"

The anger came so quickly, came so hot, that I didn't have time to understand where it came from. Or why. "A dating profile," I said.

Zé's silence answered me. The whole house was silent.

"I don't have time to date, Zé. I don't get to go out and fuck around at night."

The hallway was so dark. And his silence was so big.

As quickly as it had come, the anger drained out of me, and all I felt was tired. I stepped into my room, and as I shut my door, I said, half-apology and half-explanation, "I've got to take care of my family."

10

Somehow, Zé hadn't quit and left after I'd been a total asshole to him. Even more miraculously, we'd settled back into our normal routine. A week went by. And then another. Although, it wasn't quite normal. Something was different with Zé. Maybe. A new reserve, like he was holding part of himself back. Or, maybe not, because I wasn't sure if I was imagining it.

It was so minor, if it was there at all, that it was hard to point to any specific example. He smiled. He laughed. He sent me goofy videos of him and Igz, even when they were in the other room—one, with Igz dressed in one of his Hurley T-shirts and a pair of Wayfarer sunglasses, was so fucking cute that I spent the next hour figuring out how to get it printed. He had that usual relaxed, happy Zé energy that, I'd started to realize, I was enjoying way too much. I caught myself making excuses to talk to him. I wandered out of my home office (officially, the dining room) between calls, and we'd shoot the shit while he played with Igz. I'd go into the kitchen for a snack, and half the time, he'd already have something ready for me, and I'd end up talking to him for way too long. At night, I found stupid reasons for him to stay and watch TV. I swear to God, one time I heard myself say, "You've got to see this commercial," and a tiny piece of me died. But he sat and watched, and then he stayed. It was like basking in the sun, I thought. Like it had been winter for so long. Which was a strange thought for someone who lived in southern California.

But every once in a while, it was like I turned a conversational corner too fast, and a wall would come up. I'd ask him if he had plans for the weekend, and his silence lasted a beat too long before he mumbled a vague answer. Or once, I asked him about swim lessons for Igz, and I swear to God I saw the shutters go down. But those moments were so short, and there was never any sign of them after, that it didn't take long before I convinced myself I'd imagined them. Because he was Zé, and apparently, in an entire universe of people who found me un-fucking-bearable, he had some sort of magic immunity to my assholery.

It was Friday night, my back was killing me. To be more specific, it felt like someone was stabbing me with an icepick. I barely made it through dinner, sitting on the hard kitchen chair. When I stood to clear the dishes, the sharp pain ran straight to my brain. All I could do was stand there, balancing plates in my hands, and try not to fall over or curl up or, let's face it, whimper.

Zé noticed, of course. Concern was written across his face.

"I'm going to do these tomorrow," I said. I put the plates in the sink. "I want to get Igz down."

"I'll do them."

"It's the weekend, and you're off duty, so don't you fucking dare."

For some reason, that made him smile. But when I reached to take Igz, he was slow to release her. "Are you feeling okay?"

"My back's a little tight," I said. "I'll take something after I put Igz to bed."

"Fernando, go lie down." He tried to take her back. "I'll take care of Igz."

"What part of 'off duty' don't you understand?"

His smile got bigger. "Go stretch out. Take something for your back."

"It's a good thing you're pretty," I said, "because somebody went to town on you with the stupid stick. Here, I'll say it more clearly: go have fun. Get out of my house. And don't tell me you don't have plans; until five minutes ago, you were looking at your phone every five seconds, so I know you've got plans."

He opened his mouth.

"Don't you dare fucking lie to me."

"Don't swear in front of Igz!"

I cupped her head as I held her to my chest, and finally he released her. "She likes it. She swears like a fucking sailor."

"She does not. She's a lady."

"Get out of my fucking house!"

He grinned and pushed tousled hair back. "You're sure—"

"Go!"

He grabbed his keys and wallet and then came over to where Igz and I were standing. He bent, and for a moment, the way his face came toward me, I had this panicked thought that—what?

But instead, he kissed Igz on the cheek. Then he checked me, frowned, and said, "You can't even stand up straight."

"Yeah, but I can still beat your ass. How does that sound?"

"Do you hear the kind of abuse I put up with, Igz?"

"You've got until the count of ten. If you're still dicking around, Igz is going to see me open baby's first can of whoop-ass."

"I've never heard someone say that in real life before. Only on TV, you know. Old TV."

"Ten."

"Maybe I should take Igz with me."

"Nine."

"I could go pick up smoothies and come back."

"José Teixeira, I hope you don't think I'm going to go easy on you because you've got a booboo on your knee."

Laughing, he backed toward the door, hands raised in surrender. "Call me if you need me."

"I hope you have a miserable fucking night, you selfish son of a bitch."

That only made him laugh harder. I could hear him after he shut the door.

Igz was giving me a look.

"What?" I told her. "He likes it."

Sitting with Igz, with my back screaming at me like this, wasn't an option, so we hobbled around and pretended to listen to the TV until she fell asleep. I got her in her crib, and then I retreated to my bedroom. I didn't keep anything stronger than Tylenol in the house because of Chuy, so I popped a couple of those, laid out my heating pad, and stripped down to my boxers. I cracked a window, stuffed a towel under my door, and got into bed. I even managed not to scream, cry, or moan in the process.

The initial injury had been a mountain biking accident, and honestly, it could have been so much worse. For the most part, I was fine, but I carried stress in my back, and since I was almost always stressed—well, you get the idea.

I got a joint out of the nightstand and toked up, which isn't super easy if you're lying in bed, to be honest. But, since I'm a pro, I managed. It didn't take long for the weed to hit me: pulses of cloudy warmth, like a dragon was sitting inside my chest and breathing big, smoky breaths. That image made me giggle. Maybe it was hitting me harder, a distant part of me thought, because I'd been cutting back around Igz. Maybe I was becoming a lightweight.

But maybe not. Because usually, taking a couple of Tylenol and getting blazed would be enough to help me fall asleep, especially with the heating pad. Tonight, though, the pain seemed worse, and I found myself lying there, staring at the ceiling between hits. After a while, I grabbed my phone and started watching porn. I pushed my boxers down and took my dick in my hand. It felt good, every inch of my skin alive with the contact, but most of that was the weed. I watched the girl in the video and pumped myself for a while, but the closest I got was a semi, and then even that went away. It was embarrassing to admit, but more often than not, that had been the way of things. I'd read about it online. Stress, of course. Every fucking thing in my universe comes back to stress. Oh, sure, they talked about other things. Recreational drugs like cannabis might make it difficult to sustain an erection. Well, fuck that. And they talked about depression. I'm not depressed, I thought as I looked up at the ceiling. I massively need to nut and can't get a boner. What's depressing about that?

The knock at the door made me scramble to pull up my boxers. It took me two tries to stop the video on my phone, and a part of my brain was trying to calculate if someone on the other side of the door would be able to hear the moans of "Oh, Daddy," and "I've been a bad girl." When the fucking thing finally stopped, my heart was pounding, and sweat covered me, and the weed was about to send me into a panic attack.

"Fernando?" Zé called through the door quietly. "Are you awake?"

"Uh, yeah." And that weed-soaked part of my brain told me, a moment later, I was an idiot—because why hadn't I pretended to be asleep? "One sec."

I managed to lever myself up from the bed. I found a T-shirt, and of course, it was one that Augustus, with his trademark classy humor, had given me: SAFETY FIRST it said, orange letters against black. DON'T STICK YOUR FINGER WHERE YOU WOULDN'T STICK YOUR and then a traffic cone that was clearly supposed to be a dick. It made me giggle as I pulled it on, and I was still laughing when I opened the door. It only took me three tries before I remembered the towel.

Zé stood in the hall, staring at me. I was still giggling, and he seemed to process me in stages before he said, "Good God, Fernando, are you high?"

His eyes were a little wider than I remembered, and I wanted to check, but he caught my hand and said, "My eyes are the same size they always are, Fernando."

But they looked bigger.

"They're not," he said, and I wondered if I was saying everything out loud or if he could read my mind. His eyebrows made little fuzzy mountains. "You're saying everything out loud."

Somehow, he was holding my hand again, and the corner of his mouth pulled into a smirk. He hadn't shaved for a day or two, and his stubble was thick and dark, and he looked more like a man and less like a kid.

"That's because I'm not a kid," he said in a low voice, his hand tightening around mine, and something had changed in his face. "You need to remember that, Fernando."

"You're supposed to be on a hot date."

"Why do you always think I'm going on dates?"

I was too smart to answer that.

He burst out laughing. "You're so smart, huh?"

In fifth grade, we had done a report on an animal of our choosing, and I had picked a red-tailed hawk, and I remembered the pictures: the tawny body, and the bands at the ends of their tail-feathers, the reddish-orangish brown that gave them their name. And that final, darkest band of brown. And that was the color of his eyes.

He shushed me and said, "Fernando, please." He swallowed. "Stop talking."

I didn't need to talk. It felt good enough to stand there, every inch of me loose, happy that he was here, enjoying the unfamiliar roughness of his hand around mine. A distant part of me was aware that I was still rattling off everything like I was reading from a teleprompter. Aware, too, of the distress growing in his face.

"I wasn't going on a date," he finally said, cutting across the flow of words. "I was—it doesn't matter, I guess. I was doing something dumb. And then I thought about your back, and I decided you might be doing something dumb too. So." He took a deep breath. "How's your back?"

It hurt like a motherfucker, but I didn't say that.

"Are you always like this?" he asked. "It's like a truth serum."

I didn't have anything to say to that, but I could feel myself smiling — a big, loopy smile. Because Zé was here. Zé was home.

"Yeah, yeah, I'm home," he said. He held up a towel and a small bottle, which I hadn't noticed before, and said, "Take your shirt off and get on the bed."

"You were having a night. You were having a nice night."

"I wasn't, actually. I'd like to have one now, but you're making it harder than it needs to be."

"You're the nicest person I know. Why are you sad? You're so nice, you should be happy. Assholes are the ones who shouldn't be happy. Assholes don't deserve to be happy."

"Fernando, get on the bed, please."

Having used it a time or two myself, I recognized the end-of-my-shit quality of his voice, and I shuffled over to the bed. After he spread out the towel, I lay down.

Zé rubbed his eyes.

"What? I did what you said."

"For God's sake," he said under his breath. And then, with a definite tone: "Take your shirt off. And lie on your stomach."

He had to help me sit up, and he turned me out of the shirt. Then, his hands warm on my shoulders, rolled me so that I lay facedown on the towel. It was a regular towel, one of the ones we'd had forever, and it had been washed a million times and was nice and soft. But right then, with every inch of my skin hypersensitive, I thought I could feel every single thread scratching pleasantly against me. Against my chest. Against my belly. Against my nipples.

"How in the world am I supposed to take you seriously the next time you yell at me," Zé asked, "after listening to you go on and on about your nipples?"

I had an answer for that, but before I could dig it up, the mattress dipped under new weight as Zé sat. His hip bumped mine. Then the soft click of a lid opening broke the silence, and Zé touched my back.

I flinched.

He drew his hand back. "I think this will help your back, but are you okay with me touching you?"

"I'm okay with everything. I'm okay with everything you do. You're the best, and everything you do is perfect." And then, because it seemed like pertinent information, I added, "I'm ticklish."

I thought I heard a soft, amused breath, but all he said was "You didn't think I was so perfect when I made you eat those baby carrots for a snack." But his hand moved in a long, slow stroke up my back. Then his hand lifted away, and I heard a liquid sound. "In fact, I'm pretty sure I saw your eye twitch when I told you I'd thrown away the potato chips."

I opened my mouth to tell him I wasn't a nut-rabbit and didn't eat carrots, and I was already starting to giggle. Before I could get the words out, his hands returned to my back, warm and slick with oil. The pressure was light, and the strokes were slow and long, and the oil smelled like pine and sage. An earthy smell. And I thought about how he smelled, coconut wax and the driftwood earthiness—not quite the same, but blending pleasantly with the scent of the oil.

I groaned. I heard myself, and even high, I was shocked at the noise I made. But not shocked enough to stop. Because it felt good. It felt so good. It had been—God, I didn't want to think about how long it had been since someone had touched me like this, more than accidental contact or—rarely—a hug from Augustus.

"How does that feel?" Zé asked in his quiet way.

"How the fuck do you think it feels?"

He laughed. "I guess the other Fernando is still in there."

"There's me," I said as he continued to move his hands lightly over my back. Another moan escaped me. "I'm me."

Zé made a considering noise. "I think there's a lot to Fernando Lopez that I don't know. Maybe nobody knows."

For a while, neither of us said anything. The light, soothing touches made my body light up in ways that I'd almost forgotten—a rush sensation and pleasure that, combined with the weed, turned me into putty. Then the movement of his hands changed. He kneaded my muscles, applying more pressure, lifting and pulling at sore muscles. I groaned again at the pleasurable discomfort of it. His hands were so strong, and he was so quiet and calm, and I thought about how his face looked in the morning, the light coming in through the kitchen window, the stark clarity of it: his jaw, his mouth, the brown of his eyes, that stupid hair that somehow managed to look windswept when he hadn't been anywhere but bed.

His hands moved lower. He said something under his breath, and he gripped me by the sides, fingers curling around me to press against my belly, and he adjusted me on the towel. And it happened. It fucking happened, okay? One minute, I was lying there, half-asleep as the pain in my back faded. And the next, I was wide awake, feeling like I was sixteen again, my dick hardening. It was trapped between my thigh and the mattress, and now it seemed to have a mind of its own. Every time Zé touched me, I got harder—or that's what it felt like, anyway. And he was constantly touching me. Years ago, weed used to make me horny, but for a long time now it had had the opposite effect. Maybe we've come full circle, I thought. Maybe we're back where we started.

"What are you mumbling about?" Zé asked.

Please God, a tiny part of me thought. Please, if there is a God, please do not let me talk about my boner.

Somehow, I managed to slur, "Feels good."

"It's supposed to feel good. How's your back?"

I didn't trust myself to open my mouth, so I groaned again, and Zé laughed.

My situation didn't improve. He was so strong, and he was touching me, and he was so gentle. I thought about how careful he was with Igz, but that only made things worse. I told myself not to think about anything, and instead, I saw him, those mornings I'd walked in on his yoga, and seen him doing downward dog, seen his ass in those tiny shorts pointing up in the air. I thought about how he looked when he fell asleep on the couch, how long his eyelashes were, about the time when we'd both been moving in the kitchen, dancing around each other, and he'd put an arm around my waist without even seeming to think about it. It had only lasted a heartbeat, long enough for him to keep me out of his way while he got a bowl out of a cabinet, but it had been—well, I remembered it, didn't I? It had been something I'd never had. The casual intimacy of people who shared a space with no inhibitions.

And now, every time he pressed and rubbed and pulled, my body shifted in tiny increments against the mattress, and I realized, with a kind of growing horror, that I might actually be able to get off like this.

"Okay," I said, the word syrupy in my mouth as I raised my head. Drool made a shining strand from my lips to the pillow, and I wiped it away, but I was sure he'd already seen. "That's good. My back feels better."

"I just started."

"Yeah, yeah, I'm good—"

"Knock it off. Jeez, why are you so tense?"

He pushed, and he was strong—I let him force me down, his hand flat between my shoulder blades. I had seen that move before. All he had to do was bring my hips up, spread my legs, curl his fingers around my nape. His fingers probed my back again, and I whimpered.

Once again, his technique changed. He dug into sore, tight muscles with fingers and thumbs, and now the discomfort bordered on pain. It was like walking a tightrope, and somehow, Zé seemed to know exactly how to balance between too much and not enough. I still embarrassed myself a few times with grunts and little, shocked noises, but the intensity was actually a relief—my dick went down to a semi, and I didn't appear to be in danger of messing my shorts in the immediate future.

"We should do this more often," Zé said as he worked. "You have to be consistent with massages or you're right back where you started."

I would die. If we ever did this again, I would die. Hell, at this point, I'd probably die if I ever had to be in the same room with him again.

After a while, he returned to those long, gentle strokes. The bulldog in my pocket perked right up again. Then Zé shifted his weight, and the mattress moved under me, and I wanted to groan because it wasn't fair. But I was so caught up in my determination not to hump the mattress like a teenager that I didn't notice, until it was too late, Zé swinging one leg over to straddle me.

He weighed more than I expected. And I was painfully aware of how our bodies lined up. If I hadn't been hard before, I was ready to drill down to China now. The new position must have given him a better angle because now he ran his hands from my shoulders to the small of my back.

When he broke the silence, it startled me, and I flinched. "You realize these are the straightest of straight guy underwear, right?"

And then, before I could process what was happening, he slid a slick finger under the elastic of my boxers and snapped it.

If you thought I'd flinched before.

But Zé didn't seem to notice. He sounded amused as he said, "Blue plaid, Fernando? Seriously?"

I mumbled something.

"I expected something a little more interesting after those booty shorts I saw you in."

A groan escaped me that had nothing to do with the massage. The night Igz had been sick. The night I'd panicked about her breathing and rushed out of the house in those stupid, cock-strangling shorts. I had been trying to forget about that. I'd definitely been hoping Zé had forgotten about that.

"Sorry," he said. "That was inappropriate."

I shook my head, but it probably didn't look like much with me melted into a puddle on the bed.

"How's your back?"

My back, I thought, is definitely not the problem. But all I said was, "Good," and I could hear myself from a long way off, how I sounded, like I was drunk on his touches.

But all Zé did was rub my back again, a caress this time instead of a massage, and it felt like long moments passed before he whispered, "Good."

He shifted his weight. The mattress sank. My body, pulled by gravity, moved fractionally. And my dick, hard as fucking steel, touched his knee.

My personal hell lasted for approximately an eternity.

And then Zé got to his feet, the movement awkward because of his bad knee. We made eye contact (which is always, under every circumstance, a terrible fucking decision), and he gave me a weird, waffling smile with a bug-eyed level of freaked-the-fuck-out-ness. With exaggerated slowness, he picked up the bottle of massage oil, put it down again, grabbed a second towel, dried his hands. He still had that awful smile on his face. He straightened his tee. He looked around the room. I looked around the room too. It wasn't a mess, but it was—well, I was suddenly ashamed that it was drab and dusty and had an echoing emptiness. Although, of course, that was secondary under the topcoat of panicking humiliation. All in all, I thought it would be nice if somebody would shoot me in the head.

"Well," he said.

"Uh, thanks."

"Uh huh. Uh huh. Uh—" He seemed to catch himself. "Yup."

Yup, I thought. Where was a home intruder when you needed one?

We stared at each other. Fucking eye contact again.

"Let me get you some water," Zé finally said.

"No!" It came out more sharply than I intended. "No, I'm good. I feel so relaxed, I'm going to go to sleep." I smiled, and I thought I probably looked like I was insane. "My back feels great."

"You need to drink some water, Fernando."

"I'll drink some, I promise." And then I thought I should say sorry, but then I thought an apology would only make it so much worse. Maybe Hallmark made cards that said, *Sorry about my raging accidental erection.* "And then I'll go straight to sleep."

He twisted the second towel in his hands. His eyes still looked a little wider than usual, and his lips were parted, and it took me longer than it should have to realize that he was genuinely freaked out—and, worse, that he didn't know what to do.

"Zé," I said.

He started.

"Thank you."

He let the towel hang from one hand. "Fernando—"

"I'm going to call it a night."

"Right. Right, gotcha. Okay. Your back?"

"My back is fine. Thank you again."

"Good." He smiled, and it was his real smile, slow and sweet. "I'm glad, Fernando."

"Goodnight."

"Night."

He shut the door on his way out.

I waited until the sound of his steps had moved away. His door clicked shut. Then I got out of bed, turned off the lights, and locked the door. I used the towel to get as much of the oil off my back as I could; I hadn't been lying when I told him my back felt better. It felt great, in fact. Better than it ever had since the accident. Then I spread out the towel and lay down again. I closed my eyes. I told myself to go to sleep.

I lasted about five minutes.

I dragged my boxers down around my thighs. My dick was still hard, and my hand was slick with oil. I found my phone. I was already right on the edge, so I just held my dick and scrolled.

It wasn't the first time I'd watched gay porn. Sometimes, it hit right. Maybe that made me bi. Maybe it made me curious. I didn't know, and I didn't particularly care. One afternoon, when I'd been twelve and babysitting Augustus, I'd beat off with Cesar Davila, and I'd let him finish me. He'd liked it, liked the way I came in his hand. And even back then, I'd been smart enough to know it didn't matter if the other person was a guy or a girl as long as you liked it, you wanted it.

When I settled on a video, I refused to think about why. One of the guys was white, muscular, a daddy type. The other was Latino, with a mop of dark hair and full lips and a smile that spread across his face like honey. It started with a blow job, and when the daddy type pulled the Latin kid off his cock, the younger guy looked blissed out, his lips swollen and shiny, his chin glistening with spit and pre. The daddy turned him over, held him by the back of the neck, and fucked him hard.

I wasn't even sure I moved my hand. One second, I was holding myself, fingers aching. The next, I started to come, my oily fingers tight around my dick, giving stiff, frantic jerks as I moved too late into the orgasm.

I caught the edge of it and wrung myself through the finish. For a moment, every inch of me was alive and shining. And then it was past, and I felt loose and relaxed, the smell of my load mixing with the piney-sage fragrance of the oil. The video was still playing, the bottom whimpering. His voice was too high, I thought as I fumbled to turn it off. He doesn't sound like that at all.

After cleaning myself up, I didn't last long. Sleep trickled in, filling all the quiet spaces around me. My last clear thought was: You are a fucking idiot.

11

"Because if I wanted a human-sized pile of dickcheese stealing my shit," I shouted, "I'd put a call out on Prowler!"

"You're being ridiculous, Fernando." Mom was doing one of her better tricks, putting on an earring as she stepped into her heels. "Cannon didn't steal anything."

The dickcheese in question was hiding behind her, shoulders hunched. "Like, bro—"

"The adults are talking," I told him. "Shut the fuck up!" To Mom, I said, "That was my watch. Mine. And now it's gone because this little fuck-funnel hocked it!"

"Please don't be so dramatic." She did the next earring. "Cannon didn't take your watch."

"Well, it's gone! What the fuck do you think happened? Did it grow a pair of legs?"

"Don't be so dramatic, dear. It'll turn up." She pulled her hair over one shoulder and gave Cannon a smile. I recognized that smile. It was the see-how-hard-my-life-is smile. The look-what-I-put-up-with smile. "We'll get you a new one. That watch was ancient, Fernando. We'll find you something much nicer."

"Augustus gave me that watch."

Frowns meant frown lines, so Mom didn't frown. But she did purse her lips. "I don't remember that."

"Big fucking surprise. You were probably at Camp Vicodin!"

The sound of TV voices, some sort of children's program, filled the chasm between us. Mom's eyes welled with tears.

"Bro," Cannon said apologetically, "now I'm going to have to fight you."

"Do it, jizz lips. Take one fucking step."

Mom put a hand on his chest. "Don't. Please don't."

Cannon's face melted into sympathy, and he clutched her hand.

I slammed the door on my way out of the room.

Zé was out on the deck, walking Igz. His eyebrows were drawn down. His mouth was tight.

"Get your shit," I said.

The wind pulled at his hair. Behind him, sunlight caught the haze over the valley. He rubbed Igz's back, his eyes moving over my face.

"Are you deaf?" I waited, but he still didn't say anything. "We're leaving."

I left him out on the deck. In the kitchen, I packed Igz's diaper bag. The sound of Mom's crying filtered in from her bedroom, competing with the cartoon voices from the TV. The door behind me opened. Zé padded barefoot across the kitchen. When he came back, he'd slipped into his cracked Hurley slides. Today's outfit was a graphic tee with a stylized wave. I'd seen him wear it at least a dozen times; the hem was frayed to tatters. The board shorts were turquoise and printed with birds of paradise, and he had to knot the drawstring because if he didn't, they'd slide right off his ass. He watched, and when I slung the bag over my shoulder, he settled Igz against his chest and followed me out to the SUV.

We drove for a while in silence. The May afternoon felt hot inside the car, so I lowered the windows, and the air smelled like exhaust, so I put them back up again. Zé didn't say anything. He faced forward, but he had one arm contorted behind him so he could keep a hand on Igz's leg. In the rearview mirror, her little face was unreadable, but I could tell she wasn't thrilled with this change of events.

"He's a mile-long trench of boy pussy," I said. "And I swear to Christ he stole that watch."

We rocked over an uneven patch of asphalt. I looked at Zé.

"Maybe," Zé said. "He's insecure. You're older, smarter, more established. You're much better looking. He's competing with you for your mom's attention."

I had to pretzel my brain around that one before I said, "What kind of hot-dogging psycho-bullshit is that?"

"Is that something Americans say? Hot dogging?"

"I am not trying to fuck my mom."

Zé wasn't bitchy, which was a real downside in his character, but he did do something dramatic with his eyebrows, and then with his eyes, and then I thought maybe he secretly was bitchy, and I needed to work harder to bring out this side of him. With exaggerated patience, he said, "He doesn't think you're trying to fuck your mom. He doesn't like how much attention you get."

"What attention? Here's how my conversations with my mom go: either she talks nonstop about herself and whatever new mumbo-jumbo horseshit she's trying, like coffee enemas, and her flavor of the week—sorry, Cannon—or she's asking me for money. That's it, Zé. That's the deep, rich relationship I have with my mom. You know what? If that goose-fucker wants all that attention, he can have it."

Igz began to fuss, and Zé turned around in his seat to murmur to her, his hand rubbing her tummy. I drove, taking us out of our neighborhood and toward—well, I hadn't decided yet. The beach, maybe. Laguna Beach. I started in that direction. I figured if I changed my mind, I could always drive us off a cliff later.

After a while, Igz settled down, and Zé turned forward.

"You don't have to say anything," I said.

He looked at me.

"I shouldn't have raised my voice."

I zipped through a yellow light. He still hadn't said anything.

"I'm an asshole."

"You don't need to apologize for getting angry." His hand rested on my forearm, the touch light, casual. I thought about his hands on my sides, pulling my body. I saw, in my mind, the cock-drunk look of that kid in the video. Oh no, I thought. Abso-fucking-lutely not. Zé was still speaking. "Anger is important. Anger helps us set boundaries. Your mom crossed an important boundary, and it's good that you let her know how you feel."

I was still so fixated on not thinking certain things—like how that messy, tousled hair would feel if I plunged my hand into it—that I forgot to watch my guard, and the words slipped out. "Augustus gave me that watch."

"I heard you say that."

I shook my head as Zé rubbed my arm, and I was surprised that my eyes stung. "I don't even know why I care. It wasn't a great watch. And it was my fucking money; the little wiener just picked it out. But he wanted to give me a Christmas present, and what was I supposed to tell him?"

Traffic thickened as we made our way to the beach, and our progress slowed. In front of us, a Bentley idled at a red light. A bumper sticker said STUDENT DRIVER.

"You have got to be shitting me," I muttered.

Zé laughed. Then he said, "It sounds like he loves you a lot."

"He's an unretracted foreskin. Who the fuck knows what he's thinking?"

We drove some more. Zé's hand moved lightly on my arm.

"Sorry," I said. "I shouldn't have dragged you out of the house. It's your day off, and you've got stuff to do."

"Not really."

"I can drop you off at the house."

"I'd like to spend the day with you."

Not Igz. He'd said, *With you.* Not *With you and Igz.* Which didn't mean anything, I told myself. He felt sorry for me. But it was a nice thing to say.

"I practically raised Augustus," I said. Once again, the words seemed to slip out before I could stop them. "There's almost eight years between us. His dad was out of the picture before his cock was dry; we have different dads, in case you hadn't figured it out."

"What about your dad?"

"He died."

"Oh, Fernando."

"It was a long time ago."

"I'm so sorry."

"Yeah, well, I'm sure if he'd lived longer, I would have realized he was a tremendous disappointment. My mom's taste in men is un-fucking-real." I adjusted the vents even though they didn't need adjusting. "I was only three or four, I think, so I don't remember much about him. He'd take me to the park; I remember that."

"He must have been a good dad because he raised a good son."

I shrugged. "He did stuff for me. All the stuff Mom didn't want to do. And when he was gone, somebody else had to do it."

When I looked over, the expression on Zé's face was too intense, and so I focused on the road.

We drove around Laguna Beach for a while, looking for parking. It was crowded—it's always crowded—but after a while, we lucked into a spot as a Honda Pilot was pulling out. I parked the Escalade, and we got Igz into her stroller. Zé did it, I mean. No fumbling with the buckles. No messing around with the straps. I tried to set up the stroller, and he was kind enough not to laugh as I made a jackass of myself. He made a gimme gesture with one hand, since he had Igz in the other, and then he did some sort of twist-yank-shove movement, and the stroller popped open.

"Are you a fucking ninja?"

"Fernando, I don't have a lot of life goals, but I would be happy if Igz's first word wasn't fuck."

I grinned. "Too fucking bad."

He gave me a look as he got her settled in the stroller, but I was starting to be able to tell the looks apart. This one made me grin harder.

The buildings around the beach itself were a mix of styles—a lot of concrete and glass of Late Modernism, but some holdout, squat brick mid-century stuff, and, even older, Craftsman bungalows with shake roofs. They weren't homes anymore, but now they housed coffee shops and bistros and little art galleries. There were microhotels and tiny two-story strip malls. There were yoga studios and places that did a million kinds of facials and clothing boutiques the size of a box of rubbers. All very charming. I fit right in.

We took our time walking toward the beach, stopping to window-shop, stopping again to get coffees, stopping because we found a little park, and the shade was nice, and the smell of the ocean mixed with the perfume of the trees in bloom. Something was bothering me (not, for a change, Mom), and it took me a while to put my finger on it. A pair of guys in expensive shoes and matching shorts stared at us as they passed. An elderly man smiled and nodded and made way too much eye contact. A woman in an enormous floppy hat stopped to coo over Igz, and as she straightened, told me—us—"You have a beautiful daughter."

"They think we're a couple," I said out loud.

Zé laughed. He laughed hard. He laughed so hard, in fact, that he had to stagger in a circle, and then he winced and rubbed his knee, but he kept laughing.

"Go on," I said. "Enjoy yourself. This is going to be a great fucking memory when you have a peg leg."

Eventually, he stopped laughing. Not that I minded much. He had these perfect laugh lines that bracketed his mouth. He was usually so calm, so tranquil, and I enjoyed the way happiness made a riot of his face. And listening to him laugh reminded me how long it had been since, well, that had been part of my life. Since Augustus had left. And that had been years ago.

"I'm sorry," he said as he rubbed his knee. "It's, I thought you knew— I mean, that old guy winked at you."

"He didn't—"

Zé had a tiny, hidden grin.

"You assclown!"

"They think we're a couple." He repeated my words with what sounded like despair.

"Well, I didn't know, weasel-dick. How the fuck was I supposed to know?"

But at the same time, it actually hadn't been a surprise—more of a revelation, if I had to put a word on it. Like the pieces had been there, and my brain had been trying to put them into place. The way we walked next to each other. The way he caught my arm when he wanted to show me something. How he asked for something out of Igz's bag, and I got it for him. How I'd put my hand at the small of his back to steady him when we went up the stairs to the coffee shop, and the feeling of firm muscle and warm skin. Everything, in fact, about how we moved around each other, shared each other's space, talked and laughed. And then the part of my brain that was one hundred percent Fer added, Everything except fucking.

"I'm sorry," he said again, but I could tell he still wanted to laugh. "Does it bother you?"

"Of course not. It should bother you. And you should definitely have higher standards."

He smiled, but it was a strange smile, the amusement tempered with something else—something that, on anyone else, I might have registered as hurt. But all he said was "Why would it bother me?"

"I don't know. I'm old. I'm out of shape. I look like I just rolled out of the laundry hamper. Should I go on?"

And I didn't think, until it was too late, that I could have said—might have said—*Because I'm straight*.

But then, was I?

I'd told Augustus once that sexuality was a buffet, that you could try a little of everything. Because even back then I'd suspected. In elementary school, and in most of middle school, his friends were mostly girls. And although that had changed in high school, it was hard not to notice the rest of it: the horsing around with his friends, the excessive physical contact, the videos of them all going shirtless and pretending to make out. And that was fine; whatever made him happy, that was fine.

I'd always stuck to one side of the buffet, though (if you didn't count that time I'd let Cesar spank it for me, or that insane chicken-choking episode from a few nights before, which I blamed entirely on that damn massage). I'd considered, at various times, the possibility that I was bi or pan or that I didn't need a label. But that had always been theoretical. It was moot; it didn't matter. Except now, of course, it did. Or I thought it might. If I wasn't a complete and total moron, which, I know, was probably giving me too much credit.

Too late, I realized Zé had said something, and I'd missed it. What? What had he said? I'd been saying—*I'm old. I'm out of shape*—and he'd said something, and now he was looking at me, his eyes asking me something.

The silence had gone on too long, but for some reason, it only made him smile more. He touched my cheek and said, "Good God, Fernando," and he laughed.

"What?"

He shook his head and raised the brakes on Igz's stroller.

"What?" I asked again.

"You might be the definition of impossible," he said as he got unsteadily to his feet and started to push the stroller out of the park.

"What the fuck is that supposed to mean?"

We were getting close to the beach when we passed a clothing boutique, and the idea hit me. When we went inside, the bell jingled. It smelled like patchouli and something resinous, and rows and rows of clothing racks and mannequins and shelving units made the space so cramped that the stroller barely fit.

A fancy boy with flawless skin unlimbered himself from a stool and slunk over to us. He gave each of us a long look, and then he settled on me. He gave me a smile with lots of beautiful teeth, and it registered at only slightly warmer than frostbite. With a hint of camp, he said, "Welcome to Into Summer. How can I help you gentlemen today?"

Zé was busy with something in the diaper bag, and, because he truly was a petty little bitch underneath all the saintly kindness, he was hiding a smile.

I knew I'd have to do it carefully. I knew, from how he'd responded when I'd basically had to blackmail him into accepting a place to live, that it wouldn't be easy. But I thought, if I were careful, I could do it.

"I need some clothes for work," I said. "Business casual stuff."

"Of course, sir." He made it sound like *Daddy*. "Right over here."

"I didn't know you needed clothes for work," Zé said in a low voice.

"Is this okay? We're not on a schedule or anything, are we? I want something new for that interview with Lou's team."

"Of course it's okay."

"You don't mind helping me pick something out? I've lost some weight, and I want a few things that fit better." That wasn't a lie; Zé, for all his easygoing, surfer bum hair, for all his meltingly soft eyes, turned into a nutritional dominatrix the minute he set foot in the kitchen. Ten pounds in four weeks was a lot, but when this leather-and-stiletto bitch threw out all your ice cream and potato chips and, I shit you not, inspected your takeout for contraband, it wasn't actually all that hard. In fact, it was kind of easy to lose weight with Zé in the house. All I had to do was not murder him every time I got hungry. "Normally," I said, "I buy everything and then FaceTime Augustus. I put it on mute for the first ten minutes, and then I turn the sound back on and get something helpful out of him."

The smile only touched his eyes. "I don't mind."

"You're sure?"

"I'm sure, Fernando."

"It's not weird?"

The smile in his eyes deepened, and he pushed me to get me moving. "You're starting to make it weird."

The fancy boy walked us through the men's section, and at Zé's advice, I got a pair of polos, a couple of button-ups, and two new pairs of chinos. They had a dressing room, and Zé refused to let me buy the clothes without trying them on. As I changed, I heard him making small talk with the fancy boy, although I couldn't make out the words. Something made Zé laugh, though—more of the low, quiet, rolling laughter that I couldn't seem to get enough of.

When I stepped out of the dressing room, Zé took one look at my face, smirked—an actual, honest-to-God smirk—and said, "None of your business."

"Fuck you, you dicked-down horse dildo."

The fancy boy gasped. Like, a Broadway-quality gasp.

Zé, though, only smirked some more and went to work inspecting the clothes. He ran his hand down my chest, smoothing the polo. He fixed the sleeves. He ran his fingers inside the waistband of the chinos and tugged, and for a moment, I had this weightlessness in my gut, and I remembered how he'd gripped my hips the other night, how easy it had been for him to move me. Zé pronounced the clothes acceptable and sent me back to change.

I took extra long, but I only managed to get myself down to a semi, and I was pretty sure the fancy boy noticed. Sue me. They were mesh shorts; what the fuck was I supposed to do?

"You'd look good in this," I said, picking up a T-shirt at random. I handed it to Zé. "Try it on."

He held it, and he was still as he looked at me.

I grabbed a pair of shorts. They weren't board shorts, but that was a purposeful decision on my part. Zé had great thighs, and what the fuck good were they swimming around inside a pair of board shorts? These were black, and they had a nice cut, and they'd hit him mid-thigh, which was about perfect. "And these."

He took the shorts. He still hadn't said anything.

"Okay, I know it's getting close to summer," I said as I picked up a lightweight hoodie, "but you're always cold in the mornings."

"Fernando," he said quietly. Not his usual quiet. This was ultraquiet, so low I was sure he didn't want the fancy boy to hear us.

"I bet they have slides."

"Fernando."

His voice pulled on me. I looked him in the eye.

"This is sweet of you," he said. "And I appreciate it. But I don't need you to buy me clothes."

"I didn't say you needed me to buy you clothes."

He was holding the T-shirt and the shorts all wrong, letting them hang from his hands like he didn't know what to do with them.

"You helped me out," I said. "The fashion advice, or whatever you want to call it. Let me pay you back."

"Fernando," he said again, this time with a note of exasperation.

"I want to do it."

"Thank you, but no."

"Why not?"

"I appreciate it. I do. You're a generous person."

"You wear the same shirt three or four times a week."

"Fernando."

"Your clothes all have holes in them."

The fancy boy was drifting closer, drawn to the bloody chum of my rising voice.

"If you don't like the style, fine. Pick out something else. Or we'll go to another store."

Zé turned to the fancy boy. "We're ready to check out."

"No," I said. "We're not. We're having a conversation."

"Igz and I will meet you outside." He leveled a cool challenge of a look at me. "Unless you didn't need to buy new clothes."

I paid. And the clothes cost a fucking fortune.

Zé and Igz and I covered the last hundred yards to the beach in silence. The waves crashed. A gull cried. People thronged the beach, and their voices competed with each other—and, of course, with the music from portable speakers. Since this had been an impromptu trip to the beach-slash-escape from the house, we didn't have any of the right gear. No blankets. No sunscreen, which I didn't think about until Zé tugged the stroller's little awning into place to cover Igz. Not even my sunglasses from the car. Zé was shading his eyes.

"Can you watch Igz?" His voice was its usual even calm. "I need to pee."

I grunted and tried to find a way to stash the new clothes in the stroller's cargo area—which was a losing battle because that diaper bag was so damn big. Zé moved off toward the public restrooms. He was limping. We'd walked a lot, and of course, I hadn't thought about what that might do to his knee. He never said anything about it. He never complained. But the way he moved now—the unsteadiness, the stiffness—told me he'd been actively working to hide the strain.

Because he didn't want to be a burden. That thought rang clearly in my head. Like he hadn't wanted to accept the offer of room and board. Like he hadn't wanted to accept the new clothes, even though I thought I'd done a pretty fucking fine job of making that seem casual. You do so much for—

I caught myself almost thinking *our family*. And that's what I meant, of course. Igz and I were family. But it sounded different in my head. Like that wasn't the family I was thinking of.

You do so much for all of us, I tried again. You cook and clean. You get up with Igz when you don't have to. You gave me that massage (although the less said about that, the better). You found those weird taro chips and tried to convince me I'd like them, even though they tasted like cardboard ass. You make me laugh. I wake up in the morning thinking about things I want to tell you.

I texted Zé, *We're running a quick errand.* Then I wheeled Igz around, and we crossed the street to a strip of shops facing the water. The closest one was a sunglasses store, and the guy working—white, twentyish, with a great tan and long, blond hair and off-the-radar fuckboy vibes—was happy to sell me a pair of sunglasses. I bought myself something cheap, another pair I could throw in the glove box, but I picked out a nice pair of Ray-Bans for Zé. They were the right shape for his face, I could already tell. As the guy put everything in a bag, I ran through my list of reasons. This is a gift, I'd say. I want you to have this because I'm grateful for all the things you do for our family. It wouldn't sound as weird, I was pretty sure, when I said it out loud.

Igz and I found him in front of a surf shop. He was staring at a longboard in the display window—an elegant piece with a wood deck and impossibly perfect lines. We got closer, and he stood there, staring. A woman bumped him, and he shifted his weight, but otherwise he didn't even seem to notice. I recognized the look on his face. I had one junkie brother and another I'd spoiled shamelessly (well, once I could afford to). I knew what pure, unadulterated desire looked like, and I was seeing it right then on Zé's face.

"Do you surf?" I asked.

He startled, turned, and for a moment his face was blank. Then he looked like Zé again, and he bent to check Igz as he said, "It's been a while."

"Because of the surgery?"

His voice was guarded when he said, "Yeah."

"Do you like that board?"

Zé's laugh tried a little too hard. "Anyone would like that board. It's one of the best longboards out there."

"Let's go in and look at it."

I turned Igz toward the surf shop's door, and he grabbed the frame of the stroller.

"What?" I asked. "It'll be fun."

"I think Igz might be hungry," he said. "And I could use something to eat."

"We're going to look." And then I grinned. "And maybe get an idea for your birthday present."

"No."

A couple of middle-aged beach bums, shirtless and leathery, passed us. One of them, I shit you not, was talking about "that gnarly wave."

"It was a joke," I said.

"I know. Why don't we find somewhere to eat?"

"But if I want to buy you something for your birthday, I'm going to."

He looked out at the water.

For some reason, that only made me angrier. I took the Ray-Bans out of the bag and tossed them, still in their case, toward him. He caught them reflexively.

"I bought you those," I said.

"I don't want you to buy me anything."

"Too fucking bad. It's my money, and I already bought them."

Zé shook his head and held them out toward me.

"Then throw them away."

He was looking at the ground now. A hint of red showed under the dark brown of his skin.

"They're a gift," I said. "Because I like you. And because I'm grateful for you."

His voice was small when he said, "I don't need you to buy me anything."

"That's the whole fucking premise of a gift, dick-drip." It was hard to make a dramatic exit with a stroller, but I think I kind of managed it. "I'm going to change Igz."

By some miracle, the public restrooms had a changing table in the men's room. Igz fussed a little as I got her changed, and I thought Zé was probably right—she was hungry. When I came out of the restroom, Zé was standing there, still staring at the ground. He managed to look both miserable and pathetic. I started down the sidewalk. The jingle of a bell as someone sold ice cream out of a handcart. Children laughing. A gull screeching. Movement in the corner of my eye made me turn—the damn bird was flying straight at me—no, straight at Igz. I ducked, shielding Igz as I waved an arm, trying to knock the bird off course.

It didn't come anywhere near us. I understood that as soon as my brain caught up with my body. The gull veered off, shrieking as it flew away. But my body didn't care about that. My adrenaline was still up. I was starting to shake.

"Are you okay?" Zé asked. He was limping worse than ever, but he tried to jog to catch up.

"I'm fine," I snapped. But the anger was fading along with the fear. "Jesus Christ, these fucking birds."

"One time, one of them took a hot dog right out of my hand. I screamed like a girl."

I laughed, and after a moment, Zé laughed too. He was still holding the sunglasses, but with his free hand he touched my arm, and then he leaned over the stroller to check Igz.

"You're sure you're okay?"

"I'm fine," I said. "Apparently, I'm a flincher when it comes to seagulls. And I'm starving. And I'm mad at myself because I ruined our day."

"Our day started with you yelling at me to get my stuff because you were in a fight with your mom."

"You understand how that doesn't make me feel better, right?"

That got me a real Zé smile, the slow one.

"Asshole," I muttered. "Come on. How about there?"

There was a beachside cantina—barely more than a wooden frame, with three sides open to the beach. Inside, the aesthetic was driftwood and Modelo, and lazy ceiling fans spun overhead. I ordered a Modelo—hey, advertising works—and Zé got water.

As I unbuckled her, he said, "I'll do it."

"No," I said. "It's your day off." And then, because Augustus comes by his pettiness honestly, I said, "I don't need you to do extra work for free."

Unhappiness etched his face, and he wrapped both hands around his glass.

Once I had Igz contentedly sucking down a bottle, I took a sip of my beer.

Zé held up one finger.

"What's that supposed to mean?"

"You know what it means."

I took a longer drink.

"I'm serious, Fernando. You're driving."

I set the bottle down. It clinked against the wood.

"I'm sorry about earlier," Zé said, and his voice was so quiet that over the whoosh of the fans, I barely heard him. "It's...hard for me."

"You'll have to be more specific, dick-drip. What's hard for you? Because it sure doesn't seem hard for you to boss me around and tell me what I can drink and, let me guess, what I can eat."

"Either the shrimp tacos—grilled, not fried—or the beach salad."

In spite of my best efforts, I smiled. "That's got kind of a controlling vibe."

"Or I guess it could be your cheat meal. You want a burger, don't you?"

"I want you to tell me what's going on. I'm not exactly a master of communication, but believe it or not, I picked up on some weird fucking energy a few minutes ago." I took another drink of my beer and, after a minor struggle, added, "I'm sorry for shouting at you."

For some reason, that made him smile, and he relaxed—those long limbs loosening, his shoulders opening. "Fernando, I don't care if you yell at me. It's kind of cute, actually."

"No, it's not. It's terrifying."

"If I cared about you yelling at me, I would have quit, like, the second day."

"I was nice to you on the second day! I was nice to you the whole fucking time, right up until I caught you living like a sneak-ass bitch out of your car!"

"I was playing the xylophone with Igz, and you screamed—screamed, Fernando—from your office that you were on the phone, and maybe it could be musical playtime literally at any other point in the day."

"Oh my God, I forgot about that."

Zé wiped condensation from his glass with his thumb.

"But I didn't swear," I said.

"But the xylophone ended up in the trash."

I burst out laughing. "I didn't think you noticed that."

He gave me those fuzzy, quirking eyebrows again, and I laughed harder.

"I don't mind you yelling," he said again. "Honestly, it doesn't bother me. Or the language, although I wish you'd watch what you said around Igz. I—I've worked hard to be independent. That's important to me. This isn't about you. You're such a good person. You're so generous, so kind. I appreciate that you want to give me something. But I need to live life on my own for a while."

I ran my thumb around the mouth of the bottle, tracing the ridges in the glass. "God, you ended up in the worst fucking family, then."

"That's another reason: you have all these people who need things from you. I don't want to be another one of those people in your life. You're already giving me a place to live—"

"That's part of the job," I said. "That's your compensation. You earned that."

He gave me a sad smile.

It took me a moment; my throat was tight, and I didn't trust my voice. "I…appreciate that. Honestly, I do. You don't know—" But I didn't know either. Didn't know how to finish that sentence. Didn't know how to put into words how hard it was sometimes, or what it meant to have someone who didn't want something from me. Didn't know how to explain, even to myself, why Zé's stubborn refusal to accept anything from me also awoke a baseline panic in me, why it made me feel, with doubled urgency, the need to find something, anything, to give him. I managed to add, "I'm sorry again. Sorry I ruined the day. I was having a nice day."

"Even though people thought we were a couple."

"Real fucking funny."

That slow smile was spreading across his lips again.

I pointed my beer at him. "You should be so lucky, with that badger-fucker excuse you call a face."

It only made him laugh, of course.

When the waiter came, I ordered the shrimp tacos. Grilled, not fried. Zé got ceviche. Igz was asleep in my arms, and I thought about putting her back in the stroller, but she felt good where she was, the weight of her grounding me. And maybe someone will think, again, that we're together. That thought came out of nowhere, and when it did, I didn't know what to do with it.

"You didn't ruin our day," Zé said, and it took me a moment to track the words back to what we'd been saying. He was playing with the napkin-wrapped bundle of silverware, tearing little strips off the paper. "We had an argument. But we worked it out, right? I mean, that's an important part of any relationship. If we're going to be in each other's lives like this, we've got to know how to work out disagreements. And it's good that we're, you know, compatible. You can yell at me, and I don't care. And then, when we're both calm—well, you're good at making me feel...safe. So we can talk. Even when I might not, you know, want to talk."

"That was excruciating to listen to," I said. "You know that, right?"

He threw some of the wadded-up paper at me.

"And give me a break. You're the kindest human being in existence. Get into disagreements, Jesus Christ. I was an asshole. I'm always the asshole; I know that."

"No, you're not. I acted badly today." Before I could respond, he rushed to ask, "But we're okay, right?

"I don't know. What are you going to do with those stupid sunglasses?"

The look he shot me was genuinely distressed, and I almost relented. But he was right about being in each other's lives, and this was another thing we needed to figure out.

"Fernando."

"I should be able to do something nice for you. I understand that you want to be independent; that's great. I respect that, actually, because I had to do it, and I know how hard it is. But you do all sorts of things for me that go above and beyond your job, like—" And it almost slipped out: that fucking massage. Instead, I scrambled to course correct. "—taking care of Igz even after I get home, or waking up with her in the middle of the night, or watching her on weekends."

"I'm happy to do those things. I like doing those things."

"And I like doing nice things for you, dipshit!"

It was about a six out of ten on the roar scale, and Igz startled in her sleep but didn't wake. People turned to look. I threw some dirty glances in every direction. One white lady who was up to her tits in rosé spritzes said, "How rude."

When I turned back, Zé ducked his head to hide a grin.

"Oh," I said. "That's funny?"

The ceiling fans—and the white lady with her spritzes—made it hard to tell, but I was pretty sure he giggled.

"I will try," I put emphasis on the word, "to keep the gifts to a minimum, because I know they make you uncomfortable. I hear you, okay? But it's my money. And if I want to spend some of it on you, I'm damn well going to."

He nodded, and although it looked like a struggle, he said, "Thank you."

I watched him for a moment: that big, sprawling body; the long, strong lines; the way he'd giggled, and how young that had made him sound. I shook my head and smothered a smile. "Jesus Christ, Teixeira."

He wrinkled his nose at that. "Oh God, the straight-guy last-name thing. No, no, no. We're not fraternity brothers or golf buddies or high school football players."

"Of course not," I said, and for some reason, I picked up my beer, and it was empty now, of course, and I was thinking about how badly I needed another when I said, hearing myself from a long way off, "We're friends."

12

When we got home, Mom and Cannon were gone. I pulled into the garage and got out of the Escalade. Zé limped around to meet me, pain shadowing his face until he saw me. Then it vanished like a magic trick, and I wondered how long he'd been doing that, how long he hadn't been letting me see.

"Go sit down," I said.

"I'm fine."

I worked on the buckles. Igz was staring up at me with her dark eyes.

"It stiffened up on the ride back."

"Go sit your ass down before I have to yell at you again!"

Four on the roar scale.

He was laughing as he went inside. Not loud, but I could hear him.

But when I rescued Igz from a million straps that seemed like they were actively trying to behead her, I found Zé in the kitchen, pulling out a cutting board.

"Hi," I said. "You might remember me from such tender moments as shouting at you in the garage and screaming at you in front of a surf shop."

"Don't forget that time I made you eat radicchio."

"It's purple, Zé. Nobody in their right fucking mind eats things that are purple."

"Actually—"

"Go sit down!"

That one was closer to a seven. Igz started to fuss, and Zé frowned. He reached for her.

"Believe it or not," I said, "I can take care of her for five minutes. Let's get you on the couch—do you want an ice pack?"

"But I'm fine—"

"Love to hear it," I said as I steered him—gently—toward the living room.

When I planted him in front of the couch, though, he didn't sit. "How are you going to make dinner while you're holding Igz?"

"In the first place, you do that every day."

He opened his mouth.

"Every day, Zé. And in second place, she's got a swing, or I can put her in her pack-and-play, or I can even put her on a blanket on the floor. See how resourceful I am?"

"I'm getting a lot of masculine energy from you right now. Is this how you sound when you talk about tools?"

"And in the third place, I'm not making dinner, pigeon-dick. I'm going to order us dinner. On my phone. Which I can use with one hand." I took a deep breath and smiled. "Sit down. Igz and I will get you an ice pack."

The struggle showed in his face. Finally, he said, "Maybe I'll soak it in the tub for a few minutes."

"That sounds great. Now I won't have to murder you."

"Somebody else might find this confusing, just so you know."

"José, I swear to God, I am this close."

That slow smile, the one I thought of as mine, spread across his face. He put a hand on my arm to steady himself, bent to kiss Igz, and then limped toward the bathroom. I watched him go. I wasn't a card-carrying member of *Homo eroticus* like Augustus, but let me tell you, those board shorts weren't doing his ass any favors.

You might be shocked—shocked!—to learn that Zé had thrown away all my takeout menus, even the good one from Imperial Kingdom, and that one still had a coupon on the back I hadn't used. I thought about getting Imperial Kingdom without the coupon—or, maybe pizza, since it had been approximately an eternity since I'd had pizza. (Okay, to be fair, that's not including all the meals with doctors when I cheated, which Zé didn't need to know about, although, come to think of it, he probably did.)

After a few minutes of pulling my pud, though, I found a Greek place that delivered, and I ordered us some salads and, because I'm a hardass motherfucker alpha male, and nobody tells me what to do, a side of falafel.

I was rocking Igz when I heard the thud from the bathroom, and then Zé's pained cry.

It took me approximately ten seconds to get Igz into her swing and sprint down the hall. I swear to God, I'm not sure my feet touched the floor. When I threw open the door, Zé lay on the floor. He was wet and naked, and whatever I'd seen (and, more vigorously, imagined) during my spank sessions, it was nothing compared to having the real thing in front of me. His body was defined and masculine and healthy and young. He had muscles that would probably never see the light of day again on my body. Everything seemed to register at once: the hint of tan lines, the dusting of dark hair on his thighs, the rose-brown of his nipples. And his dick, yes, because God help me, I looked.

But it all happened in an instant, because he sounded like he was hyperventilating, or about to cry, each inhalation ragged, and he was still lying on the floor.

"Are you okay? What—"

That was when I caught a look at his face, and I remembered the night I'd figured out he was sleeping in his car: when he'd stumbled and, for a moment, he thought he'd hurt his knee. That was nothing compared to this. This was unadulterated panic, his face blank and registering only that all-consuming fear as he lifted his head, trying to get a better look at himself.

I yanked a towel down and dropped to my knees next to him. He was still doing that awful breathing, still trying to sit up, so I said, "Hey, hey,

Zé!" His eyes cut toward me, but I wasn't sure he was seeing me. I shook out the towel and laid it over his waist—I mean, the cat was out of the bag, so to speak, but I figured I didn't have to sit there and drool over him. He was still trying to sit up, so I put a hand on his chest. He was warm, his skin still slick with water from the bath, and I thought I could feel his heartbeat going a hundred miles an hour. "Hold on," I said. "Don't move for a minute."

After another moment, I could see him behind those glassy eyes. He was still sucking in those panicked breaths. "My knee—"

"In a minute," I said. I slid my hand behind his head and probed around. "How hard did you hit your head?"

"Oh God, my knee."

"José," I snapped. "How hard did you hit your head?"

He squeezed his eyes shut. I couldn't find anything worrisome on the back of his head. Not even a bump, actually. I rubbed his chest with my free hand.

"Slow down," I said. "Slow, slow. We're going to take care of your knee in a minute."

He nodded, and slowly, his eyes opened. Tears spilled down his cheeks, and his voice was thready as he said, "I didn't hit my head." He gestured. "I caught the toilet like this—" He threw out his arm. "—and it slowed me down."

"Okay, that's great. Where'd you take the fall, then?"

"My arm," he said. "And my ass."

I checked his arm. There was no visible sign of a broken bone, but since I'd loaned my X-ray specs to Augustus when he was seven and (big surprise) never gotten them back, I couldn't tell for sure. "Do you think something's broken?"

He shook his head.

"Do you want me check your ass? That was a joke, sorry."

"Fernando, my knee. Oh God."

I shushed him. Together, we got him into a sitting position, propped up against the tub. I looked at his knee. Aside from the scar, though, there wasn't anything I could see. I took out my phone and then realized I had no idea what to Google. "What was the procedure?"

He had both hands over his face, and his chest was still rising and falling more rapidly than I liked, but he sounded surprisingly steady when he said, "ACL reconstruction."

"Okay. Let's see what Dr. Google has to say."

Well, it turned out, not a whole lot. Most of the articles were about the actual process of injuring your ACL, which usually involved a fall.

"Let's get you to the ER," I said.

He dropped his hands. "Fernando, no."

"Zé, yes."

"I can't."

"Why not?"

"Because I can't afford it."

"Don't worry about that right now; we'll figure it out."

"No."

"It won't be charity. We can find a way—"

"No!"

It was the first time he had yelled at me. He was trembling—and, I noticed, about to cry again.

"Okay," I said. "No hospital."

"I need to—" He twisted around like he wanted to get up. "I need to get to my room."

"What the fuck do you think you're doing?"

"I'm—"

"It was a rhetorical question." He reached for the side of the tub, like he might push himself up, and I caught his hand. "Unh-uh. Nope."

"Fer—"

"If you don't want to go to the hospital, that's fine. Actually, it's not, but I'm quickly running out of fucks. But I don't want you dragging your lanky ass all over the house, fucking up your leg in the meantime."

He wiped his eyes. I wasn't sure a single word had made it through his panic.

"Just wait a minute," I said, squeezing his hand. "Okay?"

He nodded and wiped his face again. He clutched my hand.

I found Kennedi James in my contacts and placed the call. It rang a few times, and then a woman's husky voice said, "You'd better not be trying to make an appointment."

"God, I wish. I'm sorry to bother you, but I need some advice. Do you have a minute?"

"I've got hundreds of them. I'm stuck at the clubhouse playing nice while Duncan schmoozes on the golf course. I swear to God, if this bitch tells me one more time about how hard it is to find the right nude for her skin tone, I will not be liable for my actions."

"Uh huh. Sorry, listen, I'm in a weird spot and I'm kind of in a rush. My friend had an ACL reconstruction—how long ago?"

I could see it in Zé's big brown eyes when he thought about lying to me, but then he sagged against the tub and whispered, "Five and a half months."

I repeated it into the phone.

"How's his recovery going?" Kennedi asked. "How much is he using his cane?"

The question didn't seem to make any sense. And then I saw the look on Zé's face, the way he closed his eyes like that might make him invisible, and I knew.

"He's not using a cane," I said. I thought about all the days we'd gone on walks. All the times I'd come home and found him and Igz nesting in the living room, with everything they might possibly need gathered in one spot. So he wouldn't have to get to his feet. I thought about how I'd dragged him up and down Laguna Beach today. I felt like I was listening to myself from a long way off when I said, "At all."

"Well, that's stupid. I mean, he should be weaning himself off it, but it's not like he needs to go cold turkey. Okay, what's going on?"

"He fell, and we're worried he damaged the reconstruction."

"Take him to the ER."

"Right, I know. We're working on that. But is there anything we can do to check, you know, right now?"

Her silence lasted a beat longer before she said, "Does he have any pain in his knee?"

I asked Zé.

After a few tentative movements, shifting around, he shook his head.

"All right," Kennedi said. "What about his range of motion?"

Zé raised his leg, flexed his knee, extended it, and repeated the whole process a few more times. Finally, he said, "I think it's okay."

"What about looseness? Does he feel any instability?"

It took both of us to get Zé to his feet (and, yes, you pervert, he managed to keep the towel around his waist). He took an experimental step. Then another. I've never seen somebody facing a death sentence, but watching hope rise in his face, I thought I might have an idea what a man being pardoned might look like. He smiled at me, and it was like the sun coming up. And then the tears came again, and he leaned against the sink and covered his eyes.

"Those would be my main areas of concern," Kennedi said, "but you should still get him checked out." She hesitated. "Why don't you bring him by the office on Monday?"

"That would be amazing."

"I'm charging you an exorbitant rate."

That made me laugh.

"And I want lunch, Fer. At Di Bello's."

"Done. You got it."

"Wonderful. Now stop bothering me; I've got to go accidentally tell this bitch we bought a villa in Tuscany."

"You bought a villa?"

"God, no. Duncan is way too cheap. But she won't know that."

The call disconnected. In the silence that came after, Zé's ragged breathing seemed to take up space in my head. He was wiping his cheeks now, trying to get himself under control. He wouldn't meet my eyes.

"Let's get you in your room," I said.

"I can—"

Whatever he saw on my face made him stop.

I kept an arm around his waist as we shuffled into his room. I sat him on his bed.

"Clothes?" I asked.

"My joggers," he whispered, face turned down, but he pointed to the dresser. "Bottom drawer. A tee."

The joggers had split at one seam, of course. The tee showed a shark eating a surfboard. I threw them on the bed, and he flinched.

"Do you want help getting dressed?"

He shook his head.

"Where is your cane?"

"Fernando—"

"Where is your fucking cane?"

His voice was even smaller when he said, "In my car. In the trunk."

"Keys."

I thought, maybe, he was going to argue. Going to try to tell me he didn't need it. Maybe say something stupid like, *I'm fine*. But he pointed to the dresser again, and I scooped the keys off the top.

In the doorway, I paused. "Do you understand what's going to happen if I find your ass anywhere but on that bed when I get back?"

He nodded.

I found the cane in his trunk. He needed this. He was supposed to be using this. And instead, for weeks now, he'd gone without because—why? Because he'd thought I'd fire him? I stood there, holding on to the car, as black spots whirled in my vision. I couldn't get enough air. My heart pounded. Sweat broke out across my chest and back. What if he'd hurt himself? What if he'd made it worse? What if it wasn't the fall that messed up his reconstruction? What if it was a month of pushing himself? And then, more clearly, I thought, What about PT? Maybe he'd gone on the weekends, maybe, but I knew he hadn't.

When I got back to his room, he'd managed to pull on the joggers and the tee. The wet towel hung from the headboard. I put the cane next to him and stepped back.

He still wasn't meeting my eyes, but he opened his mouth.

I spoke first. "I'm going to tell you a few things, and I don't want to hear you talk." I struggled to master my voice. "We're going to Kennedi's on Monday, and she's going to look at your knee. She's an excellent orthopedic surgeon."

Zé's head came up. "No—"

"What did I say about not talking?" He shrank back at my shout. A few more long moments passed as I fought for control. "After that, you're going to PT. Regularly." I could hear myself, how short and shallow my breaths were. Once more, I tried for control, but it slipped away. "You could have gotten hurt! You could have hurt Igz! What the fuck were you thinking?"

He wiped his eyes again, but I couldn't tell if he was crying. The silence grew and grew.

I left and shut the door.

13

I walked Igz around the house, fed her, burped her, and then somehow, I wasn't angry anymore, just tired. We both fell asleep on the couch. The doorbell woke me, and I put Igz in her swing and paid the delivery guy and carried the food into the kitchen. I fished out Zé's salad and a fork, and I found a bottle of water and the Tylenol, and I carried it to his room. I knocked.

His voice was rough when he said, "Come in."

He was sitting up, but it was clear he'd been lying down until I'd knocked. His hair was standing up in back where it had dried against the pillow. His eyes were red, and I thought that he'd been crying, and then I thought how stupid a motherfucker I was because, of course it made me feel bad.

"Dinner," I said. I shook the bottle of pills. "If Tylenol isn't strong enough, my mom probably has—"

"No," he said quickly. He tried for a smile. "Tylenol is fine. Thank you."

I was still standing there in the doorway like an ass-muffin.

"Could I eat with you and Igz?" he asked.

I grunted and made my way back to the living room. I laid out the meal on the coffee table, set the table at an angle to the sofa so Zé would be able to sit down, and got myself a beer. When I went back to the living room, Zé was lurking in the hallway. Apparently he did have a tiny bit of brains, because he was using the cane.

"Sit on the fucking couch, jizz-for-brains," I said. "What the fuck are you going to do? Be a creep over there and eat your dinner telepathically?"

"I was waiting for you to come out of the kitchen so I could do that scene from *Willy Wonka*. He's walking on that cane and then he does that big surprise roll, and everyone is amazed."

"This is because you didn't have a big brother to bully the shit out of you."

I don't think I was supposed to see it, but a tiny smile darted across his mouth. Then his expression was carefully neutral again. He sat on the sofa. He kept his injured leg stretched out in front of him, and I was glad I'd angled the coffee table.

For a while, the only sounds were the television (CNN), the crinkle of plastic and foil as we went to work on our salads, the motor of Igz's swing. I felt like I could hear everything. When he wiped his mouth with a napkin. When a piece of lettuce crunched between his teeth. When he shifted his weight, trying to get comfortable, the springs of the sofa protested. His thigh ended up pressed against mine. I thought I could smell his hair. I thought I could smell his skin. I thought I was going out of my fucking mind.

"I'm sorry," he said and set his fork down. "Fernando, I am so, so sorry."

There didn't seem anything safe to say to that, so I grunted.

"Could we talk about this? Please?"

I turned the television up. They were talking about the president's dog. Fascinating stuff.

"Okay," Zé said and grabbed the remote and turned the TV off.

I looked at him. Slowly.

"I know you're angry at me. You're right to be angry at me."

"Anger is about boundaries," I said. "Isn't that what you told me? Here's my fucking boundary: you making the stupidest fucking decisions I can think of. You hurting yourself—"

"I didn't hurt myself."

"—instead of telling me what the fuck is going on!"

"I'm okay, Fernando. I am. I promise."

"Because you were lucky!"

Zé took a deep breath. "I'm trying to tell you something. And it's scary for me."

I forked salad around in the plastic container. I stabbed the fork down. I looked him in the eye. "What?"

"Remember how I told you I dropped out of college because nothing caught my interest? Well, that wasn't true. Not exactly."

"So, you lied to me."

"No, I—I left something out."

"That's a lie."

"Fernando, please." When I didn't say anything, he went on. "I did some surfing. Professional. That's why I came from Brazil. My whole family moved up here when I was twelve."

"I'm sorry, what? You came to California to surf? Your whole family came?"

"Of course they came," he said, and I couldn't tell what that was supposed to mean, but then he said, "They wanted me to go pro. That was their dream. My dad's dream; he loves to surf, and he was pretty good himself when he was younger."

I had no idea what to say to that, and the quiet built slowly between us.

Zé broke it by saying, "Do you know what we did when we got here? I mean the very first thing."

I shook my head.

"I made my parents take me to Surfrider—the beach, you know? We'd been here like, eight hours, and I made them drive me out to the beach. I had to see it. I had this idea—" He stopped himself. "Have you been there?"

"A couple of times."

"That's where it all happened. That's where modern surfing was born. It felt like I was supposed to go there. And my parents would have done anything for me." His eyes were in the past, and then they came back to me. "Anyway, I went pro when I was sixteen."

Okay, the surfer bit wasn't exactly news. I mean, I saw how he dressed, and there wasn't any way to misunderstand the look on his face when he'd been staring at that longboard. But professional—

"What does that mean, professional? You were making money."

His lopsided grin surprised me. "Fernando, I was making a lot of money."

I couldn't help my laugh. "Okay, so—" Questions crowded forward in my mind. "I want to say why haven't I heard of you, but I don't know any professional surfers. If I look you up, what am I going to find?"

"God, please don't look me up."

Which meant, of course, I had to take out my phone right then. It didn't take me long to find out about José Teixeira, professional surfer. The pictures were unmistakable: it was Zé, although in some of them, he was a kid, slender because he hadn't added adult mass yet, which made him look gawky with that long frame of his. In others, he was a man—close to the one in front of me, but not quite the same. In some, the hair was longer. In others (yes, I lingered over the shirtless ones), he had more mass and definition. Zé had certainly put on weight while he'd been living with me, in a good way, but he was still much thinner than he'd been—I almost said *at his prime*.

"You look like such a hardass," I said, angling my phone so he could see the photo. It was in black and white, and he wasn't smiling. It was clear that the photographer had a good eye; the picture was stunning, capturing Zé with a wetsuit rolled down to his waist, the chiseled lines of his body raked by sunlight. A hint of his vee lines showed, or maybe it was my imagination. It was hard to tell. In the photos, that's where the shadows lay deepest.

He groaned and tried to push the phone away.

My next question was hard to formulate. What I wanted to say was, Not one of these pictures looks like you, not the real you. Or maybe, Where's the stone-cold badass who keeps popping up in my search result? Or even more clearly, You giggled for almost an hour after you put those octopus-leg socks on Igz, and I'm having a hard time imagining that's the same guy in these pictures.

What came out wasn't great: "You don't act like a professional surfer."

Instead of getting mad, though, I only got that slow smile.

"What?" I asked.

"Well, no," he said. "Because I'm not."

"That's a fucking annoying thing to say."

His grin spread, but then it faded. "I mean, I'm not anymore." He put his salad on the coffee table and pushed back his hair. "I hurt my knee."

"I figured that part out. Sorry; that was habit. What happened?"

"It's stupid. God, it's so stupid, sometimes I can't even believe it. I was out with some friends one day. Just hanging. And I fell. It was a freak chance. I've fallen a million times. But this time, the board moved the wrong way at the wrong time, and my knee twisted, and pop. There goes my ACL." He was silent for a moment. "There's this part of me that thinks it would have been better if I'd done it during a competition, you know? If I'd been about to win, and I'd gambled, taken a risk, and that's how it happened."

"Sounds like that would have felt even shittier."

"Maybe. It feels pretty shitty to have ruined my whole life because we were showing off for each other, messing around."

Igz was fussing again, so I got her out of her swing and held her against my chest. Zé reached over to play with her hand, teasing her fingers with one of his. He wasn't looking at me.

"But you had surgery," I said. "And didn't you have money saved, or — I don't know."

His mouth moved, but it wasn't a smile. "I've had three surgeries, actually. And every time I get out on the water, pop. I had some money saved, but you wouldn't believe how fast it goes, especially when —" He stopped, swallowed, and whatever he'd been about to say, he replaced with a shrug. "I had to give up my apartment. I sold my car and bought, well, that junker. I sold my boards." He stopped. His throat moved when he swallowed. "I have zero skills because all I've done is surf since I was ten. I can't even get a job teaching kids to surf because of my stupid knee. I didn't graduate high school—my parents made me take the GED so I wouldn't have to be in school." He had nice hands, big hands with strong fingers, and he rubbed one of them gently over the down on Igz's head. "It was like I had a disease. People I'd known for years, people who'd been my friends for years, they didn't want anything to do with me. At the beginning, I tried. I heard about this beach party. It's not like anyone invited me, but I heard anyway. I made my way down there on crutches. I—" He shook his head and closed his eyes for a moment, and when he opened them again, they were glossy. "I was so dumb. People pretended not to see me. If they saw me coming, they moved away. I guess a few of them took pity on me and tried to talk, but what do you talk about when the only thing in your life is surfing, and the guy standing in front of you is everybody's horror story."

"Zé, God. That's fucking terrible."

He shrugged. "I was angry about it for a long time. I think—I don't think it helps, being angry. And if it had been me on the other side, I don't know if I'd be any different."

"Of course you would have. You're the kindest person I know. Fuck those giant sacks of dogshit."

"I'm not a particularly nice person. I'm trying to be better, I guess. I…I didn't like who I was. Not for a long time. So, I'm trying not to be that person anymore."

Some of his hair had fallen into his eyes, and I caught myself the moment before I reached up to brush it away. Instead, my voice gravelly, I asked, "What about your family?"

His hand fell away from Igz. He straightened her onesie, and then he sat back. He had one arm low across his belly, and a part of me recognized the instinctive defensiveness of the pose. But when he spoke, his voice had a reined-in quality, like he was holding it tight.

"You said I didn't act like a professional surfer."

"I didn't mean it that way. I don't know what I meant, I guess."

"God, Fernando, of course you do." But a smile opened on his face for a moment, and he touched my arm. "Did you know that people talk about surfing like it's an addiction?" I didn't say anything, and he spoke into my silence. "I don't know if there's any science behind it, but that's how people talk about it. And it makes sense. It's all about that rush. A great wave. A great sesh. It's dopamine. It's better than sex." Then his mouth curved. "Better than any sex I've had in a long time, anyway. Part of it's the uncertainty, wanting that big wave, but maybe the whole session is mediocre. It's like gambling. You don't know if you're going to score big or bust or whatever you're supposed to say. And, as with any addiction, you build up a tolerance to the thing that gets you high. The best waves don't hit the same way. You've got this itch you can't quite scratch."

He was silent for so long that I didn't recognize my own voice when I said, "What are you trying to tell me?"

Something flickered on Zé's face. But all he said was "That there's this toxic culture in surfing, and the higher you get, the worse it becomes. Even at a casual session, people are always talking trash, making fun of each other, trying to tear each other down. Most people have this picture of surfing like it's a bunch of long-haired beach bums chilling like they're in a beach commercial, but the reality—at least, my reality—was that it was a lot of middle-school bullshit. I know professional surfing isn't on the same level as other sports. I know it doesn't get the same attention as the Super Bowl.

Nobody's wearing jerseys with our names on them. But when you're doing it, when you're living in that tiny bubble, you're a big fish in a small pond, and it feels like every eye in the world is on you. You have to play the part. You have to look the part. You have to be a surfer." He played with Igz's foot, and something softened in his face. "You can't play the xylophone with a baby."

Then I understood. "You weren't out."

He shook his head.

"At all?" I asked.

"Nope. I wanted endorsements. I wanted to be a star. I wanted all of it. And I don't know how much you know about surfing culture, but there is so much toxic masculinity, so much homophobia. It's kind of crazy, you know? And it's not what anyone thinks about when they imagine surfing." He released Igz's foot and flexed his fingers like they ached. "So, I played the part."

I gave him a look.

He burst out laughing. "Yes, Fernando. To answer your question—"

"I didn't say anything."

His smile flowered again. "—I did manage to hook up with guys occasionally. But it was always a huge risk, and I always hated myself after. I hated myself all the time, actually, if I'm being honest. I was killing myself. And I didn't know how to stop." He cleared his throat. "So, I try to be grateful about it. My ACL, I mean. Because I'd still be there, still be drinking poison every day, if I hadn't had that accident. After that, I had to face some hard truths. My friends weren't my friends. All the things I'd thought I wanted in life were bullshit. And I'd been living a lie. That was a lot to process."

"What about your family?"

"My loving, devoted family, who gave up everything so I could pursue my dream—and who were happy to help themselves to my money—weren't happy when the surfing was gone, when the money dried up, and when they found out I was gay. They're super Catholic, and not the tolerant kind, and you want to talk about toxic masculinity—my dad and brothers practically invented it. Never mind that they'd been living on my winnings for years. Never mind that they hadn't done jack to 'manage' my career. I wasn't valuable to them anymore, so they left me. Literally, Fernando. In a hospital room. I had to get an Uber back to my apartment when I was discharged."

"Fuck that. But, I mean, you had to have known that's how they were going to react when you came out to them, right?"

"I didn't come out to them," Zé said, and a hint of color rose in his cheeks. "They walked in on me getting jerked off by a patient tech."

The laugh exploded out of me. It startled Igz, and she began to cry, but even as I soothed her, I couldn't stop laughing. Zé made a face, but he was smiling, and his cheeks were redder than ever.

"God, talk about trauma," I said when I'd finally recovered.

"You have no idea," Zé said. He was blushing even harder, but his voice was dry. "At this point, I might as well become a monk."

"Come on, you didn't get out there and hump everything with a dick?"

"Good Lord, Fernando."

"What?" I laughed again. "You deserve some action."

"Nobody under thirty calls it action. And no, I didn't." He didn't meet my gaze as he said, "I went through a rough patch, actually. I kind of hit rock bottom. The second surgery. The third. The money going up in smoke. I had to sell my condo, my boards, anything I could. And then, you know how I was living." His shoulders curved in. "And now I'm here. So, I wanted you to know. That's why it's so important for me to do stuff on my own. Because for a long time, I didn't. I believed other people would take care of me. I believed other people would make sure I was okay. And that wasn't true, and I'm not going to make that mistake again. And I'm sorry I didn't tell you. It's embarrassing, and it's a part of my life I want to forget, but you deserve to know."

I bounced Igz and thought about what to say. I settled on: "I'm still pissed."

He rubbed his eyes.

"What? I am. You lied to me. And you scared me. And honestly, Zé, did you think I would fire you for using your cane? I mean, I get it, you didn't know me that first day. But once you'd spent some time with me—am I such a piece of shit that you thought I'd throw you out?"

"No." His voice was soft, and he studied a seam in the upholstery, rubbing his thumb along the stitching. "I don't like using the cane. I'm twenty-five, Fer, not an old man. And I like you. And I wanted you to—" He gave another of those helpless shrugs.

Wanted you to what?

I said, "You're using that goddamn cane from now on. And if I find you not using it, there is going to be some serious shit going down. When Kennedi says you can start easing up on it—"

"Fernando, I don't want your friend—"

"Don't argue with me. I'm still mad at you." I waited until he'd subsided and said, "When Kennedi says so, you can start weaning yourself off it. Until then, you're going to use it. Understood?"

He gave a miserable nod.

"And whatever Kennedi tells you for PT, you're going to do. Understood?"

He opened his mouth.

"I swear to Christ, Zé, if the next word out of your mouth isn't yes, I'm going to lose my shit. I don't want to hear about how much it costs. I don't want to hear about you being independent. This is about you getting better. If it makes you happier, we'll call it a loan, and you can pay me back."

He opened his mouth again.

"Think long and hard," I told him.

That familiar struggle played in his face again. And then it was gone, his expression soft and tired, and he said, "Thank you."

"You're welcome. Now eat your damn salad."

That slow smile spread across his face again, but he didn't say anything. He picked up his salad, and I picked up mine—well, I had to balance it on my lap because of Igz—and we ate. I turned the TV on. Neither of us said anything, but that was okay; the silence was comfortable, especially once I turned the TV to a Dodgers game. When we'd finished, I let Zé hold Igz while I cleaned up (meaning, I threw away the trash).

When I got back to the living room, he was trying to get up from the sofa while holding Igz.

"You have got to be fucking kidding me."

His laugh straddled outraged and bewildered. "I'm putting her to bed—"

"Sit down, dumbass. Jesus Christ. This is why you can't get a man. You realize that, right? Because you are a giant fuckknob."

"I don't know what that means," he protested as I took Igz from him.

"It means sit the fuck down. Do I have to make a sign?"

He sat down, and I put Igz to bed.

When I got back, he was sprawled on the sofa and taking up way too much room, which meant I had to fight and jostle for my own space. We ended up pressed together, with Zé still managing to take up most of the sofa, but it wasn't all that bad. He was warm, and he smelled nice—not the coconut wax and earthiness of whatever he liked to use, but him, Zé. I watched the Dodgers game. Or I did a decent impression of watching it.

The problem was that he fell asleep almost immediately, and his head drooped onto my shoulder, and his breathing was soft in my ear. No wonder, I thought. A long day, pushing himself on his knee as we walked around Laguna Beach. Then the emotional exhaustion of his fear, of telling me the worst things that had happened in his life, of the grief and pain he must still be carrying, even if he didn't let them show. No wonder, I thought again. No wonder he seems like a kid sometimes. Because he was never allowed to be one. Never allowed to be himself. And now here he was, and he was goofy and silly and loved babies and sometimes got a raging case of the giggles, after all those days of being Butch Cassidy on a surfboard. And that position had to be uncomfortable, so I got my arm around him and helped him shift until we were better aligned, his head on my chest.

I should have known it would happen. I should have fucking known. I started to get hard.

And of course, because it was consistent with everything else in my life, it was about the most excruciating boner of my life. It happened slowly, my dick fattening, lengthening, even though I was screaming at it to stop. The baseball on TV didn't help. Running sales pitches in my head didn't help. Zé's breath whispered against my neck, and my dick kept going. Worse, the way it was trapped by my jeans meant that it didn't have anywhere to go, and the discomfort added to the intensity of the experience.

I don't know how long I lasted. Then I gave up. I lifted my hips, adjusted myself, and settled back onto the sofa. Zé moved with me, his head rocking as I jostled him. And then his breathing changed.

Maybe, I thought.

But I didn't know maybe *what*.

Maybe.

Maybe he'll go back to sleep.

His breathing was slow and even. The Dodgers went to commercial. Car insurance. They were driving around all over the place, which I guess was supposed to show you—

Zé raised his head and kissed me on my neck. It was barely more than pressing his mouth there. Even the movement of his head was tiny. His breathing continued soft and slow. Then his hand came up to cup the side of my face. Rough hands, I thought. A man's hand. He was still nestled against me. He kissed my neck again. And then, slowly, he sat back and looked at me. He was still cradling my cheek.

"Zé," I whispered.

That windswept hair had fallen in his eyes, but he didn't brush it away. He didn't do anything.

"You're having a hard day." I cleared my throat. "You're hurting, and you're vulnerable, and you're not thinking about this."

"I am thinking about this. I've been thinking about this since the day I met you."

TV voices filled the empty air between us.

"I can't," I finally said.

He leaned forward. He drew me toward him with that hand still cupping my cheek. He was strong, but at that point, I couldn't have fought him if I'd wanted to. His mouth brushed me, and then his lips parted, and he kissed me.

My first jumble of thoughts was impressions: the scrape of stubble, the softness of his lips, the taste of his mouth. And then comparisons: he was so much bigger than any girl I'd been with; in those relationships, I'd been the bigger one, and it felt strange to have that reversed. The calluses on his hand. Even how he tasted. But even as my brain was processing all of that, my body was responding. My mouth relaxed, and I kissed him back.

It didn't last long. It lasted forever.

When he broke the kiss, he pulled back. His eyes were that deep, endless brown, and they left me no place to run as he said, "I want you to hear me when I tell you I want this. I want you. You're kind, and you're funny, and you're smart, and I am so attracted to you that the last four weeks have been killing me." That slow smile spread across his face, and he touched the corner of my mouth with this thumb. "If you don't feel the same, that's okay. But I think you do. I hope you do."

It took a long time for him to get himself upright, and all I could do was sit there, as useful as a box of dicks. He gave me a final, considering look, and then he took a limping step toward the hallway.

"Zé," I said, and my voice cracked like I was thirteen years old. I swallowed. "Your cane."

That made him laugh. He grabbed it, and he made his way down the hall. The door clicked shut.

The Dodgers won.

I turned off the TV.

I made my way around the house, shutting off the lights. I caught a glimpse of myself in the window over the sink. Again, in the glass of the sliding doors out to the deck. Where I had seen him all those weeks ago, the broad span of his back, the definition his body, that intense resolve as he made his way through the poses. I stood in the dark in the kitchen, alone with my ghosts.

When I got to my room, I shut the door behind me and stood there. I knew what would happen. I'd climb into bed. I'd try to fall asleep. I'd find a video, as close as I could come to the real thing, and I'd rub one out. And tomorrow. And the next night. And then, maybe not anymore, because I remembered how it had been before Zé came. The stress. The weed. The feeling that everything in my life was winding me up like clockwork, and I was too numb to get hard, too numb for anything. Because they need me, I thought. I love you, I told Zé inside my head, but they need me.

It wasn't Zé who answered me though.

You're going to be here forever. That voice sounded like mine. You're going to be here forever, doing this forever, taking care of Mom forever, bailing Chuy out forever. It's never going to get better. You're never going to get away. I could see it: the endless days stretching out into the future. The impossible days. A whole life of impossible days.

Before I could think about what I was doing, I stepped out into the hall. I walked the short distance to Zé's door. I stopped.

And that was as far as I could go. My face was hot. My legs were shaking. I was, a part me realized in a high-altitude observation, about to cry.

Selfish, I thought. This is selfish, and it's not fair to him. I'll go back to my room, and—

The door opened. Zé stood there. His eyes were red, his face puffy, and it was like an out-of-body experience, to understand in an instant that he'd been crying. Everything else ashed away in my mind. He opened his mouth, but I didn't give him a chance.

I stepped forward and kissed him.

14

The first kiss wasn't, maybe, my smoothest move. We bonked heads—only a little. And our mouths didn't quite line up. He was off balance because he tried to move back as I moved in. And I tried to catch him, only he was taller, and then we both almost went down.

But then he caught his balance, and I slid an arm around his waist, and my other hand was at his nape. The second kiss was a lot better. By the third kiss, when he made a little sound and moved into me, I was hitting my stride.

We stumbled across the room—being as careful of his knee as I could while we moved, locked together, through the dark. When we reached the bed, Zé sat, and I sat next to him. He took my head in his hands and kissed me again, and this time, his tongue pressed against my mouth, and I let him in.

He's a dude, a part of my brain kept saying. His hair, his mouth, his skin, his size, his strength. This running catalogue of his maleness. I was used to being the assertive one (well, back in the day, when I'd had time, I'd been the assertive one)—and while that was probably some patriarchal bullshit, and there was no reason the girl couldn't be the assertive one, that wasn't how it had happened for me. So, this, with Zé moving me closer, his hands strong and possessive on me, was new. And there were no boobs to play with; that was new too. And the way he thrust his tongue into my mouth, the demanding certainty of it, was like being fucked, and a part of my brain lit up as the words played in my head, He's fucking you. He's fucking you with his tongue.

Maybe Zé sensed it because he eased back from his next kiss and considered me.

I tried for a smile and landed somewhere near nervous desperation. "So, uh…"

"Oh. Oh! Oh God, Fernando, I'm sorry. It's your first time?"

"It's not my first time, donkey-cock." But I had a hard time meeting his eyes. "It's my first time with a guy."

The silence stretched out.

"If that's—" I began.

"That is the hottest fucking thing of my entire life."

I wasn't used to Zé swearing. I definitely wasn't used to the heat in his voice, the gravel, the unabashed desire. The way he looked at me, like he was eating me with his eyes, was something I'd gotten a few times from Augustus's friends, and I'd gotten it in clubs back when I still went to clubs, but I'd never needed to acknowledge it.

"Sorry," he said almost immediately. "I'm not trying to fetishize or objectify or, um, I don't know. I shouldn't have said that."

"No, I like it. That you like it. I mean—I don't know what I mean. I'm sorry if I'm making this weird."

"You're not making this weird." He ran his fingers through my hair and gave me the slow smile. "And I definitely don't want to spend all night apologizing to each other. How about this? What would you feel comfortable doing?"

"I thought we were doing pretty good making out."

The corner of his mouth twitched. "We were doing great."

"Let's try that again."

Zé went slower this time. He didn't grab me. He didn't haul me around. His tongue touched mine, but the demand was gone.

"Are you kissing me," I asked, planting a hand on his chest, "or your grandmother?"

He burst out laughing. "I'm trying to be a gentleman."

"I liked how you were kissing me before. And I liked that you were handsy. I mean, I'm not used to it, so maybe go slow, but I liked it."

Zé nodded. "Are you not comfortable touching me? Because you keep putting your hands on the wall."

"Well—" I had to think about that. "I mean, normally I'm touching boobs."

He wasn't much of one for rolling his eyes, but right then, he made an exception.

"Then tell me what to do, you horse's ass."

He shucked his shirt and leaned back. Then, taking my hands in his, he brought them to his chest. That was all: he spread my fingers and pressed my palms to his pecs. He was warm and solid. Velvet skin and dense muscle. He had a little bit of hair around his nipples, which I hadn't noticed when I'd seen him naked before. More hair at his happy trail.

"Okay, I'm figuring out one downside to being gay is the comparison thing."

He slid his hands to the small of my back. "What?"

"Zé, you're like, jacked." I wasn't ready to move my hands, but I flexed my fingers against his well-developed chest. "God, I don't think I could look like you if I tried."

"I thought Augustus was gay?"

"Yeah, so?"

Zé brought one hand around to caress my stomach through the shirt. I was painfully aware that there was, uh, some excess there. "You've got no idea, huh?"

"No idea about what?"

"How hot you are. When you told that twink to move today, the one who was blocking the sidewalk, you didn't hear him say, 'Yes, Daddy'?"

"He was—I mean—" I stopped. "He was being sarcastic."

"No, he wasn't. Jesus, Fernando. When I saw you in those booty shorts with those daddy thighs…" He made a sound like he'd tasted something he liked. Then he smiled again and rubbed my stomach again. "So, the comparison thing happens, sure. But I'd recommend not making that a big part of your focus. On the one hand, it's not healthy. On the other hand, you don't know what your partner likes. For example, I like you. I think you are, without exaggerating, the most attractive guy I've ever met. And I want you to take your shirt off, and I think I'm showing a lot of restraint by not tearing it off you right now."

"A lot of restraint, huh?"

"I don't want to rush you." He wrapped his hands around mine again and, his voice lowering, said, "We're spending a lot of time talking, Fernando. I want you to touch me. And I want you to kiss me."

"I can do that."

We went slow, and he let me take my time exploring his body. I knew part of that was because he was Zé, and he was so easygoing and comfortable, but I'd never gotten to do that with any of the girls I'd hooked up with—probably because most of those encounters had been so rushed. With Zé, I took my time. I traced the definition of his chest. I ran my hands over his back. He let me touch his arms, following the swell of his muscles. He flexed, and he looked like such a goof, but God, the man had arms. He liked when I touched his nipples, arching his back and making a low, guttural noise. And slowly, minute by minute, I started to feel—well, comfortable wasn't the right word, but relaxed, maybe. Or more relaxed. Because yes, his body was different. But he was still a person. And he wanted to be touched and admired and caressed.

When I kissed a line up his neck, he made this broken, yowling noise, and I thought, for a moment, I'd hurt him. I pulled back and saw the glazed look in his eyes, and I realized he'd liked it, and a swell rose in me because

I'd made him make that noise, I'd made another guy make that noise, and I dove down again and made him make it again.

"Fer," he whispered shakily, pawing at my chest. "Oh shit, oh God, that's too much, that's too much."

When I pulled back, he was trembling, his chest rising and falling rapidly. His nipples had hardened, and his pupils were huge.

I turned myself out of my shirt. I wasn't thinking about it; I was ready to have it gone, and as soon as I tossed it on the floor, Zé's hands were all over me. His mouth too, latching on to my nipple a moment later. None of the girls I'd messed around with had ever done that, but I'd seen it in videos, and I heard my own shocked exhalation of breath, and it sounded like somebody else said, "Fuck, fuck, fuck."

When my back started to hurt, I leaned against the wall and pulled Zé onto my lap. He grinned and rocked against my dick, and I swatted him on the ass. This position made it a lot easier to touch him wherever I wanted, and more importantly, it gave me easy access to his neck. I never lingered, but I went back again and again, leaving hickeys, chafing the sensitive skin there until it was red from my stubble. A few times, Zé took the initiative, but more and more, he seemed happy to let me lead. I was sucking on his neck when he brought my hand down between his legs.

His dick was hard and hot even through the board shorts, and he moaned as he wrapped my fingers around the fabric-clad length. I'd never touched another guy's dick, but I figured they all worked on the same general principles, and I stroked him through his shorts. We did that for a while until he reared back, breaking the kiss with a gasp, and said, "Help me." I figured out what he meant when he started fumbling with his shorts, and together, we got them down around his knees. I pulled them the rest of the way off. He was commando underneath, big surprise.

For a minute, I looked. He had a great dick; I'd seen enough in porn to have something of a scale, and his was a ten out of ten: long, thick, straight, foreskin already pulling back slightly to reveal the purplish-red head. I'd handled my own equipment enough to recognize somebody who was close. He had big balls, no surprise there either, and as he noticed me looking, he spread his legs. The smell was dick and balls, but somebody else's dick and balls. A dude smell. But not, like I had been half-expecting, a locker room smell. Zé, but a more intimate part of Zé. I didn't think I'd catch myself sniffing his shorts anytime soon, but I liked the smell, and more than that, I liked that it was Zé's smell, liked the intimacy of it.

"Touch me," he whispered hoarsely.

I chafed his thigh and nudged him to slide off me.

With a groan, he did, rolling to bury his face in the pillow. He had a full, muscular ass, by the way. Not much hair. Another learning point: apparently, I liked a guy with some junk in the trunk. As I scooted off the bed, I slapped his ass, and he squawked and flopped onto his back to scowl at me. If anything, though, his dick looked harder than ever.

I stripped: jeans, boxers, socks. It should have been nerve-wracking, I guess. I should have hesitated, felt awkward about being in front of a guy like this. But by that point, my dick was screaming to be free from my jeans, I was so horny I would have gotten naked in front of the Pope. Zé lay there, drinking me in. He reached up to touch my belly again. Then his hand slid down, skating over my thigh. He cupped my balls and then tightened his grip and used them to tug me forward until my knees hit the bed. Propping himself up on one elbow, he brought his face to my cock and inhaled. When he looked up at me, his eyes were hooded.

"I want to suck you off," he said in that throaty whisper. After a beat, he added, "Please?"

I must have answered—technically, making a whimpering noise in your throat is an answer—because he pulled me forward again. He brushed the head of my dick against his lips. They were soft and wet, and I was wet, and my dick glided across them. I'd had blow jobs before, but not all that many; lots of the girls I'd hooked up with either hadn't been interested in doing it or hadn't enjoyed it. I'd always taken it as a stereotype of porn that gay dudes loved sucking cock and got off on it, but for Zé at least, stereotype or not, it was true. He was lying on his side, legs stretched out because of his knee, still rubbing my cock back and forth, back and forth, and he didn't seem to be in any hurry to get it over with.

When he opened his mouth, I thought he was going to take me down, but instead he started licking. Little licks at the head, where I was sensitive enough that it was almost too much. Longer licks from the base to the tip. He took my balls into his mouth, one at a time. He tried to do both and couldn't, and when he finally gave up, he shot me a sheepish grin and went back to my dick.

For some reason, that grin made me relax. I eased my weight forward, one knee on the bed, bringing my dick in closer for him—and at a better angle. I planted one hand on the wall for stability. The other, without letting myself think about it too much, went into his hair. I'd had fantasies, literally, about this: his mouth on my cock, my hand in his hair. It was softer than I expected, but the texture was exactly what I'd imagined—slightly coarse from salt and sun and whatever he styled it with, and so abundantly thick that half the pleasure was sinking my fingers into it, gathering a handful of his mane, giving the slightest tug to control his head. He moaned the first time I did that, and his lips opened, and I slid inside.

Hot. Soft. Wet. He bobbed up and down frantically, continuing to moan. He had a lot of sharp teeth.

I tried to ignore the teeth. I tried to think about how this was Zé, how I'd fantasized about this, how that young guy had looked in what had quickly become my favorite video—drunk on cock. But the reality was that plenty of girls, interested or not, had given me better BJs than this. Mostly because it hadn't felt like I was going through a meat grinder. It was almost like—

Almost like he'd never done it before.

Using my hold on his hair, I eased back. His lips were puffy. Saliva slicked his chin. But he didn't look blissed out. He looked frustrated. And then, to my surprise, like he was about to cry. "I'm sorry."

I hadn't thought about the fact that, although Zé might have had more experience with guys, he didn't have much experience in general. Especially not outside of frantic, secret hookups. And while, admittedly, I'd been going through a dry spell (I could hear Augustus laughing halfway across the country), I'd done all right for myself before, well, I'd stopped taking care of myself (if anything, Augustus was laughing harder).

"Don't be sorry," I said. I sat and pulled his head onto my thigh, and he rolled onto his back and looked up at me. I finger-combed his hair.

"No, that was horrible. I could tell."

"Zé, stop." I gave another little tug on his hair, and he looked at me. "I'm here. With you. I want to be here with you. I'm enjoying being with you. In case this hasn't made it clear." I pulled my dick and let it slap against my belly. "I'm enjoying it a lot."

I went back to running my fingers through his hair. After a while, he said, "I've never sucked anybody's dick before."

"I'm honored."

He slapped my side.

"I'm serious, Zé." But I did press my tongue against the inside of my cheek so it bulged out. He slapped my side again, and I laughed. Some of the tension in his face eased. "I love that you wanted to try that with me. I'm trying a lot of things tonight too, and I'm grateful you were willing to be vulnerable."

"What's going on? Why haven't you called me a turkey turd or a dick bobbin or a blue-balling jackass?"

"I'm being a good sexual partner, pecker-lips." Sliding out from under him, I eased his head down onto the mattress. Then I moved down the bed. As he propped himself up onto his elbows, I spread his legs and knelt between them. I ran one hand lightly over his scar. I thought that knee still felt hot, inflamed from the strain of the day and the fall. But maybe that was my imagination. I felt hot all over. I felt like I was burning up, actually.

"What are you doing?"

"We're breaking a lot of new ground tonight, bozo."

"No, Fernando, don't. Please don't."

"Why not?"

It was hard to concentrate on his words when I was staring up the length of his body: his hard dick, his defined abs and chest, those powerful arms and shoulders, and then his face. In porn, there was never this much talking, so how could this be so much hotter?

That was why it took me a moment to process the words when he said, "Because you're more, um, straight, I guess."

"I'm straight?"

"Well, you know. This is your first time with a guy, and I don't want you to do anything that's going to freak you out or that you don't like or…" His voice faltered. "I want it to be good for you."

Because if it wasn't good, what? I'd give up on him? I'd fire him?

I slapped the inside of his thigh. Hard.

He let out a noise that wasn't quite a shout and sat up on his elbows, eyes wide.

"The internalized homophobia is a real boner killer, okay?"

"Fernando! Caralho!"

"Don't be a baby."

"That hurt!"

Rubbing the sting out of the red mark on his thigh, I eyed his dick. "Mr. Happy seems like he's doing okay."

"What is wrong with you?"

"What's wrong with me is I don't like hearing bullshit. I'm here with you because I like you. I'm not here because I expect five-star servicing. This is not a fucking car wash, and it's not a fucking Taco Bell, and you're not some escort I hired because I can't get laid."

"You think Taco Bell has five-star service?"

I smacked his thigh again, but more lightly this time. "No more bullshit. Do you hear me?"

He was trying to glower; he had the right bone structure for it, and I remembered those dramatically brooding pictures of him framed against the ocean. But now that I knew the goofball inside, it wasn't effective.

"Good," I said. "Now give me that dick."

"There is something seriously wrong with you." But he spread his legs and lowered himself to lie on the mattress again. Then he raised back up again. "Fernando, you don't have to—"

"Jesus Christ," I said and pushed him back down.

I lowered my head between his legs. The smell was familiar—sweaty dick and balls. I'd smelled it on myself before. But it was different. It was Zé, and I recognized his body as part of the mixture. Maybe raunch wasn't my thing because the smell wasn't a huge turn-on, but I didn't mind it either. Dudes smelled like dudes. That seemed like Gay Shit 101.

I slid my hand under his dick, and Zé shivered. I wrapped my fingers around it, and his whole body tensed. He was definitely hard. I mean, this was the first cock besides my own I'd touched, but I'd had a lot of boners in my life, and Zé's fell in the drill-through-concrete category. I slid my hand down his length, rolling the foreskin away from the head of his dick. It was reddish-purple, nicely shaped against the long shaft. He shivered again, and I used my free hand to stroke his thigh. I bent and licked the tip, and it tasted salty, a little bitter. Zé moaned.

Well, I thought with something like a hysterical laugh growing inside my head. Here we go. All those jokes about swinging on knobs. Get ready to watch me swing like a motherfucker.

On my first try, I took the head and a little of the shaft into my mouth. The taste was stronger—not as bitter, which must have been the pre, but salty and musky, and my brain made an automatic connection to why one of the slang terms for dick was meat. Different from eating out a girl, I thought. Different taste. And definitely different having something inside of me, taking up my body. Again, I thought, this is what it's like to get fucked. But it wasn't, not really. I remembered that video, that daddy type railing the younger guy's mouth. What would it be like to get into that headspace? No control. Just taking that dick as it invaded you again and again.

I closed my lips around the shaft and sucked, but I realized almost immediately that wasn't what I was supposed to do. I pulled off him and went down again. Too far, this time. He hit the back of my throat, and I started to gag. Okay, I thought, as I fought down the reflex. Okay, he's got a big dick, and you've got a gag reflex like a motherfucker. I tried to remember what I liked. How I liked it. I ran my tongue around his knob. I lapped at that ultrasensitive spot below the head. He was leaking more; that bitter taste flooded my mouth. Maybe that should have grossed me out, but it made things hotter. He was moaning, his hips restless as he tried to lie flat, and he was leaking in my mouth, and I was doing this to him. I was making Zé feel this way.

Reaching out, I searched for his hand. When I found it, I laced our fingers together. His tightened around mine. I picked up the pace, taking as much of him into my mouth as I could, building up a good rhythm, and then breaking to lick and suckle and tease his head. I felt the change when it began to happen, and it blew my mind. His whole dick hardened like it had gone to the next level. I could trace the veins with my tongue. It was insane: like he was steel, like every piece of him had been tightened to its breaking point. He was muttering in Portuguese, sounding like he was stoned, and then his head came up, his eyes glassy and blind, and he made the unmistakable grunt of a guy about to nut and slurred, "Fer! Fer!"

I sat back and pumped him twice, and he came all over himself. A huge load. Thick, white jets of come against the rich brown of his belly and chest. One of his legs jerked, and as the orgasm subsided, I realized he was shaking. I relaxed my grip, released his dick, and took myself in hand. It was easy, looking down at the wreckage of him, to bring myself off. One, two, and my load was flying too, spattering all over his dick and balls and thighs. I rode the crest of the orgasm, and when I came down, I felt like someone had taken me apart joint by joint. I propped myself against the wall and, for a while, enjoyed looking at him.

He had one arm over his eyes, and he mumbled something in Portuguese.

"A little louder," I said.

When he peeled his arm away, his eyes were wet. His smile was tremulous, and it made me think of butterfly wings, like it might flutter away at any moment.

"Hey," I asked softly, "are you okay? Was that too much?"

He shook his head.

I rubbed his leg.

"Oh my God," he whispered.

"That's me."

He made a face and tried to kick me, and I laughed and caught his leg and rubbed it some more. His breathing slowed in increments. Then he raised himself on one elbow and said, "Fernando, that should be illegal."

The embarrassment caught me by surprise; I ducked my chin, shrugged, my face heating.

He scooted toward me, took my head in his hands, and moved in for a kiss.

"I, uh—I probably taste like dick."

"You're hot," he said, "but you're not bright, are you?"

I had an answer for that, but his mouth was on mine, and after a while, it didn't seem important.

When Zé finally pulled back, he looked me in the eye, held my gaze until it felt like too much. Then he turned his face into his shoulder to wipe away another tear and whispered, "Thank you."

It was on the tip of my tongue: I love you.

But I knew it was the rush of hormones, the release, the fact that I'd gotten off with another human being, a real live honest-to-God person, instead of my hand or a toy.

So, when Zé laughed quietly and said, "God, I needed that," I knew I'd done that right thing, not saying anything. Maybe he saw something on my face because he said, "Are you sure you're okay?"

"Am I okay?" I asked. "You looked like you went into a coma."

He gave me that slow, beautiful smile. Taking me by the hand, he lay down again, and he pulled me down next to him. He opened his mouth. Then he closed it again. He opened it again, and the struggle played itself out in his face.

"For fuck's sake," I said, giving him a push to roll over. I pulled him to my chest, and we squirmed around until we were settled: his head pillowed on my arm, his legs slotted with mine. Maybe he should have been big spoon, but my last thought, as sleep rolled in, was that he fit right in my arms.

15

Zé, it turned out, was a lot of things. He was sweet, obviously. He was kind. He was patient. He was a world-class doofus. He had that lazy smile that turned me inside out. He was hot, okay? In bed, he was thoughtful, generous, and exciting. And, it turned out, he had moved into my head and was taking up a lot of space.

After getting up to feed Igz, I stayed awake a long time, thinking. A year from now, we'd be...what? I mean, what was this? A onetime thing? A meaningless hookup? Neither of those captured the fact that we lived in the same house and saw each other all day, every day. Fuck buddies? Maybe. I mean, we were friends, certainly. Good friends, actually, especially since we hadn't known each other for long. But we'd clicked from the beginning: I was an asshole, and he was Zé, and that meant we worked perfectly together. And the best part was that nothing ever felt complicated or messy or difficult. He was so easy to be with. So easy to spend time with. He wasn't a talker, but when he did, I could listen to him for as long as he wanted to talk, and he could tell me about what Igz had done that day, or something interesting he'd read (I was going to have to get a subscription to *The Atlantic*), or something funny he'd seen on a walk. Or we didn't have to talk at all. We could sit there and watch TV. Or we didn't even need TV. We could be together in the same space, and I didn't have to do anything, and every once in a while, I'd look up and think about how his hair was hanging in his eyes again, or he'd be looking up too and he'd smile before he went back to his phone, and he had this way of raising his hips and straightening his shirt, and sometimes I could see the ridges of his abs—

Well, I thought as I heard my own thoughts, that answers one question: I'm definitely bi.

So, we could do this. We could be together. Fuck buddies who were also amazing friends, two guys who wanted to spend time together, wanted to spend every minute together, who worked together and lived together and were raising a child together, who had mind-blowing sex and shared a bed.

Sure, I thought, and the voice in my head sounded a lot like mine when I was about to drop a particularly devastating truth bomb on Augustus. Or you could nut up and admit that you're in love with him.

My first reaction was to push it away. And then…not. Because was it so scary? From ten thousand feet up, it probably sounded like a lot—I mean, I'd known him a little more than a month. But we'd been together so much of that time. Gone through so much together. Everything with Igz, the good and the bad. Lou and the job and the interview. Mom and Cannon. He'd even listened to me talk about Chuy and Augustus. He'd seen me lose my shit, and a couple of times, he'd lost his. And instead of going our separate ways, here we were. Together. That meant something, right?

In the other room, Igz began to cry.

Zé stirred, but I pressed him back into the mattress and kissed his nape. "I'll get her."

His hand snaked around and caught me as I was trying to rise. He turned and kissed me. Then he flopped back onto the bed and, to judge by his breathing, was asleep again instantly.

"You could have at least pretended to fight me on it," I whispered as I got up.

He started to snore.

Igz wasn't happy with me, and she let me know it. I changed her and got her a bottle, and she was a pleasant weight in my arm as I made coffee. Then we sat at the table, and I got out my phone, and I said, "Since you're a girl, feel free to help me out at any point. And don't internalize that. And don't attribute this to casual sexism."

Fortunately, she was in a milk coma and couldn't tell me what she thought about me.

What was I supposed to do now? That was the question I was hung up on. I mean, I liked him. Okay, no denying that. The sex had been fantastic. Check that box. We already lived together, so… That was where it got weird. I mean, did I ask him on a date? To our living room? To watch *SportsCenter* together?

Igz told me what she thought about that with a loud belch.

"Everyone's a critic," I said. "But you haven't given me a single idea."

What about flowers? Or breakfast? Or breakfast in bed with flowers? I could call in an order right now, go pick it up, and be back before he got out of bed. That would be some romantical shit, right? I almost called Augustus, and then I slammed on the brakes. First, because it would mean telling him everything I'd kept from him—all the bullshit with Chuy, Igz, Mom and Cannon, all of it. And second, because—

Why?

Because I didn't want to tell him, not until I knew it was more than a fuck-buddy sleepover.

"Sure," I told Igz. "That sounded good, right?"

Igz did not agree.

But maybe breakfast in bed and flowers would be way too much? Zé was so cool. So relaxed. Maybe he'd wake up, and his eyes would get a little wider when he saw the food and the flowers and me, the sex-deprived, affection-starved loser who, after a night that had barely gone beyond heavy petting, had fallen head over heels in love.

"I am not pathetic," I told Igz.

She closed her eyes. The queen could not be bothered with such horseshit.

Maybe a date. But a cool date. Like, something impressive, something that would make him think, Okay, Fernando might have his shit together sometimes, occasionally, when he needs to be clutch. I had a vague picture of a hot air balloon. Or—maybe pay an Italian guy to sing to us? That was a thing, right? On a boat? In a canal?

A voice that sounded a little too much like Augustus when he was trying not to laugh said, *You're thinking of Venice, dumbshit*.

"Well, I don't know," I growled at Igz. She turned her face into my chest and snuggled into me. "You are being zero fucking help."

Footsteps alerted me, and I looked up as Zé came into the room (with his cane, because he's a smart boy). He wore a pair of trunks and a baggy, threadbare tee, and his hair was a riot. He looked at me, and the panicked thought flashed through my head that he knew, that he could tell with one glance that I was totally out of my head for him, and he was going to get weird or act differently or—just kill me—laugh. But that lazy smile rolled across his face, and he bent and kissed me, and he kissed Igz, and he scruffed the back of my head as he moved to get coffee. "Who are you talking to?"

"Igz."

He did laugh at that. "What's she telling you?"

"Nothing. She's being withholding. She gets that from my mom."

Zé kissed me again as he sat at the table. He curled those big hands around his mug, and his eyes floated away, and then they came back, and the lazy smile turned at the corner with a hint of self-mockery.

"I'm nervous," he said.

"Oh. Uh, yeah."

That made him laugh again, and he relaxed and sipped his coffee. "I don't want you to think I'm playing games or that, I don't know, I was messing around. I like you. I wouldn't have done that if I didn't like you. And I know it's complicated because of our situation, but I wanted you to know that I want to see where this goes. If you're interested, you know. In me. Or in a relationship. So, I was wondering what you think and how you're feeling." He looked like he tried to stop, but more slipped out. "Oh God, are you freaking out?"

"You can't do that!" It came out a little louder than I intended, and Igz woke with a start. I shushed her and rocked her as I lowered my voice. "What the fuck is wrong with you?"

"What?"

"I've been going crazy out here. I've been turning myself inside out trying to figure out what you might be thinking and what you might be feeling and if I'm a colossal dope and how am I supposed to tell you that I think I might possibly I don't know be in love with you and if breakfast in bed would make you go running for the hills. I was thinking about—" It threatened to rise into a shout, and I only half managed to strangle it. "—Venice!"

"Uh—Venice?"

"Yes! And then you come out here, and you say exactly what you feel, and you—you make it so fucking easy, and now I'm ten times as much in my head because why couldn't I have done that, why couldn't I have been mature and self-possessed and acted like a fucking adult. I'll tell you why: because I am taking advice from a goddamn infant."

"There is so much happening right now," Zé murmured.

"Didn't your family ever teach you not to talk about your emotions? Good Christ, Zé. We're supposed to play mind games, go full psych ops, have a million different misunderstandings and be absolutely fucking miserable because that is still better than being totally, fully emotionally available and vulnerable and all that fucking shit."

"Just want to check: did you tell me you love me?"

"I said I think I love you!" It was a whisper-shout because of Igz. "And I didn't mean to say it out loud."

The slow smile unfurled again.

"And I'm feeling exposed right now," I said. "And this is Igz's fault because she wouldn't give me any good ideas for a date."

"I think I love you too."

I groaned. "Zé."

"What?" His laugh mixed outrage and confusion. "I'm trying to make you feel better. There. Now I said it too."

"Don't you understand that I have spent my entire life with a narcissist mom and two walking loads of come I have to call brothers? I cannot handle an emotionally healthy partner. I need someone seriously fucked up. Maybe you should tell me you taped our sex last night and you already posted it to your blog."

"I don't think anyone has had a blog since 1999."

"That's good. That was borderline bitchy. Say something like that again."

He took my hand. "Fernando." He kissed my knuckles. He looked into my eyes. After what felt like a long time, he said, "Good morning."

"Good morning," I said and tried to pull my hand back.

Zé held on. "Lots of big stuff, right? Last night. And now this morning."

"Yes." I tried again, but he was like a terrier. "I'm not happy about it."

Those fuzzy eyebrows went up.

"Uh, I mean, I'm happy about the part with our dicks."

"Good God."

Since he wasn't letting go, I decided to hold on to him too, and I squeezed his hand. "I mean, I wasn't joking about all that stuff, Zé. Not totally. You've seen my family. I meant what I said. I feel strongly for you—"

"You think you love me."

"Yes, God damn it. Can I please finish a fucking sentence?"

He kissed my knuckles again, maybe to hide a smile.

"I am seriously fucked up." I tried to soften my tone. "I want to see where this goes, but—"

The sound of the door opening interrupted me. Then voices moved into the house.

"I said I'm done talking about it," Mom snapped. Her voice was high and tense, like she was at the edge of her control.

"Well, I'm not done," Cannon said. "I didn't kiss her, she kissed me—"

The crack of a slap rang throughout the house.

"You fucking bitch!"

I was out of my seat, passing Igz to Zé, before Cannon had finished the words. When I reached the living room, he froze mid-step as he advanced on Mom. The cute little white boy had a red cheek now, and he looked like he hadn't slept: his eyes were bloodshot, his stupid blond-broccoli hair was a mess, and even from across the room, I could smell the pot and booze on him. Mom didn't look much better. She still wore what she must have had on when they went out the night before, her little black dress and a new pair of heels, but her makeup was smudged, and it made her face look strangely skewed, as though she were a portrait of herself, and the paint had smeared.

"What the fuck is going on?"

"Nothing," Cannon said. Then, to Mom, "I want to talk to you in your room."

Mom laughed and turned to me. Cannon caught her arm.

"Get your fucking hand off her!"

Cannon drew his hand back like he'd been burned, and his face got redder. I saw the indecision in his body: the little dry-humper thinking about if he wanted to take a swing.

Before he could, Mom said, "Don't talk to him like that."

"Talk to him like that? He called you a fucking bitch."

"This isn't any of your business."

"You're my mother!"

"Fernando," Zé said from the kitchen.

I shot him a look and turned back to Mom. "You don't want me getting involved?"

"I'm handling this," she said.

"Yeah," Cannon said. "Stay out of this."

"Whose fucking house do you think this is, pencil-dick? Get over here and say that to my face."

"Fernando!" Mom took a deep breath and straightened her hair. "Chuy called me last night. He wants to come home. And he's ready to do rehab."

The pivot in the conversation threw me off-balance. "What—Chuy called you?"

"He's in a halfway house in Oakland."

"He called you? Hold on, that piece of shit has a phone? I thought he was dead. Where the fuck has he been?"

"I don't know, Fernando. He's sick."

"And now he wants to come home?"

"Lower your voice," Mom said. "You're scaring the baby."

"The baby? That baby?" I pointed. "That's his baby, Mom. His. And he left her here. Abandoned her. And I've been picking up his shit again. Like always. Now he wants to come home?"

"He's your brother, Fernando. He wants to get better."

"Fernando can't go today," Zé said. The sound of his voice startled me; I'd forgotten, for a moment, he was there. "He has an interview."

Mom turned an icy look on him. Then her attention came back to me. "Well, I can't do it. I'm a wreck. Look at me, I'm shaking. I need to take my medicine, and you know I'm not supposed to drive on my medicine."

Your medicine, I thought.

"Is that what you want? Do you want me to drive up there? Because I will, Fernando. Even though you know Dr. Gould told me not to drive after I take my medicine. Fine, I'll do it. Fine."

And she would. She'd get in her car (that I paid for). And she'd pop her zanies (that I paid for). And she'd maybe make it to the other side of LA before she pulled into a strip mall and had a meltdown and called me, sobbing. And I'd go. I'd go pick her up. I'd get her home. And then I'd drive to Oakland, but only after I'd added an extra three hours to my day dealing with her bullshit.

"I am not paying for his fucking rehab again," I said.

"Fernando," Zé said.

Mom touched her eyes—perfectly dewy with tears. "I'll get a job. I'll pay for it."

"He can live in this house," I said, "as long as he's clean, but I am not throwing my money down the fucking drain again."

"I said I'd do it! Why are you always so awful to me?" Mom's tears came faster, and she turned and headed down the hall. Cannon shot me a dirty look and went after her. A moment later, her door shut, but it didn't stop the sound of her sobbing.

I tented my hands over my nose. I took a few deep breaths. Tried to, anyway.

"Hey," Zé said.

When his hand touched my back, I flinched.

"Hey," he said again more softly.

I shook my head. I'd only had a couple of migraines in my life, thank God, but I remembered the auras. This was like that. The way my vision seemed to shrink. The way the light seemed too bright. I headed for my room. I opened the door too hard, and it bounced back from the wall.

Clothes. I was pulling on a pair of jeans when Zé appeared in the doorway. He held Igz against his chest. She was crying softly. Had been crying, I realized. For how long? I tried to think back and couldn't remember.

"I know it's your day off," I said, "but can you watch her?"

"Of course."

"Did you have plans? You probably had plans."

"Fernando, you can't go to Oakland today. You're meeting with the senior management team at Lou's grow."

"Apparently, because I have a jerkwad excuse for a brother, I'm not." I buttoned the jeans and dug around for socks. "It's fine. I wouldn't have been able to pay for his rehab on what they were going to offer me anyway."

Zé's silence seemed to take up all the space in the room. I pulled on a pair of socks. Igz was settling into her last hiccupy cries, curled into his shoulder.

"Where's your cane?" I asked.

"This is your dream job. That's what you told me."

"The key word there is dream."

"Lou loves you. She's so excited for you to work together. And you're wonderful at what you do; you'd be a huge asset. It's something you're interested in and excited about."

"This is nice. Twist the knife a little more, would you?"

"I know you're hurting right now, and I know you're scared and worried about your brother and your mom, but I think you need someone to tell you that you don't have to go running off to Oakland today. Chuy has been fine on his own for weeks. He'll be fine for another day. You can get him tomorrow."

"I can't, actually. You heard my mom. She'll drive up there herself. Try to, I mean." I looked around. Keys, wallet. But my phone. "Where's my phone?"

"So, let her."

"You don't understand."

"I do, actually." He adjusted Igz on his shoulder. His voice was soft and low, and he stroked her back. I knew how that felt, those broad hands moving slowly, calmingly. "Every time your mom has an emergency, she calls you. And you fix it for her. Because you're a good son. You're a good man."

"She'll fall apart halfway there. Less than half."

"So, let her," he said again. "She won't die from it."

I laughed, but I've always had a dark sense of humor. I'd been fourteen when they had to pump her stomach. She'd been fine, but I remembered the doctor sitting me down, this stern-faced old white guy with a cap of iron-gray hair. His hand heavy on my shoulder. *You saved her life*, he said. *If you hadn't been there...*

"Zé, I appreciate the pep talk, but you don't know what you're talking about."

"You deserve to live your own life, Fernando. This isn't an emergency. Nobody's in danger."

"Chuy—"

"Chuy can come down on a bus. You can book him a flight. You've worked so hard to be where you are, Fernando. You've given so much up for everyone else. You deserve to be happy. Please don't throw this opportunity away."

"You know what will happen if I try to put him on a bus? He'll get to the station, and he'll score. Or he'll score in the Uber on the way to the station. He'll never get on the bus. Or if he does, he'll score on the bus, and he'll get off somewhere between here and there, and I won't find him again for six months. He's an addict."

"You want to know something about people with substance abuse disorders?" Zé asked, and his voice was shaky, and his eyes looked liquid. "You can't fix them, Fernando. No matter how much you love them. No matter how hard you try. You can't control them. You can't make them be who you want. You can't. And I know you love him, and I know you want to save him, but you can't."

Mom had stopped crying. Igz was no longer fussing. I put my finger to my ear; it felt like when the pressure changed, like I needed to pop it.

"I'm sorry," Zé said, "but someone needed to tell you that."

I found my phone in the kitchen and left.

16

I called Lou before I left LA.

"Let me guess," she said. "You've got a sore throat from all those big doctor knobs. You're going to sound funny because somebody's been stretching your vocal cords, and you wanted to warn me in advance."

"I've got to cancel."

"What the fuck, Fernando?"

"Something came up."

Traffic. Light on glass. A horn.

"You have got to be shitting me," Lou said and disconnected.

I dropped the phone on the passenger seat and drove out of the city.

The drive, in theory took six hours, but it ended up being almost seven and a half because first there was roadwork, and then there was an accident that shut the 5 down to a single lane, and apparently everybody and their mother had to be in Oakland today because the closer I got to the city, the worse the congestion became, until the freeway was a parking lot. I pulled off and, because Zé wasn't there to say no, I got a massive burger with bacon and mayo and I picked the lettuce off. Large fries. I only ate half of it and then I felt sick.

When I called him, he picked up on the first ring. "Is everything okay?"

"I ate this thing called a Bacon Slayer."

His silence ran for five seconds. Then ten. And then, like a miracle, I could hear the smile in his voice as he said, "You're out of my sight for one day, Fernando."

"I had to tell you."

"Was it good?"

"Yes. And then it was disgusting. And now I'm disgusting, and I think I'm going to puke."

"Let me guess: large fries."

I laughed. And then I said, "I didn't like how we left things."

"Neither did I."

"I know you were looking out for me."

"No, I was out of line." Zé's breathing sounded funny. "I don't like seeing you unhappy."

"I'm not. I mean, I'm pissed. But I'm fine."

But even as I said it, I thought: that empty bed in that empty room in that empty house, and all the years I could see stretching ahead of me, and what it had been like before Igz, before Zé.

Zé still hadn't said anything.

"Are you okay?" I asked.

"Fine," he said.

"I'm sorry I ruined your weekend."

"You didn't ruin my weekend, Fernando."

"I'm sorry you have to watch Igz today. I'll pay you double or overtime or whatever it's called."

"Do you want to think carefully about what you just said to me?"

"Uh, thank you for doing it out of the goodness of your heart?"

He muttered something like *Meu deus*.

"Thank you," I said. "And I'll find a way to make it up to you."

"I've got an idea about that," he said, and I laughed again. "It's fine, I promise," he added. "Your mom offered to watch Igz while I run some errands."

"God, don't let her give Igz eyelash extensions."

Zé laughed.

"You think I'm joking," I said.

"Goodbye, Fernando," he said. And then I could hear that lazy smile unrolling again. "I think I love you."

"I think I love you too," I said as I disconnected.

I think.

You, I told myself, are a goddamn moron.

The halfway house was on a rundown block. Flattened Burger King cups and FoodMaxx bags carpeted the street, and dusty weeds grew in the sidewalk cracks. An enormous pair of panties was tied around a lamppost like a bow, and I had as many questions about the size of the underwear as I did about how they'd ended up there. Most of the houses had faded paint, missing shutters, even a few boarded-up doors.

But the halfway house looked fresh and clean: crisp white paint, royal blue trim, more of the same royal blue for the door. White curtains hung in the windows. Even the metal fence had been painted white. The yard was free of litter and well-kept. Maybe that was part of the program. Maybe all Chuy needed to keep him clean was a weed wacker.

I parked and got out of the Escalade, but before I could reach the gate, Chuy emerged from the house. All he had were the clothes on his back: an oversized Cal State sweatshirt, a pair of joggers, dingy white sneakers—a brand I didn't recognize, but I pegged as a Walmart special. They might have been clothes he'd traded for. They might have been clothes he stole or borrowed. The halfway house might have given them to him and, if they'd been smart, burned whatever he'd been wearing. With Chuy, you could never tell. He looked like shit. His hair was longer, falling past his jaw, and although it was clean, it was raggedy, like he'd tried to trim it himself. He was so thin that he looked sick. He needed a Bacon Slayer or eight. His dad was this white guy who'd gone to prison before Chuy was born, and that meant of the three of us, Chuy had always been the lightest. Now his skin was sallow, and dark circles hollowed out his eyes. Not drugs, by the way—his dad, I mean, in case you're wondering. He tried to rob a Valero, and he shot the attendant, who happened to be pregnant. She was fine. The baby was fine. Daddy went away for a long time.

I watched Chuy let himself out the gate, and I thought, I'd been too young. We were only two and a half years apart. I'd been too young to get his head on straight. I'd done my best with Augustus, and even then, I'd only been reasonably successful—but a little runt of a cockhound was better than how Chuy turned out. I tried, I thought, and I didn't know if I was telling myself or telling him. I tried, but I was too young, and I didn't know what to do.

He didn't look at me; he walked straight to the Escalade and jiggled the handle. I unlocked it with the fob, and we climbed in. Then I turned the Escalade around, and we started home. We inched our way out of Oakland. We made it onto the 5. Some banger in a Honda Civic almost clipped us, and then we were merging into traffic and headed south.

And he still hadn't said anything.

Fortunately, being in sales means you learn how to start conversations with charm and aplomb.

"You stupid, selfish, self-centered, egotistical spoiled little fuck of a dick-drip. What the fuck is wrong with you?"

He leaned his head against the window.

"I asked you a question!"

Nothing.

"You're not going to talk to me?" I asked. "That's all right. I can talk for both of us. You left an infant in our kitchen, you piece-of-shit excuse for a human being. You abandoned a baby. What if I hadn't come home that night? What if Mom and Cannon had stayed at a hotel?" My voice was rising, but I couldn't rein it in. "She could have died!"

"You were in your room," he said in a low voice. "I checked."

"You checked? Oh, fantastic. Fucking wonderful. You're the fucking father of the year. Grabbing your shit and running off like you're a fucking child. What the fuck is so screwed up inside your head? What the fuck happened to you that you can't do one fucking thing right?"

"I was doing the best I could," he snapped. His head came up, and his eyes were dry, but they still looked a little red around the edges. Normally, I'd have attributed that to weed, but not when he'd just gotten out of a halfway house. "I didn't want to fuck her up any worse than I already had. I was trying to give her a better life."

"What about my life, you piece of shit? Do you have any idea what the last six weeks have been like? I had to change everything. I had to change work. I had to change my schedule at home. I had to hire a fucking nanny to take care of her so that I didn't lose my job. I get up two, three times in the middle of the night to feed her. I can't go out, can't see friends, can't do anything because I'm raising your fucking child because you can't give two shits about her."

He set his jaw and stared forward.

"You know what this little fuck-parade today cost me?"

His eyes were blank; I didn't think he was seeing anything as he looked out the windshield.

"My dream job, ass-weasel. The job I have wanted since I was in college. And I had a chance, you know that? I finally don't have Augustus hanging onto my pubes. Mom is going to marry Cannon, and then she'll be his problem. And you—Jesus, Chuy, even if I wanted to do something, you're the fucking disappearing man. They had an opening. I'm a great fit. I finally had a chance. And you fucked all of it, you fucking junkie piece of shit."

The Escalade rocked over uneven pavement. He looked at me from out of those deep, dark circles around his eyes. "Let's see. This is the part where I'm supposed to say, 'Thank you, Fer. You're amazing, Fer. You're so special and wonderful. You're the only thing holding this family together. I love you so much.'"

"I am the only thing holding this family together."

"Why?"

"Because look at you—"

"Don't give me that bullshit. You know what I'm asking. Why?" And before I could say anything, he said, "Because you're the one who saves everyone. Saint Fer. You gave up your whole life for us, and now I have to feel so fucking grateful every time you save me again. You know what? I'm sick of you saving me. Go fuck off and fuck yourself."

"Fuck you."

He laughed, the edge of it jagged. "It's unreal, you know that? When you went to college, I thought, 'He's out. He made it out. He's going to have his own life now.' And instead, you came back. And I know—" He stopped, and some of the heat left his voice. "I know Gus-Gus needed you. I know I wasn't taking care of him, and Mom…" He clicked the button for the window, but it couldn't roll up any more. He clicked it a few more times. Now he sounded like he was trying to ask a question. "But when he got to high school, I thought you'd leave. And when he went off to college, I was sure you'd leave. And you stayed, Fer. And you know what I figured out? You like it. This is what you want. It took me a long time to figure that out about the world. People always do what they want."

When I finally spoke, my throat was so thick I could barely get the words out. "You have no fucking idea what you're talking about."

Chuy slumped back against the seat and shook his head. It must have been an hour, driving in silence through long, empty valleys, the blue of the sky graying at the horizon until it was almost the same color as the asphalt.

"I don't want you to do this anymore," Chuy said. "I don't want you to keep giving up your life for me. I want you to be happy. I want you to have a good job. I want you—Jesus Christ, Fer—I want you to be done with Mom. I know you do it because you love us. But you've got to stop. Please stop."

"Sure." My face prickled, and I fought to keep my eyes clear, to focus on the road. "Great fucking idea. And the next time you OD, the next time you hit a dealer's stash and somebody puts a knife in you, what, Chuy?"

The tires hummed.

"It's my life," he finally said. "You've got to live yours."

I couldn't say anything. If I did—if I said, do you remember how we made our own Voltron out of cardboard boxes, and when the Serrano assholes kicked it to shit, you went berserk. If I said, do you remember when you made me a birthday cake out of Graham crackers. If I said, I remember when you got a fever when you were two, and I've never been so scared in my entire life. I remember how you looked your first day of high school, I remember how nervous you were when you asked me what to do with a girl, I remember when you told me you were going to be a rock star, and we spent every Saturday for a month trying to find you a guitar. If I said any of it, the dam would burst, and I'd probably drive us into a power pylon.

Instead, I blinked until I could see, and we drove on.

We stopped for food, and I got a wrap. Chuy got the Bacon Slayer, and I couldn't help it. I laughed.

"What?"

"I had one on the way up."

He grinned. "These things are fucking amazing."

"Talk to me after you're a half a pound of mayonnaise into it."

We ate as we drove, and Chuy broke the silence between bites. "How's, uh, the baby?"

I grunted.

He picked at his fries.

"Is she yours?" I asked.

"We did a test."

"Where's her mom?"

"She's gone." When I looked over, he had pinched one of the fries into mush. "OD'd. Kaliyah was like that when I got there, and the baby was there, and I didn't know what to do. I knew you'd know what to do." He cleaned his fingers on a napkin. "I had to get out of there."

Which meant getting high. I tried to think of what to say. The best I could come up with was "I'm sorry."

He nodded.

Grief wasn't what I'd been expecting, but I could feel it, the raw wound of it. For a girl named Kaliyah, yes. But maybe for himself, too.

"We call her Isabela."

For a moment, I thought he was going to cry. He wrapped up what was left of his food, and his hands were shaking as he did. "Isabela. That's nice. That's a nice name. Kaliyah would have liked that."

"What about Kaliyah's family?"

"Her parents are dead. I don't know if she had brothers or sisters; she's not from here, you know?"

I nodded.

He dropped his head against the window again. After a while, he said, "Isabela."

"Zé calls her Igz. And don't get me started; I already know it's a stupid nickname."

"Igz. I like it." A grin flashed and went out. "Zé's the nanny?"

"Yeah. He's good with Igz."

Chuy turned his head, his expression unreadable as he studied me. But what he said was "So, Mom and Cannon?"

"Jesus fucking Christ, it's a fucking shitshow."

That made him laugh.

"Are they really going to get married?"

"Who knows? One minute, they're screaming at each other, the next—" I made a gagging noise. "He's not even half her age, the little pisser, but he bought her a ring. I guess if she doesn't fuck things up like she always does, it might actually happen."

"What are you going to do with all that free time on your hands? Take Gus-Gus to Disneyland?"

I flipped him the bird, but he grinned. "Apparently, I'm going to raise your child, you giant badger-fuck."

"No, Fer. I don't want you to—I'll figure it out."

"Uh huh."

"I mean, you're definitely going to have to help."

"There it is."

"Probably do most of the heavy lifting."

"Sure," I said. "Why the fuck not?"

"First thing, though is get rid of that manny. Mom does not like that guy."

It took a moment for the words to process—for me to wrap my head around the fact that, for some reason, Mom had talked to Chuy about Zé. "Get rid of Zé? Are you shitting me? Zé's the only reason this family isn't a flaming shit-fire."

"Aren't all fires flaming?"

"What the fuck did Mom say about him? Zé is a fucking saint. What's wrong with him? Tell me one fucking way he's not perfect."

"Whoa." Chuy tried for a laugh, but it fell off uneasily. "Cool it. I'm not the one talking shit about your boyfriend."

"He's not my boyfriend!"

The words came out too loud and too fast, and I heard the half-buried shrillness of my panic.

Chuy's eyes got huge.

I sank into my seat.

"Holy shit."

I shook my head.

"Holy fucking shit. Are you kidding me? You're banging the babysitter?"

"We're not banging, jack-hole!"

Although, I mean, technically...

"Your face! You are totally doing the babysitter." Chuy burst out laughing, "Jesus, Fer."

"All right, fine! We hooked up. Or something."

"Oh my God, do you like him?"

I wrapped my hands around the steering wheel and stared out the windshield. "Maybe I do. Is that a problem?"

"Do you mean, is it a problem that you like to double dip? Uh, no. I've known that about you since you were fourteen and you forgot to clear the cache on the computer."

"What the hell—"

"On the other hand, if you mean, is it a problem that you're boinking the person responsible for keeping your life from turning into a flaming shit-fire, the answer is: it depends on whether you're going to fuck it up."

I wiped my forehead; sweat dampened my hairline. It was hard to get my voice to sound normal when I said, "I don't want to fuck it up."

"Then don't." A grin lolled across his face. "It would be a real fucking shame if Gus-Gus were the shining example of a healthy relationship in this family."

"Good Christ. Did you see that fucking video when his pet dinosaur hugs him from behind? I swear to God you can see him chub up."

It was easy, after that, to spend the rest of the drive talking shit about Augustus.

By the time we got home, it was dark. The living room lights were on. Zé had waited up, I thought. Or maybe not. Maybe he was just reading on his phone. Maybe he couldn't sleep. But maybe he'd wanted to make sure I got home. Maybe he'd been a little worried. And we'd have to stay up for a while so I could tell him about the drive. Tell him everything, actually.

When I stepped inside, he was sprawled on the sofa, head pillowed on one arm. His head came up, and a red mark on the side of his face told me he'd been sleeping. He pushed back his hair and said muzzily, "You're home."

"We're home. Chuy, this is Zé. Zé, Chuy."

Chuy was giving him a once-over. Then he wolf-whistled and gave me a thumbs-up.

Zé groaned.

"Dumbass," I said, giving Chuy a shove. "Do you not have two fucking brain cells to rub together?"

"What?" Chuy said, and he was laughing. "You did a good job. For once."

"Where's Igz?"

Zé rubbed his eyes. "Your mom still has her. She and Cannon are—"

A door opened down the hall, and a moment later, Mom and Cannon appeared. Mom was clearly in her comfy clothes—matching sweats and only sixty percent of her usual amount of jewelry and makeup—and carrying Igz, who looked fussy and tired. That made sense, since she should have been in her crib hours ago. Cannon was in a tank and shorts, and he was practically bouncing at her heels. He gave Chuy a long, considering look. Judging his fresh competition, I figured.

"Why isn't Igz—"

"I want him out of this house." She pointed at Zé and then, of all things, covered Igz's ear. "I want him out right now. I want you to make him leave. And we're going to need to change the locks."

Zé's fuzzy eyebrows drew together, and he looked at me.

Unhappiness settled over Chuy's face. "Mom—"

"Right now, Fernando. Did you hear me? I want him out of this house."

"What—" Zé began, and he started trying to rise.

"What the fuck are you talking about?" I asked. To Zé, I said, "Sit down. You're not going anywhere."

"Yes, you are." Mom rounded on him. "Get your stuff and go. I want you to leave." Her voice rose, taking on an edge. "Right now!"

"Are you out of your fucking mind?" I asked. "Zé, sit down! Zé is the best thing that's happened to this family in a long time. What the hell crawled up your ass?"

"The best thing that's happened?" From the pocket of her sweats, she produced my watch. The watch Augustus had given me. "I found this in his stuff."

"You went through my stuff?" Zé asked.

Everything was happening too fast. I held up a hand. "Hold on—"

"And some of my jewelry," Mom said. "Pieces I didn't even know were missing."

"That doesn't make any sense," I said.

Zé was trying to get to his feet again. He seemed to have forgotten about his cane, and he was using the couch to lever himself up. "That's not true."

"I found it!" Mom screamed at him. She had a great set of lungs; she'd been taking vocal lessons as long as I'd been alive. Igz startled in her arms, and then she began to wail. Cradling Igz's head, Mom brought her voice back down as she said to me, "He stole it, Fernando."

I shook my head and looked at Zé. "No, this is some kind of misunderstanding."

He was pale, and he leaned on the couch like he couldn't quite stand upright. "I didn't touch her stuff. I never went into her room. I wouldn't steal anything."

"Wrong family, sweetheart," Mom said and glanced at, of all people, Chuy. "We've played this game a time or two before."

Chuy leaned against the wall, his body closed. His eyes met mine only for a moment before skating away.

"What does that mean?" Zé asked. No one said anything. "Fernando, I swear to God, I wouldn't steal."

"I know." I shook my head again. "Mom, Zé is the last person—"

"He's an addict, Fernando."

She delivered the words with cool pity as she adjusted Igz, still wailing, against her shoulder. Cannon hovered behind her. It looked like the broccoli-haired bro was trying not to smile.

Zé looked awful: his face washed out, his body contorted as he tried to prop himself up on the couch, braced like he was cowering under a blow. His breathing was rapid and shallow.

"No." I started to shake my head again, but that hadn't seemed to work, so I stood there. After a moment, I knew I had to say something else, but all I could come up with was "No."

"Yes. We followed him tonight. I knew something was wrong. I knew he was hiding something. All those nights he had to leave, and he couldn't explain where he'd been."

My brain was automatically doing the math. I remembered those nights too. The nights Zé left, and when I asked where he was going, he'd say, *I have something to do,* and when I asked when he got back, he'd say, *out.* All the nights I'd wondered if he'd been hooking up. But he hadn't been hooking up; he'd told me that—unless, a part of me observed, that had been a lie too. So, what had he been doing? I didn't know. He'd never told me. He'd always found a way not to tell me.

Zé wasn't moving. I didn't even think he was breathing, except I could hear those softy, raspy breaths.

"Mom," Chuy said, "why don't you and Cannon and I—"

I turned toward Zé, and he flinched. He looked gray. He rubbed his mouth, and his eyes found mine and darted away again.

"He was at an NA meeting," Mom said. "He went straight there. I heard him. I listened to him talk about pills, Fernando."

I nodded. A part of me thought, NA is good. I've been trying to get Chuy to try NA for a long time. But it was hard to think clearly because there was this high-pitched noise in my head, and it drowned everything else out.

"I know you asked," Zé said, his voice drawn so tight I thought it might crack. "I know, Fernando. But I'm sober. I haven't used in almost a year—"

"So," I said. "It's true."

"Fernando."

"I asked you," I said.

"I know."

"I told you what I was dealing with. I told you—" Everything, I almost said; I told you everything. But I managed to change it into "—how important that was. I told you I didn't want anyone who'd been in that life."

"I know," he said, and he sounded like he was about to cry. "I'm sorry. But I'm not using, and I swear to God, I didn't steal anything."

I rubbed my eyes. When I'd first started working—a real job, I mean—and we'd been behind on every bill, and even treading water had seemed like a miracle, on bad nights, I'd started doing the math in years. It would take a year of my life, working full time, if I didn't pay for anything else, to pay off Mom's credit cards. It would take two years, if I didn't use a single cent for anything else, to clear the car loan. Four years to get Augustus through college. And now, I did that math again. Another year to put Chuy through residential treatment. A year to get Zé his PT. Who knew how many fucking years, I thought, and I wanted to laugh, to pay for Mom's fucking wedding?

"He's not leaving," I said to Mom.

"He stole my jewelry!"

"Half your boyfriends steal your jewelry! He's not leaving."

Zé was shaking his head.

"Come on," I said. "We're moving your stuff into my room."

"I don't want him in my house!" Mom screamed. Igz was screaming too. "I want him to leave!"

"It's not your house! I pay the bills. I pay the mortgage. The deed is in my name. If I say he's staying, he's staying."

Mom looked like I'd slapped her. For a moment, her whole body was so lax with shock that it looked like she might drop Igz. Then she recovered somehow. I saw her put on the mask. "I am your mother, and I am telling you I am terrified. He's a thief. He's an addict. I am worried about myself, and this baby, and your brother. And you don't care. It doesn't matter what I say or how I feel. As usual."

What would it be next, I wondered. Tears? Or would she lock herself in her bathroom with a bottle of gin? Would she take Igz in there with her? Would she take her into the tub? I tried to soften my voice. I'd learned a long time ago that she did better when I was calm. "Mom, I would never put our family in danger. If I thought Zé—I'd never let him—if I thought he was a problem, I'd make him leave."

Mom made a scoffing noise.

"What is that supposed to mean?" I asked.

"You know what it means. It means I'm not an idiot, Fernando. It means I'm not blind. I'm begging you right now, pleading with you, and you won't see reason. Because I'm not important enough. No, you've got bigger things to worry about."

"Mom, Jesus," Chuy said.

"You're going to put this whole family in danger because of your little crush. Your family, Fernando. Your father raised you better than that. But who cares, right? Your father doesn't matter. Your mother certainly doesn't matter. Nothing matters anymore because this boy enjoys stringing you along."

I couldn't move. I couldn't look at Zé. I couldn't do anything. I felt like my head had separated from my body. It was like someone else speaking out of my mouth when I heard the words, "I don't know what you're talking about."

Zé was pushing his hands through his hair. Now he froze.

Cannon laughed, the sound short and full of an ugly happiness.

"You think I don't see how you follow him around, how you stare at him, how you talk about him." She rocked Igz and shook her head. "He's using you, Fernando. And one day, you're going to wake up, and he'll be gone, and all you'll have left is your embarrassment." She waited again, like this was a conversation, like she was listening. And then she said, "Come on, Cannon."

They retreated to her room. The door clicked shut. The night was windy, the sound high and whistling against the house. Chuy was looking at the floor.

Zé was the first to move. He lurched toward the hallway, his steps uneven, and he had to put a hand on the wall as he tried to move faster.

I picked up his cane and went after him.

In his room, he was throwing clothes in his suitcase.

"You don't have to do that," I said. "We'll move them to my room."

He opened a drawer, took out an armful of clothes, and hobbled to the suitcase. Then he dropped them in.

"Zé."

He shook his head and opened the next drawer.

When I caught his arm, he shook me off.

"What are you doing?"

"I'm leaving."

He opened another drawer, and I took a step back reflexively.

"What do you mean you're leaving?"

Zé stood in the middle of the room. He glanced around, but I didn't think he was seeing anything. He zipped the suitcase shut and picked it up.

"What the fuck is going on?"

In the next room, Igz's sobs sounded uncontrollable.

His voice was thready as he repeated, "I am not going to do this again. I'm not. I will not, Fernando."

"Do what?"

"Get out of my way."

"Don't listen to her. She's being a bitch."

"Move."

"I didn't say you had to leave. I said you're staying. Hey, did you hear me?"

"I heard you." He nodded. "I heard you, Fernando."

"What the fuck does that mean?"

"It means get out of my way, or—or I'm going to call the police."

I stared at him.

"Move!"

I took a step back, and Zé pushed past me into the hall. He was limping worse than ever. He needed to get off his knee for a while. He needed his cane. I was still holding it, and I went after him.

When I caught up to him at the door, I grabbed his arm. "Where the fuck do you think you're going?"

He looked at me. He had those dark eyes that made me think again of that final band of brown on a hawk's wing. "You know, Fernando, you're a special person. You're kind. And you're loving. And you're generous. And you deserve so much better than what you let yourself have. And I feel sorry for you."

Igz was still screaming. She'd take forever to calm down, I thought. She's terrified.

When I spoke, my voice didn't sound like mine. "You feel sorry for me?"

"Let go of my arm," he said in his low voice.

"You feel sorry for me?"

He stared back at me.

"Who the fuck do you think you are?"

"Okay," Chuy said, his hand closing over mine. He pried my fingers away. "That's enough."

"Go fuck yourself with your sorry," I said. "Fuck off, you lying sack of shit. You have no idea who I am or what I've been through or what I've done. Fuck yourself with that shit. You've got no fucking idea how hard I've worked or how much I've sacrificed."

He didn't say anything.

"I'm proud of who I am. I'm proud of what I've done. All of this, my family, everything, that's me. I did that. And what have you done?" I waited, but he still didn't speak. "You're sorry for me? How fucking dare you? Get the fuck out of here."

And nothing, still nothing but the wing-tip brown of his eyes.

"Get the fuck out of here!"

He dragged his suitcase out of the house, and I slammed the door.

17

That night turned into the next day, and somehow, I didn't die. That was a good reminder: no matter how much it hurts, it won't kill you. Life had taught me that a long time ago, but at some point, I'd forgotten.

I canceled my appointments that day. And the next day, too. I rotted on the couch in between bouts of robotically taking care of Igz. She was fussy, of course. I'd forgotten that babies can be in a bad mood too.

I didn't see Mom and Cannon; they'd left at some point during the night. I got a text telling me they were going on a cruise. Good for them. Mom needed to recover from the trauma and my abusive behavior. Cannon probably needed somewhere fresh to wet his willy. Chuy rotted on the couch with me. I showed him how to change a diaper, but after that one time, I did everything myself. Igz wouldn't settle down when Chuy held her. And Chuy, for his part, didn't seem all that interested. I kept having to tell him to support her neck. And he kept forgetting to hold her bottle for her.

I wrote out texts to Zé: *I'm sorry* and *Can we please talk?* and *I fucked up*. But I deleted all of them without sending them. I thought maybe he might text me, or call, or something. Let me know where he was. That he was safe. I tried to think of something happy—a goofy picture, like the ones he used to send. Zé on the beach dressed like he was in a mariachi band. When that thought came into my mind, I had to go to the bathroom and turn on the water, and I cried like I hadn't since I was twelve years old.

One day turned into another. And then another. We settled into something like a rhythm. I moved Igz into my room and got up with her at night. I got her ready in the morning. Chuy watched her when I had to leave for work. He got better about holding her correctly. And he didn't drop the bottle anymore. But he watched a lot of TV, and sometimes, when I picked her up, her diaper needed changing, and I wondered how long she'd been wet.

By the end of that first, horrible week, I remembered the first days with Igz: the unrelenting demands on my time and energy, the hazy days, the broken sleep. It was like walking through a cloud. I found my memories mixing with when Mom had first brought Augustus home, when I'd realized how much he needed and how little I could do. Memories of when I'd been older. When I'd started working. Throwing newspapers before school. Picking up mismatched shifts after school wherever I could. Going home to fall asleep doing my homework. The impossible days. That's what I'd called them, later, when I'd been far enough away from them to look back. And they were here again. I could see them stretching out ahead of me, the rest of my life a string of one impossible day after another.

But it was better, I knew, than the alternative. Because I felt like I was moving through a cloud all day. Because I didn't think—couldn't think, even if I'd wanted to. Because I was so tired that, against all odds, I was able to sleep. A gray, grainy sleep. But sleep. And before I could sleep too long, before I could dream, Igz would wake me, and we'd start all over again.

Somehow, it eventually became a routine. Sleep and work and a bag of tacos or DoorDashed burgers and TV and a few empty words with Chuy and then sleep again.

Igz wasn't happy. She wasn't sleeping well, which meant I wasn't sleeping well. She fussed all the time. She went through a bout of colic one night when the only thing that would keep her from screaming was for me to walk her, and so I shuffled through the night singing every song I knew by Sublime. I figured it had worked all right with Augustus.

When it started, I recognized the signs. Chuy began keeping strange hours. He'd stay up late. He'd sleep in, and I'd have to wake him at ten, eleven, twelve—whenever I needed to leave for an appointment. He'd spend all day on the couch watching TV, with Igz either propped against him or in her swing.

"What's going on?" I asked him after the first few days of this.

"Why do you always ask me that?" he said, and then Igz started crying, and he left me to deal with her.

I tried other times, and I got the same non-answers: *I'm fine, I don't know what you're talking about,* even *You always do this,* even though I had no idea what that meant.

He started going out.

The first time he came home, I was all over him. But his eyes were clear, and I couldn't smell anything on him. I told him what would happen if I caught him using.

"I know, I know," he said as he went down the hall to his room. What had been Zé's room. He sounded like we were playing. Like this was a joke we always told each other. "You'll kick me out."

The next morning, when I finally got him out of bed (it was technically still morning at eleven-thirty), I said, "I want you to start seeing somebody."

He rubbed his eyes as he leaned into the refrigerator. "How are we out of milk?"

"A therapist."

He made a noise that could have meant anything.

"God damn it, Chuy, are you listening to me?"

"Sure, papi." He kissed my cheek, and I shoved him away. He laughed and said, "Whatever you want."

But he skipped the first appointment—left the house and went God knows where. And he didn't even pretend to go to the second.

The mood swings. The suspicious sleepiness. I checked his arms and couldn't find any marks. I couldn't find anything. And he laughed and acted like we were horsing around. One afternoon, I was trying to work, and a thump broke the stillness of the house. Igz began crying. I ran out of my office and found her on the floor next to the couch, where she'd obviously rolled and fallen. Chuy's eyes were still closed, and in a moment of disbelief, I realized that somehow, he'd slept through it.

I hit him, a flurry of blows as I bent to pick up Igz. He woke slowly, moaning, his voice thick as he said, "What the fuck?"

"What the fuck?" I checked Igz as best I could, but she seemed scared more than anything else. As I tucked her into my shoulder, she began to scream in earnest. "What the fuck? You let her fall off the fucking couch, you worthless piece of shit. What the fuck is wrong with you?"

"I fell asleep!"

"I know you fell asleep, shit-bird! It's two in the fucking afternoon! Why the fuck are you sleeping?"

He stared at me from those dark, sunken eyes, and I couldn't stand looking at him anymore. I took Igz out onto the deck and walked her. It was almost June, and the day was warm, the sun licking my skin. Below us, the valley looked like it was on the other side of a piece of smoked glass, but everywhere else, the day was clear and bright with crisp shadows. I walked Igz, and I wanted Zé. Wanted him like it was the only thing I knew how to do, every inch of me turned toward that wanting. Like I could make him appear if I tried hard enough. Like a prayer.

He'd had fans and friends and a life, I thought as I walked Igz in the sun, in the shade, making a loop around the porch, the air smelling like sage. He had a family. He believed all those people loved him. And he lost all of them, all at once. And he kept going, somehow. But you—the thought was scathing. You, the first time things get a little scary, you sell him out as fast as you can. You all but said you'd throw him out if you needed to. You said you didn't know what she was talking about.

I remembered the look in his eyes. The devastation. And how he'd said, *I am not going to do this again.*

But it happened anyway, I thought. I blinked to clear my eyes, but the valley was a smear of green and gray now. You did it. He trusted you. He took a chance on you. And you took everything away from him again.

Igz was settling down, so I carried her into my room and shut the door. We lay on the bed in the dark. My work phone rang. I turned it off.

He's gone, I thought as I stared up at the ceiling, smelling Igz's Johnson & Johnson, watching the afternoon shadows move. He's gone, and he's never coming back.

The next day, my back was killing me again. I had an opening that morning, so I booked a massage—somewhere local, a place I'd never been before. I drove halfway there in shorts and a tee, and I saw myself in the mirror and thought, What am I doing? I turned around and went home.

When I got out of the Escalade, I could hear Igz crying. I ran to the door. He let her fall again, and this time it's bad. He's high, and he rolled over on her. He's high, and he dropped her. He's high.

I found Igz in the living room. She was in her swing, rocking gently, and her crying sounded like annoyance that had escalated, over time, into genuine worry. I scooped her up, and almost immediately she began to settle into hiccups and discontented noises, telling me how angry she was with me, beating me up with her little fists.

"Chuy?"

He wasn't in the kitchen. He wasn't in the bathroom.

I stopped in his doorway. I knew what his bedroom looked like when he ran. I stared for a moment at the emptiness.

Shushing Igz, I stroked her back. Her tiny body quivered with relief and fear and whatever else was working its way through her.

"It's okay," I whispered. "It's okay. I'm here."

And then I shut the door.

18

I dropped meetings and canceled appointments and lied my ass off. Somehow, I limped to the weekend.

Saturday morning, I was half-awake as I made coffee and fixed Igz's bottle and realized that, somehow, she'd already wet herself. I started toward the living room with Igz in one arm and, in my other hand, a mug for myself and a bottle for her. Then I remembered the diaper bag was in the kitchen, and I was all out of hands. Somebody else, some genius (meaning, somebody who'd gotten more than four hours of sleep at a stretch) might have thought of putting Igz down, putting the coffee and bottle down, and then getting the diaper bag. Instead, I put my foot inside it and dragged it along with us.

When I stepped into the living room, Augustus was there.

I stared.

He stared.

It wasn't a dream, because in my dreams, he wasn't such a fucking wiener. He stood there in a pair of slides, a pair of jersey taint-tickler shorts that made it painfully clear Augustus had been cheated in the dick department by his fuck-up of a father, and a tank top that said *Daddy Said So*. It showed the silhouette of a face that was mostly a beard. He looked like a man, broad shoulders, lean muscle, even some stubble on his jaw. He looked like a walking, talking public service announcement for mandatory vasectomies.

"Is that a baby?" he asked. "Why is your foot inside that bag?"

I started to cry.

It only lasted a moment, and then I had myself under control again. But the horror on Augustus's face told me I hadn't been fast enough. I tried to wipe my cheeks and couldn't because I was holding everything in the fucking house. Somehow I managed to say, "Of course it's a fucking baby. What the fuck did you think it was? Get your ass over here and help me."

Aside from his addiction to daddy dick, he was a decent kid. He ought to be; I'd brought him up that way. He took the mug and the bottle, and he offered to take Igz, but I shook my head. I did kick the diaper bag off my foot, and he carried it over to the sofa. I sat, and Augustus sat, and he was staring at Igz and staring at me.

"What the fuck are you doing here?"

The confusion and concern on his face evaporated. "Surprising you."

"No shit."

"Hi, Fer."

I grunted.

"I missed you. Did you miss me?"

"Interesting philosophical question: can you miss an outbreak of genital warts?"

He reached out to touch Igz, and then he stopped and looked at me.

"She's not a fucking museum exhibit. Igz, this is Augustus. He's the reason I'm so screwed up, and he's also the reason you will never be allowed to date. Ever. Under any circumstances. Augustus, this is Isabela, but we call her Igz."

I couldn't read the expression on Augustus's face. He reached out and gently took one of Igz's fists and pumped it lightly. "Nice to meet you, Igz."

I had to blink rapidly again.

"Can I hold her?"

"Let me change her first."

Augustus, of course, sat there and watched and did nothing as I changed Igz. After getting her dressed again, I handed her to Augustus.

"You have to hold her—"

"I know," he said.

And, to my surprise, he did. He held her perfectly, her head supported, her body fitting neatly into the crook of his arm. I had another of those moments where I felt like I was seeing a stranger: this man with ridiculously developed biceps and zero body fat where I kept expecting to see Augustus, who had once gotten his hand stuck inside a jar of M&M's and had peed himself at a pool party because he was too afraid to ask to use the bathroom. He rocked her without even seeming to think about it, and his face was open and alight with—what? Wonder was part of it. Happiness. Pleasure. He likes children, I thought, and it was something else, something new, another thing I hadn't known about my own baby. And then, as clearly, He's going to be such a good dad. He already was with Lana—I knew that—and seeing this drove it home.

This time, I had to use my shirt to dry my eyes.

Augustus noticed, of course. His head came up, and his eyes searched me. "Fer, are you okay? What's going on?"

"No, I'm not okay, beaver-dick. I'm going through menopause, and my emotions are totally out of whack."

He rolled his eyes, and I definitely remembered that. "Do you want to tell me why you have a baby? Oh my God, Fer. Did you have a baby?"

"Yes, Augustus. I squirted her out myself."

He laughed, but his face twisted. "This is why I have issues. You realize that, right?"

"You have issues," I said. "Join the fucking club." But then I said, "She's Chuy's."

"Oh my God," Augustus whispered. "I can totally see it. Look at her nose."

"Her eyes, too. She's lucky that's all she got; I honestly don't know what I'd do if I had to tell her she looked like a giant, gaping anus because she got that from her daddy."

"Fer, I'm serious, you can't talk like that around a baby."

"Are you kidding me? She swears like a sailor. You should hear her let rip."

Augustus was silent for a long time, studying Igz, bouncing her lightly. When he spoke, his voice was painfully neutral. "Where's Chuy?"

I didn't say anything.

"Oh my God," he said again. More of a whisper, this time. He swallowed and looked up. "Fer, you've been doing this all on your own? God, I'm so sorry. Why didn't you tell me?"

"Because if I told you, you'd be out here, when you're supposed to be working and building your agency and making lots of money to keep Daddy in Botox."

"You know he doesn't do Botox."

"Don't think I missed that fucking tank top. I'm burning it before you leave."

"I swear to God I told Theo you were going to say that. I even recorded it. I'll play it for you later."

"Where is your pet dinosaur?"

"He couldn't take off work." Augustus cooed as he ran his hand over Igz's head, and because she's completely heartless and treacherous and has absolutely zero loyalty, she smiled at him. "He said I should come by myself. Believe it or not, he didn't even turn on the tracking app on my phone."

"He has a tracking app on your phone?"

Augustus looked at me.

I subsided into the couch, muttering, "I knew it was a joke."

"This," Augustus said in a baby voice to Igz, "is why we're going to have to take you to Missouri. To get you away from all the crazy."

I tried to hit him, but he used Igz like a shield (coward), and he was giggling, and Igz was smiling, and I had to think of something, so I said, "You need some coffee," and then all I could do was stand at the sink, my knuckles aching as I wrapped my fingers around the stainless-steel apron. I looked at a far-off point of dusty green on the side of the valley. I tried to breathe normally.

I didn't hear him come into the kitchen; when he touched my back, I flinched.

"Fer," he asked quietly, "what's going on?"

I told him. We ended up on the couch, coffees forgotten, and I went through all of it. As much as I could, anyway. I couldn't tell him about Mom, not all of it. And not everything with Chuy. Not that horrible thunk when Igz had fallen. Not coming home, again, and finding her crying in her swing.

I didn't tell him about Zé, either. The rational part of my brain knew that Augustus, more than anyone, would be unfazed by the fact that (it turns out) I apparently enjoyed the occasional dick. After all, I'd been the parenting genius who had once told him sexuality was like a buffet, and he ought to try as much as he wanted. He would have been annoyingly excited, of course, and unbearably supportive. He would have listened.

But the part of me that had spent my whole life protecting him with shadows and half-truths and evasions and outright lies, the part of me that had built him a better world to grow up in—that part of me wasn't ready to tell him. Because even though the rational part of me knew he'd be happy for me, it felt like too much. Like a burden. And, if I were being honest with myself, I'd already cried three times since he got home, and I was sick of feeling vulnerable.

"I knew something was wrong," Augustus said when I finished. "I knew it. I told Theo the minute I sent you a picture of those sneakers with the Swarovski crystals all over them and you didn't blow up, I knew something was wrong."

I barely remembered the message he was talking about—some sort of hideous, crystal-encrusted sneakers he'd pretended to want for Christmas. "I've been busy."

"Yeah, I get that." He bounced Igz on his knee. "Do you think that manny was stealing from Mom?"

"Jesus Christ, Augustus."

"What? I'm asking."

"No. If I had to bet, I'd say that underage micropenis took her shit while they were fighting and then tried to cover for it when they made up again."

"But the manny could have—"

"It wasn't Zé." I tried to bring down the volume of my voice. "Okay?"

"Yeah. Sure, okay." But he was looking at me differently, and I didn't know why. "What are you going to do?"

"I'll be fine, Augustus."

His smile was silver and darting. "Oh yeah?"

"Yes."

"Because you had your foot in a diaper bag when I showed up today. And your hair—uh, when was the last time you washed your hair? And you don't have any food in the refrigerator. And—"

"All right. I get it. I didn't know you were coming, you ungrateful excuse for a stool sample. If I'd known you were coming, I'd have baked a fucking cake."

Augustus gave me another of those un-fucking-bearably adult looks and took out his phone. He placed a call and said, "Hey. Yeah, everything's okay. I made it to the house. I slept a little, yeah. How are you? How's Lana?" And then the treacherous little weasel cunt said, "I'm going to have to stay out here for a while. Um, everyone's okay, I guess. Fer squirted out a baby."

"You little shit," I breathed.

Augustus grinned, and then he broke up laughing at whatever his pet dinosaur said. When he'd recovered, he said, "It's a long story; I'll tell you tonight. Are you going to be okay if I'm here a couple of weeks?"

"He's not staying for two weeks," I said loudly. "He's not staying at all. Period."

More of that fucking eye-rolling. "I love you too. Hold on, I'll tell him. Theo says he loves you."

Theo's voice sounded tinny—and wry—on the phone's speaker. "Hi, Fer."

"If he loves me so much," I asked, "why doesn't he get one of those lockable playpens and keep you from—"

"Bye, babe," Augustus said into the phone. "I love you."

"—wandering off. You know, the kind people get so their kids can't escape."

"That's called a cage."

"Exactly, why doesn't he buy that?"

"Are you going to tell me what's really going on? Or are we going to spend two agonizing weeks with me trying to worm it out of you?"

I snorted.

"How about four weeks?" Something must have shown on my face because he said, "I work from home, bitch, and Theo's the most responsible human in the world. Want to make it six?"

"Did you call me bitch?"

"Remember that time I nagged you until you told me all my Christmas presents?"

"That time? It's every fucking year!"

To hide his grin, he ducked his head and booped Igz on the nose. She was still smiling at him, which tells you something about loyalty and the next generation. "All right. It's going to be a long eight weeks."

My line was to say something like *Eight weeks? In eight weeks, you'll have drained every pecker from here to the Castro.* And Augustus would laugh, and

I'd pretend to get angrier, and eventually, the question itself would be buried under the drift of our bullshit. But this time, I didn't say anything. I couldn't.

Augustus looked up, and they were my Augustus's eyes, the one I'd raised. And at the same time, they weren't. They were more mature. They were...wiser. Wiser, I thought with a hint of manic despair. I'm about to ask the same kid for advice who went through an entire bottle of Jergens the week he discovered jerking off.

The words slipped out of me before I let myself think about them. "Do you think there's something wrong with me?"

He furrowed his brow. His knee, still bouncing Igz, slowed. His smile was a trembling question mark like he was waiting for the punchline.

"Never mind," I said.

His smile slipped. "Fer."

"Like you'd know." I tried to force my voice toward normalcy. "Good Christ, you're the one shacked up with a living museum exhibit. They could make some weird porn out of it. 'The Driest Dick: The Legend of Pharaoh's Boner.'"

Augustus watched me and then shook his head. "Don't do that."

"Something about the Nile and lube."

"Fer," he said, and there was so much authority behind it that for a moment, I forgot this was the same kid who'd reeked of Jergens. He stopped bouncing Igz, laid her against his chest, and met my gaze. "I love you. I think you're wonderful. What do you mean, is there something wrong with you?"

"He said I do this because I want to do it. Mom, I mean. And Chuy. Dealing with their shit. He said I don't let myself have more. I don't let myself be happy." And I'm not happy, I thought. It was the first time I'd expressed that thought to myself so clearly, but there it was. I'm not happy. And I'm lonely. And I want more. I might have even said that to Augustus, but by then, my throat had closed up, and I couldn't get anything out.

"Fer," Augustus whispered. "Oh my God." He scooted over and, even though I tried to elbow him off, gave me a one-armed hug. I didn't break down crying—thank. fucking. god—but Augustus's hair did get a little wet.

When he finally released me, I ran both hands over my face and shook my head. "I'm fine," I said, but my voice was gravelly. "It's been a lot lately."

"Of course it's been a lot. You've got to be exhausted."

"It's all right. Plenty of people are single parents. I'll hit my stride." I found the remote and turned on the TV. I had no idea what I was looking at: apparently a romantic diaper commercial. "Sorry I unloaded on you like that."

For what might have been the first time since he'd been thirteen and I'd tanned his ass, Augustus took the remote from me.

"Hey," I said. "Just because the dinosaur let's you watch *Barney*—"

He turned off the TV and tucked the remote behind his back. "The TV stays off until we finish this conversation."

"Excuse me?"

"You heard me."

I stared at him.

It took about ten seconds before he shrank down, hugging Igz to him. "Uh, please?"

"What the fuck is Pharaoh's boner letting you get away with?"

"Fer, I want you to talk to me. I'm your brother. I love you. I want you to be happy, and I definitely want to help you after—" His voice got thick, and he stroked Igz's fuzzy head. "—after you did so much for me. You gave up your whole life for me. I know that; I'm not an idiot."

"Oh yeah?"

His grin blossomed. "I'm not a total idiot."

I sighed and rubbed my face again.

His voice was tentative as he said, "I'm not a child anymore. You don't have to protect me."

I closed my eyes and saw her again: I'd been thirteen the first time, and she'd used a plastic bag because—the note said—she wanted to be beautiful when they found her. What was beautiful about having plastic stuck to your face, I wanted to know. What was beautiful about your kids finding you like that? I'd told Augustus she was tired from an audition, and I'd let him pick the snacks for his lunch so he'd be too excited to ask questions.

"Who said those things to you?" Augustus asked. "Chuy?"

It was another open door, another opportunity to tell him about Zé. But I nodded.

The silence lasted longer this time. "Do you think he's right?"

"Do I think he's right?"

"It's an important question."

The old, familiar helplessness welled up in me. "You know Mom has bad days. Every time one of these walking fucksticks disappears, she spirals. And even if she didn't, she doesn't even pretend to work anymore. She couldn't afford an apartment, let alone to keep herself fed. Am I supposed to say, 'Hey, thanks for giving birth to me, now fuck off and go be a bag lady'?"

"Well—"

"And Chuy. He had the fucking gall to look me in the face and tell me he doesn't want me to do this anymore. What the fuck is that supposed to mean? All these fucking years running after him, getting his stomach pumped, carrying that fucking Narcan everywhere, rushing him to the emergency room, the rehab, the nights driving the worst fucking streets because I had no idea where he was. And now he says don't bother, he doesn't want me to do that anymore. Let him die, that's what he's saying. It was a good ride while it lasted, leave me the fuck alone so I can load up in some shithole and choke to death on my own vomit!" My throat hurt, and I realized I was yelling. Augustus's eyes were wide, and he had one hand cupped over Igz's head, but I couldn't stop. "You think I don't wish they'd leave me the fuck alone? Jesus Christ, they ruin everything. Mom's emergencies. Mom's breakdowns. She needs to go to Sedona. She needs to go to Santa Barbara. She needs to go to Vail. She needs more fucking pills!" I stood and started to pace. "Every time I try to do something for myself, every time I want something for myself, she finds a way to fuck it up. Or Chuy swoops in again. I finally had a chance to live my life doing what I wanted, and he dropped a fucking baby in my lap like—"

The hurt in Augustus's eyes made me look away. All I could do was stand there, my chest heaving, my whole body hurting with the force of my shouting. From a long way off, I could hear Igz crying.

Augustus carried her out onto the deck, and the door shut behind them, and I couldn't hear them anymore.

My eyes burned. My face was hot. I went to the bathroom and splashed cold water on my cheeks. I held a towel against my face, pressing it there until my knuckles throbbed, fighting a scream. It was like something had come unplugged in me, and now, no matter how hard I tried, I couldn't stop it up again. All my helplessness. All my disappointment. All my rage. My hands were shaking so badly I couldn't hang the towel up again, so I left it hanging over the side of the sink.

The sound of the deck slider called me back. Augustus was settling Igz in her swing; she'd stopped crying. He straightened, looked at me, and his eyes were still full of pain.

I tried to think of something to say. I'm sorry. I knew I was supposed to say I'm sorry, but I couldn't even get that far.

And then Augustus hugged me. Not his awkward one-armed hug like he was a seventh-grader trying to cop a feel. He wrapped his arms around me and crushed me to him. He was still shorter than me, but the little wiener had been packing on muscle, probably so he could Tarzan his way from dick to dick out in the homo jungle.

That line of thinking helped me hold it together for about five seconds. And then I burst into sobs.

Augustus held me. I didn't hold him; he held me. And he rubbed my back. And I wanted to pull myself together, make it all okay again, tell him this was a blip. But those were old instincts, and I was too far gone.

Eventually, I stopped crying, and we ended up at the kitchen table. Augustus brought two beers from the fridge.

"So, you and Theo are day drinkers and swingers," I said scratchily. "Great role model you've got there."

"Drink your fucking beer," Augustus said with a grin.

I took a swallow. And then another. I was still hiccupping from the sobs, and my eyes had that sticky itchiness that came after a hard cry.

"I'm sorry," Augustus said, turning the beer in his hands, "that I messed up your life."

I snorted, but it was, admittedly, a wet snort. "Give me a fucking break. You're my baby. You love being my baby. I love that you're my baby. God, Augustus, I love you so much I would pull off my own skin for you. I didn't even complain when you turned out to have a raging dick addiction."

"You did complain, actually. You complained nonstop. You still complain."

"I love you, even if you are a giant billboard for free boy pussy." My throat tightened, and my voice thinned. "I have never, not once, wished you weren't in my life or that a single fucking thing with you had been different. I'm so fucking proud of you. I'm so grateful I get to be your brother."

Augustus nodded, still looking at his beer. "But you gave up so much—"

"Knock it off. I shouldn't have said that; that's not what I meant."

"But Fer, I think—I think maybe it's okay for you to feel that way. I mean, I know you love me. And I know how much you've done for me. I know you'd do it again if you had to."

"I wouldn't buy you that fucking prom ticket again if I'd known you were going to spend the whole night dreaming about going down on your boy Kris."

Another grin splashed across Augustus's face. "God, he was cute."

"That ticket cost a hundred fucking dollars, Augustus, and you didn't even get laid. You could have dry-humped Kris for free."

"I think it's okay for you to be angry. I think it's good, actually. You can be angry at the universe, or at fate, or at the unfairness of being asked to give up a life you'd built for yourself. You can be angry at Chuy. You can be angry at Mom. You can even be angry at me if you want; I can handle it."

It was a funny thing, breathing; my body couldn't seem to remember how to do it.

Neither of us spoke for a while. Augustus set down his bottle, and the glass clicked against the tabletop. "I've never heard you talk like that," he said. "About Mom and Chuy and—" He didn't say *me*. Instead, he said, "—everything."

"Yeah, well." I shrugged. Somehow, my beer was empty. "I don't know. I guess it's been in there for a while."

"I'm glad you told me."

I rolled my eyes.

That made him smile, but it faded quickly. "They're right, you know. I think they're right."

"Oh yeah? In your professional opinion, you think they're right?"

"I don't think you're happy, Fer, and you deserve to be happy. I think you feel responsible for everyone. And I think maybe—maybe Chuy's right. Maybe there's a part of you that wants things like this because—" He stopped and touched his bottle and dropped his hands in his lap.

"Because what?"

He didn't look up.

"No, please. Tell me, Augustus. Why do I want my life to be a fucking shitshow? What a profound psychological insight. Please, tell me more."

"I don't know, Fer. I think maybe that's something you could talk to someone about."

But I could hear myself answering the question—a series of flashbulbs, like my brain had been ready to go. Because your dad told you a man takes care of his family. Because your mom never had time for you, never had time for anyone but herself. Because you were a child the first time you knew she'd tried to kill herself, and you've been terrified for thirty years that she'll get it right.

"Does Mom—" Augustus's voice was small. He stopped. Started again. "Did she say she was going to do something if you—I don't know. If you did something different."

Christ, I thought. The way we talk in this family. Mom's having a bad day. Did she say she was going to do something? She didn't have to, I thought. She's never had to say anything.

I shook my head.

"Because that's emotional abuse, Fer. Even if she doesn't say it. That's manipulative and selfish and—and wrong."

I shrugged.

"And she can get therapy, medication, a support system that's not you." His voice was rising. "She doesn't have to be so fucking—so fucking self-centered all the time."

"Easy, tiger."

But Augustus's words spilled out faster and harder. "And you can't fix Chuy, Fer. You know that, right? He told you that. I'm telling you that. Any reasonable person will tell you that. He's got to take responsibility for himself. And Mom too. You're a human being, and you deserve dignity and autonomy, and your worth isn't based on how much you can help those—those two dumbshits who keep choosing over and over again not to help themselves. I am so fucking sick of it, Fer!"

The last words were a whisper-shout that it sounded like he barely managed to control. I stared at Augustus—his chest heaving, his eyes wide, a hint of red in his cheeks. And then I burst out laughing. He started laughing too, sinking back in his seat, hands covering his face.

"I'm sorry," he kept trying to say through the laughter. "I'm sorry."

I waved the words away and kept laughing.

When we'd both calmed down, though, he said again, "I'm sorry. I know it's easy for me to say. I know I'm not you, and I don't live with this every day, and I don't know what I'd do if I were you."

"You'd do something better. You've always been smarter."

He practically glowed. He'd been like that since as long as I could remember. When he'd been sounding out words in that little tent I'd made in the fucking one-bedroom. The way his whole face lit up when I told him he'd done a good job. With his spelling. The first time I'd laughed at one of his stupid videos.

"I want you to talk to someone, Fer. I don't know if that's the right thing to say. I hope you'll talk to someone."

I grunted.

"About setting boundaries."

I nodded.

"And self-care."

"Okay."

"And about this sense of obligation, and feeling guilty, and recognizing the limits of what you can control, and how important and valuable and wonderful you are as a human being, totally independent of what you do for everyone else."

"I said okay, dick-drip! Jesus fucking Christ. Why the fuck am I going to pay some fucking therapist when I can sit here and have you yammer at me?"

"And about how you deserve happiness and what you want matters and you should go after the things that you want. There. I'm done. I'm not saying anything else."

I stared at him for a long time before I said, "For fuck's sake."

He grinned.

"Come here."

"Uh, maybe not."

"Get your ass over here."

"I'm good."

"Augustus! Right fucking now!"

He took a long time coming around the table.

I hugged him. I kissed the side of his head. And then I said, "You smell like somebody used a jockstrap to clean a porn set. After, I mean. All those giant, porn-y loads."

"I hate you. You are the single weirdest human being who has ever been born."

Neither of us said anything for a long time. His arms tightened around me, and he whispered, "We'll figure this out."

I lifted him off the floor because I knew he hated it, and I kissed the side of his head one more time, and I shook him so he'd know he was still my annoying baby brother who'd probably paid for his last year of college with rim jobs. And I whispered, "Thank you."

19

In June, even on a weekday, Surfrider Beach was popping. Cars were parked up and down the Pacific Coast Highway, and as I searched for a spot, I watched beachgoers making their way down the sandy hill toward the water. I ended up having to park near the Malibu Pier. Then I got out and walked.

After the first few times coming here, I'd gotten smart. I wore my flip-flops instead of shoes. Shorts. A tank that Augustus had given me, with two cats high-fiving on the front and, on the back, two sassy tails. I was walking bait for ass pirates, if I do say so myself. But since I was, technically, an ass pirate myself—at least occasionally—I figured it was time to get into the spirit of things. Plus I thought it might make him smile.

I'd thought about that a lot during the last couple of weeks. About whether I should do this. And when I realized I was kidding myself—when I was forced to admit I wanted to do this—wondering how. I'd done a lot of thinking the last couple of weeks. It was strange what having a semi-normal sleep schedule did for your brain.

Part of that was because Augustus had been willing to stay, and he'd helped with Igz. He'd been a natural, too; I knew he was good with Lana, but seeing him with an infant reinforced it. More than helping with Igz, though, he'd been…well, weirdly close to a friend, which was hard to reconcile with the Augustus I remembered (the park-cruising, ass-hook-dangling, spank-o-rama Augustus, in other words). He talked to me when I wanted to talk. He listened. When I came home from my intake session, he didn't ask why my eyes were red, and he didn't say anything about the fact that I'd sat in the Escalade for a good half an hour after getting home, even though he must have heard the garage door. He sat me on the couch with Igz, got me a beer, and watched the last half of a John Wick movie with me. And I knew, if I wanted to, I could tell him about it. About all of it. Even now, after he'd gone home, I knew he'd be there if I picked up the phone.

I tried calling Zé; I want that on the record. But he hadn't answered my calls or texts. He hadn't called back.

A gull dove in front of me, pulling my attention back to the beach. It swooped for a half-eaten drumstick, caught it in its beak, and flapped its wings to rise again. Other gulls swirled around it, a fucking tornado of squawking feathers, and the bird dropped the drumstick. Another gull immediately dove, and the whole process started over again.

There were always gulls, of course—too many beachgoers leaving too much half-eaten food, some of them stupid enough to feed the birds on purpose. And, as I'd been coming here over the last couple of weeks, I'd started to form my mental list of what stayed the same and what changed. The line outside the organic café at the pier was always long, even if the faces changed. The number of people on the beach ebbed and flowed, but there were always people—people in bright swimsuits, people smelling of sunscreen, people laughing and shouting. There was always Joel, the guy standing knee deep in the surf, banging on a drum he wore on a strap around his neck. Going to fucking town on it. I don't even know if his name was Joel; the second or third time I came to Surfrider, I heard this leathery beach bum say, "Joel, knock it off," but if his name was Joel, he kept pounding away.

Other things stayed the same and, at the same time, were different too. The lifeguard tower was painted the same blue as the sky; that stayed the same. But the lifeguard changed. Today, he had on tiny red shorts and a white tank, and every inch of him was corded with swimmer muscle. I guess that was a change too; I guess I'd always been able to admire a guy's looks, but now it felt different, because that door was open.

The surfboards changed—dozens of them leaned against a sagging wire fence—but there were always surfboards. Always surfers too. I watched one guy trying to get down to the water. He must have slipped because he fell face forward onto his own board and bit it, hard. His friends were watching from up the beach, laughing. They kept laughing as he dragged himself out of the water and limped toward them, leaving a trail of bloody footprints in the sand. I thought about what Zé had said, about how toxic surf culture could be, but the laughter sounded friendly—even if nobody was trying to help him.

The sun was hot on my neck as I continued up the beach. The air seemed to shimmer above the sand, and on every breath, I caught that familiar cocktail of beach smells: brine and zinc and a hint of decay. The first time Mom had taken Augustus to a beach, there'd been a dog rolling on a dead seal. I'd had to tell Augustus they were playing, and we'd gone the other direction. The sun sparked on the water. A helicopter floated overhead, blades and rotors thrumming. Someone was playing *cumbia*. My heart was running wild in my chest.

If he's not here, I told myself, you'll come back tomorrow. And the next day. And the next. A part of me was vaguely aware that this was pretty much the definition of stalking. But I ignored that part and focused on my heart—specifically, on trying not to choke on it, since it seemed to be lodged halfway up my throat. He had told me about this beach, about coming here the first day he'd been in the United States. He'd told me this was where modern surfing was born. And I knew he would be here today; I knew it. He would. He had to be. Because today was different.

I found him at First Point; he was watching the surfers, of course. He wore board shorts and a ratty old T-shirt that he must have owned for a million years—this one showed a dinosaur on a longboard and said SURF-

O-SAURUS—and all I could do was try to think if I'd seen it on him before. It was easier to think about that, to try to remember, than to think about everything else: about how long his legs were, about the strong, bronzed muscles of his thighs, about the lines of his neck as he turned his head, about the way the wind tangled those thick, dark curls. He was watching a girl ride a wave to shore. She was young, maybe not even a teenager yet, and she rode the water like she'd been born to do it. He wasn't smiling as he watched her, but he looked happy.

And then I stopped because he was wearing the Ray-Bans I'd bought him, and because my emotions had been totally fucked since that intake session, and I was one hundred percent sure I was about to burst into sobs. I couldn't bring myself to keep walking. I stood there, the sun baking me, the sand working like a convection oven, sweating inside that stupid tank and wondering if I had time to run back to the pier and buy something else, anything else, anything, in particular, that didn't have two cats with sassy tails high-fiving on it.

He looked over, and I forgot how to breathe.

Surprise first. Then his brows drawing together, his face hardening, his body closing as he hugged his good knee to his chest. He looked out at the water again.

God or Jesus or Buddha, I thought, or whoever is the patron saint of high-fiving cats, please give me one fucking break in my life.

And somehow, for Zé, I managed to move forward.

He didn't look at me as I approached, even though he must have heard me squishing through the sand. He kept his gaze fixed on the water; the girl was off her board now, paddling parallel to the shore. A chunky little boy in a snorkel mask was coming in on the next wave, and he looked like only the grace of those high-fiving cats was keeping him on the board. Sure enough, he fell almost as soon as I looked at him, and the wave crashed over him. He bobbed to the surface a moment later, sputtering and laughing. Zé's mouth twitched in a reluctant smile.

"Hi," I said.

He shifted on his towel. His shoulders tightened.

"Can I sit down?"

"What are you going to do if I say no?"

"I don't know. Wait for you in the parking lot, maybe. Okay, that actually sounded way more stalkerish than I meant it to."

"How stalkerish was it supposed to sound?"

"No, I meant—" I stopped. "You ass nut."

He looked up at me. The Ray-Bans made it impossible to see those dark eyes.

"I miss you," I said.

"I can tell. I'm surprised you weren't hiding in the back seat of my car."

I winced, but mostly for show. Then I sat.

He gave me another, longer look.

"You didn't say no," I reminded him.

"I didn't say yes."

"You're not going to make this easy, are you?"

"What do you want, Fernando?"

"I want to apologize," I said. And then my voice was too thick to continue. "I want to say I'm sorry. And I want to tell you I miss you. And I think I love you. Still."

He put his hand on his forehead. Maybe like he was shading his eyes. Maybe like he had a headache. Maybe I was giving him a headache.

"You were right," I said. "About a lot of things. About me. About how I'm living my life. Or not living it, I guess. About the—the shitshow I've got going with my mom and Chuy."

It seemed like a long time before he gave a tiny shake of his head, and his voice softened into what I remembered as Zé's voice. My Zé's voice. "I shouldn't have said those things. That wasn't the time, and it wasn't kind, and it certainly wasn't my place."

"But you were right," I said. "And I needed to hear it. From you, I mean. Because it was your place, you know what I mean? You're so important to me. And you're the only person who I could hear it from, actually hear it." He didn't say anything, so I went on. "Chuy said I do this stuff—all this stuff with him, with Augustus, with my mom—I do it because I want to. God, that made me so angry. But, uh, I've been talking to someone, and I think, maybe, there might be a little truth to it. There's a lot of shit with my dad I'm unpacking. Even more shit with my mom. Tubular shit."

A startled laugh escaped Zé before he managed to stop it. His brows drew together like I'd tricked him somehow, and he said, "That's not how you use tubular."

"Well, I'm not a super-hot surfer bro, so I'm kind of playing it by ear."

He pushed the glasses up onto his head. His eyes were the exact shade of brown I remembered. The red-tailed hawk. That last, final band of brown. He was watching me watch him, and something changed in his face: color coming into his cheeks, the lines of his mouth softening. He blinked and looked away.

"I'm glad you're talking to someone, Fernando. I want you to be happy."

"Well, I'm not happy because I fucked everything up with you, and you make me happy."

He pulled his knee closer to his chest. He looked out at the water. Every inch of him was drawn so tight I thought he might snap.

"I'm sorry about everything, Zé. About my mom and how awful she was to you. About how I reacted when I went to pick up Chuy and you tried to help me see I was doing something stupid. But mostly I'm sorry that I was such a fucking shitheel when it came down to it. When my mom made that crack about us. When I found out about—" *The drugs* wasn't exactly the direction I wanted to take, so I settled for "—everything. I thought about that a lot. About how you lost all these people in your life by being yourself.

I should have made sure you knew how important you were to me. How much I care about you. I should have told you I love you."

I hadn't meant to say those words. It had been so much easier to hide behind *I think*. But they popped out, and when I heard them, a flush ran through me, and fresh sweat broke out everywhere, and I had a panicked moment that I was going to be sick, puking on my hands and knees while Zé stared at those sassy tails on my back. But then it passed, and I felt...good. Open. Relieved.

He put his hand on his forehead again. The waves came in. The swash rode up the beach. Joel was still pounding his drum.

"I should have told you about...about everything," he said, his voice clotted with emotion. "I should have told you that first day. But I was scared you wouldn't give me the job, and I needed the money, and then I was so embarrassed. Embarrassed that I'd lied. Embarrassed that I was an addict. Embarrassed to tell you how lonely I'd been, and that the pills made it easier, and then they weren't making it easier but I couldn't stop, and I kept giving up one thing after another for those fucking pills." His voice broke. His shoulders shook. I scooted closer and put my arm around him, and the T-shirt was hot against my skin. He jerked away, but I settled my arm again, and this time, he leaned into me. He kept speaking out toward the ocean, wiping his cheeks as tears fell. "And I knew about Chuy, and I knew how hard he'd made your life, knew how scared you were for him, and I couldn't, Fernando. I couldn't tell you. I liked how you looked at me. You're so kind. You always treated me like I was special."

"You are special," I said. "I love you. Not because I think you're perfect. I love you because you've worked so hard to build a new life for yourself after you lost everything. I love you because you're so strong and calm and centered. I love you because you are such a fucking beautiful person, inside and out, that I feel like a human dumpster fire when I'm around you, but that's okay, because I get to be around you, and that's what matters. I love you even though you wear the same fucking Quiksilver shirt, like, eight days in a row, and I love you even though you have the absolute worst taste in TV shows—"

"I don't even watch TV."

"Exactly! And I love you even though you are the biggest goof on two legs. I love you because you are the biggest goof on two legs." I had to blink my eyes clear. "I love you. And if you'll give me another chance, I won't let you down again."

His voice was husky when he said, "I shouldn't have run away. I'm sorry I did that. It was a lot. It brought back a lot. I've spent the last few weeks telling myself I did the right thing. I keep telling myself that I can do this on my own. That I don't need anybody. That I'm better off alone. And you know what? I spent a lot of my life living a lie, and I know what it sounds like when I'm telling myself one more stupid lie."

I opened my mouth to answer, but before I could, my phone buzzed.

"Go on," Zé said, wiping his cheeks again. "Check it."

"No."

He gave a wet laugh. "Fernando, look at your phone so I have five seconds to put myself together."

I checked my phone. Mom's name showed on the screen.

"You'd better answer it." Where Zé had smeared the tears across his cheek, they left a salt track that caught the light. There was weariness in his eyes. Resignation. He knew, I guess, this was part of the package—if we were a package.

I answered the phone on speaker.

"Cannon took my necklace," Mom said. "The emerald solitaire. The little shit has been eyeing it for weeks, and now it's gone, and he's gone." Her voice rose into a scream as she repeated, "He's gone!"

"Mom, I can't talk right now."

"Did you hear me? He stole my necklace!"

"I heard you. Did you hear me?"

"You have to find him. He's probably trying to pawn it right now!"

"Mom, I'm sorry about your necklace. And about Cannon. And I'll be happy to look for your necklace when I have some free time, but I can't drop everything and do it this minute."

"Fernando, I need you right now!"

"I understand. But I'm doing something important. I can't do it right now."

"What are you doing that's so important?"

"I'm trying to convince Zé to be my boyfriend. And forgive me. Not in that order, I guess. Oh, and we had sex when he was living at our house, so I'm bi. You can tell Shannon at your next life-coaching session that you now technically have one and a half gay sons. That's fifty percent for you."

Her silence echoed across the call.

"I'm going to go now," I said, "and I'm going to put my phone on do not disturb because Zé is important to me, and I have a right to my own time and to take care of my own needs."

"But Cannon—"

I disconnected. It took a surprising amount of willpower to look at Zé.

His eyebrows made those fuzzy peaks again.

"I'm working on setting boundaries," I said. "My therapist said I should be clear and concise and compassionate. Those are the three C's. And if I need to repeat myself, that's okay."

He nodded slowly.

"I didn't mean to tell her about the blow job," I added. "That was a spur-of-the-moment thing."

He covered his mouth, but I could still see his smile.

"Also, I know I'm amazing at playing it cool—"

Zé's eyebrows did their thing again.

"—but that was hard for me."

"I know," he said softly.

"I know I've still got a lot of work to do," I said.

"So do I."

"I know I'm not perfect."

He shook his head and whispered, "Neither am I."

"But one thing I'm good about, Zé? One thing I'm proud of? I care about my family. When Augustus decided to stay in Missouri, I told him he could always come home. If Chuy would say goodbye before he disappeared, I'd tell him the same thing. We're family, and they can always come home. And you're my family too." I had to stop. The sun was so bright, and I had to blink rapidly to clear my eyes. My voice fought with the crash of the waves, the cry of the gulls, the *cumbia* blaring on a distant radio. I fought to reach him across that vast space that had opened between us. "Please come home."

20

The afternoon sitter today was, no joke, a fifteen-year-old girl with braces. Maybe she picked up on my energy—the needle was somewhere between manic and insane—or maybe she had an insta-crush on Zé (honestly, a real possibility). Either way, she couldn't stop staring at us. I paid her for the rest of her shift and sent her home early.

Igz smiled at Zé, in case you're wondering. Her treachery knows no bounds. Zé didn't even have to work for it. He stood there, holding her, inspecting her, and Igz smiled like it was the most entertaining thing of her life.

I brought in Zé's bag, and Zé looked up from Igz and said, his voice a little choked, "How is she bigger?"

"They have a way of doing that. It's super fucking annoying, and it doesn't stop for a good fifteen or twenty years."

"Don't listen to him," Zé told Igz. "He's happy you're growing up big and strong."

"See how happy I am," I said as I lugged Zé's bag down to his room, "the next time I have to scour the clearance rack at Target for new clothes. I swear to God, she needs new stuff every other week."

"We won't buy you everything off the clearance rack," Zé said to Igz.

"You're goddamn right we will."

"No more of the hotdog onesies, I promise."

When I got back to the living room, Zé was standing there, rocking Igz.

"Do you want to sit down?" I asked.

"I'm okay."

"Do you want a drink?"

He shook his head as he touched Igz's cheek.

My heart did that Grinch thing where it got huge in my chest, and I heard myself say again, "Do you want to sit down?"

Zé gave me a look. Maybe he took pity on me, because a small smile creased his cheek, and he said, "Yes, Fernando. Thank you."

So, he sat. And I sat. And he held Igz. And I watched him hold Igz.

"Maybe you should go work," he finally said.

"I don't need to work right now."

"Maybe you should go catch up on some paperwork."

"I'm good."

"Maybe you should turn on the TV."

"Nah."

He gave me a look.

It took me a moment, and then I said, "Holy fuck, I'm staring at you."

Zé's quiet laugh rolled through the house. He kissed Igz's tummy to hide his smile.

"You want me to leave."

"Of course not."

"You want me to get the fuck out of your hair."

"I love spending time with you, Fernando."

"You know what this is? This is betrayal. Because I'm the whole reason you two even know each other, and now you're cutting me out of the picture."

This time, Zé didn't bother hiding his grin. "Why don't you tell me what's in the fridge, and in a few minutes, I'll get started on dinner?"

I stayed on the couch to make my point.

That slow smile unfurled on his face, and he touched the back of my hand—lightly, and withdrawing again almost immediately. "I'm not going anywhere."

"Where the fuck would you go?" I asked as I got to my feet. "You two are a match made in fucking heaven."

I thought maybe that being in the kitchen would make things easier, but somehow, it only made things worse. The needle on that internal dial inched a little closer to crazy. I kept wiping my hands on my shorts, pacing back and forth the length of the kitchen, straightening the towel and sweeping breadcrumbs off the counter, and feeling my heart climb higher and higher in my throat. Maybe this was what it felt like right before an aneurysm.

"What's in the fridge?" Zé called.

"I don't know," I blurted. And then, before he could ask what that meant, I said, "I'm ordering something."

Zé appeared in the doorway, all six feet of him, biceps on display as he adjusted Igz in his arms. His steps were a little too careful. "I think she's hungry."

"Where's your cane?"

"I'm weaning myself off it."

"Weaning yourself off it? You never used it like you were supposed to! Jesus Christ, Zé."

"I feel fine."

"And you didn't do your PT."

"Fernando."

"Where is it?"

He sighed.

"Try that again," I said. "I'm a little deaf when I'm talking to idiots."

For some reason, that made him grin. "In my trunk."

"You're using it until we see a doctor and you're cleared."

He sighed again.

"Speak up, son."

I thought maybe he'd fight me, but then his face changed, and he smirked. "Yes, Daddy."

"Do you see who you've chosen?" I asked Igz. "This sexual reprobate was your pick."

Igz didn't mind, though; she was still smiling at Zé like he shat rainbows.

I got the cane from the trunk. I ordered dinner. Zé fed Igz and burped her, and no fucking lie, she was out like a light. He was so careful when he stood. Careful of his knee. Careful not to wake her. He moved slowly down the hall. I stood. I moved around the living room like somebody was shooting me in the ass with electricity. I tried to stand at the window. I picked up a pillow and put it down again.

When Zé came back, his face was unreadable. He stood in the hallway, looking at me. That windswept hair. Those dark eyes. He wasn't smiling, but he always looked so kind. My knees were trembling. And he was still standing there.

"It's your birthday," I said.

A flash of surprise crossed his face. Then he smiled. "I can't believe you remembered."

That bumped the needle down a little, and I scowled.

"Of course you remembered," he said, but it sounded like he was speaking to himself.

"I—I got you something."

He frowned. "But you didn't even know where I was until—wait, how did you know where I was?"

"You told me about that beach. How important it was to you. So, I kept going there. Every day."

"Really?"

"Zé, I'm kind of having a heart attack right now, so can we please focus?" When he didn't say anything, I rushed into the silence. "Please don't be mad."

There wasn't any good response to that, so I led him out to the garage. I'd installed hangers on the wall of the garage, and the longboard fit perfectly beside the Escalade.

He stopped when he saw it. He stood totally still.

"I know you don't want me to spend money on you," I said. "And I know you want to be independent. And I respect that, and I respect you, and if you tell me you don't want it, I'll get rid of it. But after you left, I felt like I was going crazy. I felt like I had to do something. And I didn't know where you were or if I'd ever see you again, but I thought if I did see you again, maybe, if I did everything exactly right, you'd forgive me."

He still hadn't said anything. His hand drifted against his thigh like he didn't even know he was moving.

"Could you say something? Because I'm freaking out right now."

"You bought my board back."

I nodded.

"How?"

"I called a lot of surf shops." Another of those silences opened. "Are you mad? If you're mad, I'll get rid of it."

He shook his head. And then, like he was on a delay, he said, "I'm not mad."

"Did I cross a line? Was this totally inappropriate?"

He shook his head again. He put one hand on the wall like he didn't trust his legs, and he limped across the garage. He touched the board tentatively. And then he followed the length of it. It was more than a touch; it was a caress. How many hours had he spent working on this board? Caring for it? Waxing it? Trusting his body to it? And then a thought that had never occurred to me sprang into my head: was this the board he'd been on when he'd hurt himself?

"Zé—"

"Thank you." The words were flat, almost hard. He dropped his hand and turned to face me. His face was still unreadable. "That was kind, Fernando. Thank you."

"If you don't want it, we'll get rid of it."

He shook his head.

"If you want the money instead."

"No." And then, like he was struggling, he said again, "Thank you."

The moment grew longer and longer until I felt it break. And then we went back inside.

We sat on the couch, the television on, TV voices babbling. Eventually, the doorbell rang, and I got our food and carried it into the kitchen. He hadn't liked it, I thought as I unpacked the salads. He hadn't hated it. He hadn't liked it. He hadn't cared, maybe that was a better way of putting it. That part of his life was over. You should have gotten him a cute dad shirt, I thought as I got down glasses. You should have gotten him a cake—

Zé's hands on my hips caught me, steadied me. And then the length of his body was pressed against mine, his mouth against my neck. He kissed me lightly, and I shivered like I had a fever. That was how it had all started. His lips against my neck. The gentleness of it. The question in it. Like now.

"You don't have to…" But I couldn't finish that sentence.

I tried to turn, but his hands tightened on my hips, holding me in place. I remembered how easily he'd moved me when he'd wanted to. How strong he was, with that toned, masculine body hidden under baggy surf clothes. His lips brushed my neck again, lower this time. The stubble on his chin scraped my shoulder. His cheek rubbed against the strap of my tank. I was instantly, totally, no-take-backs hard, my dick trapped between my body and the cabinets.

"Zé," I said, my hands finding his.

"I love you," he whispered and kissed my shoulder again. "I don't think I love you. I love you."

"I love you too."

"Thank you for being so wonderful."

I shook my head.

"Thank you," he said again, and now his kisses were moving back up my neck again, "for being so generous."

"I should have asked."

"I can't tell you how much it means to me. I'm sorry I acted—I acted weird." The next kiss, he pressed below my jaw. I could smell him: coconut wax, and that darker, driftwood earthiness. "I got a little overwhelmed. Lots of feelings." His breath was warm on my neck. "Thank you, Fernando. Thank you so much."

I tried to say something. I couldn't.

Zé drew my face around and kissed me. It was awkward—in part because of the angle, and in part because our timing was off. But it was Zé, and he tasted like Zé, and his mouth was Zé's mouth, and I remembered the shape of it, how he was supposed to feel, and I turned and kissed him again. He parted his lips and let my tongue into his mouth, and he moaned. I could feel him now through those stupid board shorts, the hardness of his dick, and he rubbed himself against me as I kissed him again.

When we separated, we were both breathing hard. His pupils were so big his eyes looked almost black, and his lips were glossy and parted. He took my hand, and I said, "Zé."

But he smiled and nodded, and I'm not made of steel. I let him lead me down the hall. His hand was a man's hand. Callused, big-fingered, certain. When he stumbled, I put out a hand to steady him, and he looked back over his shoulder to smile at me. I pushed the hair out of his eyes and thought, I'm allowed to do this. I'm allowed to touch him like this.

We went into my bedroom, and I helped him out of his clothes, and then he helped me with mine. I spent a moment looking at him: the dark nipples, the beautiful brown of his skin that lightened below his hips, his cock. He was looking a little raggedy down there, which made me weirdly happy—it was nice to know (or to believe, anyway) that last time, Zé had cleaned himself up for me, and after he'd left, he'd let himself go.

I thought maybe we'd try what had worked for us last time, with Zé sitting on my lap so that he could keep his leg straight, but instead, he stretched out on my bed. I sat next to him and put my hand on his hip, and I watched goosebumps spread across his belly. I did that, I thought. I'm doing this, and I did that, and he's letting me. I rubbed my hand across the ripple of abs, and he flexed into me like a cat.

"Lie down," he whispered. "I want to be with you."

So, I did. We made out for a while. He liked when I scruffed him with my stubble, and I left hot red tracks across his neck and chest and nipples. I sucked and bit his nipples. He left a major hickey on my neck, and distantly, I knew I was going to have to ask Augustus about concealer. He played with my dick, and after a while, I played with his. I liked it, don't get me wrong. It was hot, handling a guy's junk. And it was hotter because it was Zé. But it was still new ground. I stuck to the basics, and to judge by the noises, I did all right.

When I slid down between Zé's legs, he stopped me.

"What?" I asked. "Do you want to sixty-nine?"

His cheeks were already flushed, but now the color deepened. "I want you to fuck me."

"Oh."

"Is that okay?"

I nodded so fast my head almost came off. Zé grinned, and I realized how that must have looked.

"I mean, I don't have to," I said. "I'm still figuring this stuff out, so if you like to top, I mean, I can definitely, um, try—"

He didn't laugh, but his grin did get bigger.

"What the fuck is wrong with you?" I asked, swatting the inside of his thigh. I ignored his yelp. "I'm being a fucking gentleman. I don't have to stick my dick in you just because—"

"Just because the only way you've ever had sex is to be the one doing the sticking?" Zé asked drily.

"Not to put too fucking fine a point on it."

He gave me his Zé smile, that lazy, surf bum smile. "I want you to fuck me, Fernando, because I want you to fuck me. If I want to fuck you, I'll ask. If you want me to fuck you, all you have to do is tell me. Although, you might have to jump straight to being a cowboy while my knee is healing."

I rubbed the red spot on his thigh, feeling the dark hair there, the thickness of his powerful legs. The way he lay, with one leg bent, exposed a hint of his hole, and I could see a scattering of more dark hair there.

"If it's too much," Zé said gently, "it's okay. I want to be with you, and I wanted to tell you what I wanted."

"No," I said. "No, I want to. I turned into a fucking bobblehead when you asked me, remember? I don't want to, uh, do it wrong. Hurt you, I mean. Or, I don't know. Be bad at it. It's different from with a girl, I mean."

"We'll go slow," he said. The dark brown of his eyes swallowed me. "You'll take care of me."

I will, I thought. I always will.

I had lube and a condom in the nightstand, and hail Mary, mother of God, the condom wasn't expired. In the videos I'd watched, sometimes the guys fingered each other to loosen up, and sometimes they went straight to the pounding. Since I figured gay porn couldn't be any more realistic than straight porn, that probably meant going straight to pounding wasn't an option. I helped Zé get into position on his side, which was easier with his knee, and I parted his cheeks with one hand.

Aside from porn, I hadn't spent much time around assholes. It was darker than the skin around it. I didn't know what I was expecting, but he smelled like Zé—a little thicker, a little muskier, but not dirty.

"You okay?" Zé asked.

I nodded and squirted lube on my fingers. I ran my index finger over his hole a few times. The texture surprised me, but even more surprising was that Zé made a little contented noise. Not going to lie, that chubbed me right up. I added a little more lube, and when I felt his hole relax, I pressed against it. The resistance lasted long enough that I almost stopped, and then my finger slipped inside.

He was hot. And tight. Both of those things caught me off guard. Then I remembered this wasn't about me and checked his face.

"I'm good," he said. And then, with a tiny smile, "You have thick fingers, and it's been a while."

"Do you want me to—"

"No, don't move." He closed his eyes, and his breathing slowed. "I'm good, Fernando. I'm good. You're making me feel so good."

I eased my finger partway out and slid it in again. I'd read enough porn to know the theory. I pressed and pulled on the ring of muscle, forcing it to relax. I'd kind of forgotten about the prostate until—

"Meu Deus," he grunted, and his whole body tightened, his hole spasming around my finger.

A smile spread across my face. He looked up at me from under hooded eyes, his expression dazed. "Hello," I said and did it again.

A groan ripped through him, and then my name: "Fernando."

I liked how that sounded.

As I worked a second finger inside him, I stretched down and kissed him. In return, his kiss was sloppy and broken. His hips jerked, and he groaned as I twisted my fingers, working the bulge of my knuckles past his rim. His leg was shaking. I stroked his flank with my free hand and kissed him again, and again, he struggled to respond, his mouth only partially sealing against mine as I found that spot inside him again and another punched-out noise escaped him.

"Fuck me," he said against my mouth. His stubble scraped my lips.

"You're still pretty tight."

"Fernando, fuck me." The words sounded dragged out of him. "Fuck me right now."

Who was I to argue?

I unwrapped the condom and rolled it on as Zé watched from under those hooded eyes. It took me two tries. I was trembling, and part of it was because this was a first (even if it wasn't *the* first), and part of it was because it had been a long time. I gave us each a little more lube, and then we shifted around until our bodies aligned. His chest rose and fell rapidly, and a flush spread across his chest, up his throat, into his cheeks. His hair was a fucking mess, and I had a vision of pulling on it, drawing his head back as I drove into him. Not today, not while his knee was still touch-and-go. But one day.

He was so tight. So tight that at first, I thought he wasn't going to let me in. But it was like it had been with my finger; right when I thought I should pull back, right when I thought we needed to try some more stretching, muscle relented, and he took me inside him. He grunted, and I stopped with barely more than the head of my dick inside him. He squeezed his eyes shut.

"Did I hurt you? Do you want me to stop?"

Zé shook his head. After several long seconds, he nodded, and I eased forward again. His hole clutched me, and even though I was trying to stay focused on him, on making sure he was okay, it was hard not to make comparisons, for my brain to register all the ways this was different and new and—yes—fucking amazing. He reached out blindly, found my hip, and urged me forward again. And then again. And then I was fully seated. His chest rose and fell with deep breaths, and then his eyes opened to slits.

"You feel so big inside me," he murmured.

I rubbed his leg, which was slung over my shoulder. I kissed his ankle.

"God, Fernando," he said in that scratchy voice. "I've wanted this for so long."

"Me too." My fingers followed the powerful muscles of his quad. His dick had softened, and I touched it, stroking lightly under the head.

Zé smiled. "That doesn't mean I don't like it. It's a lot, and my body is focused on other things right now."

"I want it to feel good."

"It does." He made a few microadjustments and then said, "Go slow at first."

I did. In porn, I feel like guys always talk about how hard it is to go slow, but that's never been true for me. Sure, there's a time and place to pound, and that can feel fucking amazing. But in my experience (I could hear Augustus and Chuy saying *limited experience* from the peanut gallery), my partners (and I) tended to get off more from slow and steady than from a nonstop bangfest. The drag and scrape of his tightness felt incredible, and Zé made soft noises that suggested he was feeling all right. I felt him relax, loosening up, accepting me more easily. I started to move a little faster. I began to find my rhythm. Like I said, it had been a long time, and I was out of practice. But my body remembered, and the way Zé watched me, with that distracted look of someone struggling to pay attention, was flattering. Hot, too. I scooted closer, changing the angle of our bodies. This time, I was doing it on purpose, looking for it.

"Caralho, fuck, damn, fuck!" He shouted the words at full volume, his hole clamping down on me, his back lifting from the mattress. I tried to keep us in position, drilling forward against that spot. His eyes were huge, but I wasn't sure he was seeing me. He moaned—if you can call a shout a moan, "Fernando!"

His hand slid between his legs, and he began jerking himself off. He still looked like he was only three-quarters of the way to hard, but he seemed to know what he was doing. I kept going, and as I watched his face and felt his body tense around me, I went faster and faster. I could feel it, how he was chasing that edge, and the intensity of my fucking kept inching it further and further away. It was the hottest thing I'd ever experienced in my life, and I fucked him like my balls were on fire.

And then, intense or not, the fucking couldn't hold him back any longer. Zé grunted. His body locked around me, his hole squeezing my dick.

He came—a few strong spurts, and then softer ones, painting his defined abs.

I slowed. I'd read enough porn to know how sensitive a guy got after he nutted.

But Zé shook his head. "Keep going," he mumbled, and he got a hand on my hip and drew me into him again. "Keep going."

Jesus Christ, I thought.

He trembled as I chased that sweet spot of friction and heat and contact. He made soft little noises that were unmistakably distressed. He looked up at me, and his half-lidded eyes were dark and dreaming. Then I felt like something was lifting me up, and blood washed in my ears, and I came.

After, he was still looking up at me. I managed to give him a fumbling kiss and then, as carefully as I could, I eased out of him. I ditched the condom and lay down, and he turned, letting me take him into my arms before I even had to ask: his back to my chest, my nose in that mane of windblown hair. He breathed slowly and softly now. I drew his hair back and kissed his ear.

"Te amo," I whispered.

"Eu também," he said, his voice all raw edges. "Te amo muito."

21

"Six months isn't that long," Zé said as I secured Igz's car seat in its base. Tried to do it. "Do you want me to do that?"

The lawyer's parking lot wasn't busy on a weekday afternoon. In the shade, the temperature was pleasant, and I could smell the carne asada from the food truck parked at the corner. Maybe Zé would say yes to tacos, I thought. Maybe, after that meeting, he'd take pity on me.

"Six months will go by so fast. You have to push down until it clicks."

"I'm pushing," I said. "What the fuck does it look like I'm doing?"

He stretched one long arm past me, made some tiny adjustment that I couldn't quite track, and the car seat clicked into its base.

"Show-off."

"Fernando," he said, and he turned me away from the car seat to settle his hands on my hips. Those big dark eyes held me. "I know it wasn't the answer we wanted, but it's okay."

"Anything can happen in six months. He might show up again. He might decide he wants to get clean."

Zé leaned his forehead against mine. "And that would be a good thing. We'd be happy about that."

"Speak for your fucking self."

Six months of no contact, it turned out, was the minimum amount of time necessary to prove parental abandonment. That was the first step in terminating Chuy's parental rights so I could adopt Igz. So we could adopt her. Even though that felt like a big *we*.

"He's your brother," Zé said.

"Half-brother."

Zé leaned his head a little more heavily into mine. "And you love him."

"Debatable."

"If he comes back, we'll ask him to give you power of attorney for Igz."

I tried not to say what I was thinking. I tried to be positive, because Zé was always positive, always patient, always kind. Unless you brought home a bag of Mr. Taco tacos, and he ripped you a new asshole because you'd been doing so good on your diet, and why do you need a bag of greasy tacos? Because they're delicious, I'd tried to explain. It hadn't gone over well.

"You don't know how Chuy is," I said. "You don't get it. He might come back and decide he wants to be her dad."

"It'll be okay."

"What if he takes her away? God, Zé, he'd lose interest in her in about a day, and he'd drag her to those filthy fucking squats, with God knows what kind of people."

Zé's arms slid around me.

"I know." I bit the words off. "I can't control what other people do."

He nudged me with his forehead again.

"I can only control myself."

He kissed my nose.

"You know this psychobabble is about as useful as shit in a paper bag."

"Fernando."

I closed my eyes and took a deep breath, and then another. I concentrated on his arms around me, the points of contact between our bodies, the feel of the ground beneath my feet. After a while, I nodded.

"It's going to be okay," he said again.

"I know." Then my eyes opened. "What time is it?"

Zé knew me well enough to be suspicious.

I checked my phone. "Shit, we're going to be late for your PT."

"We talked about this. I can miss—"

"Nice try."

"One time won't make or break—"

"We're not going to have time for dinner, so we'd better grab something fast." I did a quick scan. "How about that taco truck?"

"It would have been more convincing if you hadn't started drooling when we pulled into the parking lot. We did something important today, Fernando. We took a big first step. Let's celebrate with a nice, healthy meal instead of jamming fast food down our throats while we drive."

"You're going to PT."

"No tacos."

"You've got to eat something; you've got work right after."

Zé's face changed at the mention of his job. He looked, well, happy. It was only a few afternoons and evenings a week, and it was easy to plan my appointments and meetings around it. It wasn't a lot of money. He'd started doing surfing lessons, working with a local surf shop. They'd been understanding about his knee, and so far, Zé had been careful, mostly working with the kids on land as they learned the basics about their boards and about surfing, and occasionally helping with the lessons in shallow water. He'd promised to be careful, and from what I could tell, he'd kept that promise. It was worth it, seeing his face transform like this every single time he even thought about the job. Getting part of his life back. And, of course, he was a natural with kids.

Then his face shuttered again. "No tacos. We'll pick up protein bowls from that place near the house."

"One taco isn't going to kill me."

"I'm not worried about one taco, Fernando. That bag you brought home was literally bursting at the seams."

We got in the Escalade. I thought there was probably a Mr. Taco along the way. If I took a specific route. And if I got stuck in the drive-thru line, he'd have no choice but to let me order at least one taco.

"As soon as I save up enough money, I'll get a car," Zé said. His current vehicle had died a fiery death his third day at work, and although I'd offered multiple times to buy him something (whatever he wanted), he'd refused. I opened my mouth to offer again, and he shot me a warning look. "Me, Fernando. With the money I earn working."

I raised my hands in surrender.

"A few more weeks," he said, "and your life will get a little simpler. No more driving us around."

I turned to check Igz one last time, and maybe it was a full moon, or maybe it was a solar storm, or maybe the world was ending, but I shit you not, she smiled at me. I didn't know I was smiling back until Zé touched my cheek, his thumb at the corner of my mouth.

"You know what?" I said. "Simple is overrated."

Acknowledgments

My deepest thanks go out to the following people (in reverse alphabetical order):

Wendy Wickett, for help with repetition, for the increased clarity of the text, and, of course, for rent-a-fuck.

Mark Wallace, for spotting all those missing endmarks (so many!), for the gentle reminder about capitalization, and for keeping me from going "full hillbilly!"

Tray Stephenson, for helping with my prepositions, for adding back my missing letters (how did they disappear?), and for his kind words about, as he put it, this emotional roller coaster.

Nichole Reeder, for proofing the text, for wonderful continuity questions—Fer's vacation, the baby's car seat, and more!—and for all the help with writing a newborn!

Pepe, for editing this manuscript, for helping me clarify and smooth out the prose, and for his suggestion about Zé's age (so well thought out, even though I ended up not making that change).

Meredith Otto, for the feedback on Fer's growth in this book, for her questions about the birth certificate, and for doing all of this even after the tech gods destroyed her annotations!Cheryl Oakley, for catching so many typos that I still can't believe I missed, for her excellent questions (about Auggie's crystal sneakers, for example!), and for her kind words early on about this book.

Cheryl Oakley, for helping me revise this manuscript, for her clarifying question about Auggie's sneakers, and for her enthusiasm about this venture into contemporary romance.

Raj Mangat, for helping me figure out how much a nanny should make, for asking so many good questions to flesh out the story, and for forgiving me (I hope) for keeping *that* word (twice!).

Marie Lenglet, for asking so many wonderful questions about the timeline (the final version, including the accompanying issues, was the best I could do unfortunately), about the relationship, and about the urgent care – another problem without an easy fix, for her help with all things baby related, and for so much more!

Austin Gwin, for that local's knowledge about the 5, for covering what "wasn't covered in a creative writing class" (yikes!), and for his great feedback about the more intimate moments of this book.

Fritz, for spotting missing words, for matching up the correct body parts to the correct people, and for his excellent questions about Auggie, Zé, and the clarity of Fer's thoughts.

Savannah Cordle, for catching my missing words, for her excellent questions (some of which I even answered!), and for that amazing marginal note when she told everyone in the book to go f' themselves!

And special thanks to my patrons who provided screams (and other feedback) as the story was being serialized.

About the Author

For advanced access, exclusive content, limited-time promotions, and insider information, please sign up for my mailing list at **www.gregoryashe.com**.

Printed in Dunstable, United Kingdom